Palgrave Studies in Animals and Literature

Series Editors
Susan McHugh
Department of English
University of New England
Auburn, ME, USA

Robert McKay
School of English
University of Sheffield
Sheffield, UK

John Miller
School of English
University of Sheffield
Sheffield, UK

Various academic disciplines can now be found in the process of executing an 'animal turn', questioning the ethical and philosophical grounds of human exceptionalism by taking seriously the nonhuman animal presences that haunt the margins of history, anthropology, philosophy, sociology and literary studies. Such work is characterised by a series of broad, cross-disciplinary questions. How might we rethink and problematise the separation of the human from other animals? What are the ethical and political stakes of our relationships with other species? How might we locate and understand the agency of animals in human cultures?

This series publishes work that looks, specifically, at the implications of the 'animal turn' for the field of English Studies. Language is often thought of as the key marker of humanity's difference from other species; animals may have codes, calls or songs, but humans have a mode of communication of a wholly other order. The primary motivation is to muddy this assumption and to animalise the canons of English Literature by rethinking representations of animals and interspecies encounter. Whereas animals are conventionally read as objects of fable, allegory or metaphor (and as signs of specifically human concerns), this series significantly extends the new insights of interdisciplinary animal studies by tracing the engagement of such figuration with the material lives of animals. It examines textual cultures as variously embodying a debt to or an intimacy with animals and advances understanding of how the aesthetic engagements of literary arts have always done more than simply illustrate natural history. We publish studies of the representation of animals in literary texts from the Middle Ages to the present and with reference to the discipline's key thematic concerns, genres and critical methods. The series focuses on literary prose and poetry, while also accommodating related discussion of the full range of materials and texts and contexts (from theatre and film to fine art, journalism, the law, popular writing and other cultural ephemera) with which English studies now engages.

Series Board
Karl Steel (Brooklyn College)
Erica Fudge (Strathclyde)
Kevin Hutchings (UNBC)
Philip Armstrong (Canterbury)
Carrie Rohman (Lafayette)
Wendy Woodward (Western Cape)

Alice Higgs

Animal Fiction in Late Twentieth-Century Canada

Alice Higgs
London, UK

ISSN 2634-6338 ISSN 2634-6346 (electronic)
Palgrave Studies in Animals and Literature
ISBN 978-3-031-42611-7 ISBN 978-3-031-42612-4 (eBook)
https://doi.org/10.1007/978-3-031-42612-4

© The Editor(s) (if applicable) and The Author(s), under exclusive licence to Springer Nature Switzerland AG 2023

This work is subject to copyright. All rights are solely and exclusively licensed by the Publisher, whether the whole or part of the material is concerned, specifically the rights of translation, reprinting, reuse of illustrations, recitation, broadcasting, reproduction on microfilms or in any other physical way, and transmission or information storage and retrieval, electronic adaptation, computer software, or by similar or dissimilar methodology now known or hereafter developed.

The use of general descriptive names, registered names, trademarks, service marks, etc. in this publication does not imply, even in the absence of a specific statement, that such names are exempt from the relevant protective laws and regulations and therefore free for general use.

The publisher, the authors, and the editors are safe to assume that the advice and information in this book are believed to be true and accurate at the date of publication. Neither the publisher nor the authors or the editors give a warranty, expressed or implied, with respect to the material contained herein or for any errors or omissions that may have been made. The publisher remains neutral with regard to jurisdictional claims in published maps and institutional affiliations.

Cover image: Volodymyr Burdiak / Alamy Stock Photo

This Palgrave Macmillan imprint is published by the registered company Springer Nature Switzerland AG.
The registered company address is: Gewerbestrasse 11, 6330 Cham, Switzerland

Paper in this product is recyclable.

Acknowledgements

To my parents. Without you this wouldn't have been possible.
May we strive for relationships that centre care and empathy with those around us, both human and animal, now more than ever.

Contents

1 Introduction: Nation, Identity, Species — 1

2 Reconfiguring Animal Narratives in Farley Mowat's *Never Cry Wolf* (1963) — 19

3 Trauma on Display: Women's Wilderness Writing and Animal Ciphers in Margaret Atwood's *Surfacing* (1972) and *Life Before Man* (1979) — 49

4 Writing Bear(s): Thematising the Canadian Animal Story in Marian Engel's *Bear* (1976) — 75

5 Queership, Kinship, Careship: Adopting An Ethics of Care in Timothy Findley's *The Wars* (1977) and *Not Wanted on the Voyage* (1984) — 93

6 Unsettling Coyote: Engaging with Indigenous Concepts of Care in Gail Anderson-Dargatz's *The Cure for Death by Lightning* (1996) — 119

7 **Conclusion** 143

Bibliography 147

Index 157

CHAPTER 1

Introduction: Nation, Identity, Species

In April 2020, a young grizzly bear swam ashore on Hanson Island in British Columbia's Broughton archipelago in search of food. Fresh out of hibernation in the spring, bears in this region ordinarily begin foraging for mussels, clams, huckleberries and other seasonal resources until the salmon population picks up in the summertime. However, this young grizzly could smell something even easier to feast on—a pile of garbage that had not been stored correctly. As he appeared to make the island his new home and continued to tuck into his garbage feast, wildlife officers in the area were concerned that he had become too comfortable around humans. This is the threshold that they commonly use to determine when a bear cannot be relocated and must be killed.

However, local First Nations groups were displeased with this decision. Mamalilikulla representatives asserted their nation's right to govern their territories and the human-bear relationships within them, citing a similar incident in which a bear named Gatu had recently appeared in a community nearby on the northern tip of Vancouver Island and despite numerous requests from First Nations locals to take a proactive approach in managing the bear before his behaviour escalated, he was shot and killed. Reflecting on this, Mike Willie, hereditary chief of the Kwikwasut'inuxw Nation was one of the Indigenous persons that oversaw the campaign to relocate the Hanson Island bear alongside the non-profit Grizzly Bear

© The Author(s), under exclusive license to Springer Nature
Switzerland AG 2023
A. Higgs, *Animal Fiction in Late Twentieth-Century Canada*,
Palgrave Studies in Animals and Literature,
https://doi.org/10.1007/978-3-031-42612-4_1

Foundation: 'we don't want our bears killed any more ...We have the right to govern within our own traditional territories and we have inherent rights and we have title.'[1] In a symbolic act of kinship with the bear, he was affectionately named Mali, after the Mamalilikulla First Nations, whose territory encompasses the island. Work thus began to find a resolution to suit all parties, one which concluded that Mali be relocated to Hoeya Sound, an area of BC famous for grizzly sightings. Given that Indigenous voices were being centred in this context, the press coverage of the incident sought to frame it as an example of a successful effort towards reconciliation:

> This bear's death was averted through an unlikely partnership between local Indigenous groups and conservation officers, raising hopes of a more holistic approach to wildlife management with greater Indigenous input.[2]

Mali was subsequently captured and relocated. George Heyman, the province's Minister of Environment, declared that this was motivated by a 'desire for reconciliation' with local First Nations, which 'helped guide the process'. Certainly, the outcome does gesture towards a growing return of autonomy to the First Nations community, as Willie stated: 'it feels that this could be a blueprint to move forward—for us and for other First Nations on the coast ... it was a really good ending.'[3] Whether or not this event marked real progress in terms of reconciliation is a broader question, but what this event does tells us is that contemporary settler Canada is still engaging in a process of trying to find a means of reconciling its relationship with Indigenous Nations through its relationship with animals.

Indeed relations with animals frame much of settler Canada's cultural identity and storytelling. No animal has perhaps been more associated with Canada than the beaver, which having played such a significant role in Canada's fur trade history, was given official status as an emblem of Canada in 1975. Nicole Shukin has argued that Canada's incorporation of the beaver into a nationalist sign functions as a form of animal fetishism:

> The beaver is Canada's fetish insofar as it configures the nation as a life form that is born rather than made (obscuring recognition of the ongoing cultural and material history of its construction) and insofar as it stands in for an organic national unity that in actuality does not exist.[4]

The sign of the beaver and its institutional circulation in the 1970s serves the function of creating a new sense of national identity rather than acknowledging the history that informs contemporary Canadian identity. Canada's beaver, then, is underpinned by a settler-colonial desire for a new identity:

> In the 1970s, the institutionalization of the sign of the beaver mustered this nostalgic web of associations into the political service of a dominantly white, Euro-Canadian discourse of national culture, one pivoting on an assertion of its own indigeneity. Through the animal capital of the national symbol, a postcolonial project of national culture deeply structured by the logics of capital and "White normativity" has become the privileged content of a discursive struggle for "native space," displacing the ongoing machinations of internal colonialism and white supremacy, as well as infranational struggles for First Nations' self-determination.[5]

This new sense of national identity that is privileged through the beaver is a settler one. Whilst the choice of a beaver somewhat acknowledges the sacrifice of the species, given that beaver pelts helped establish Canada's economic presence on the global stage, it overlooks the vast Nations and peoples that lived and thrived on Turtle Island before the arrival of European colonisers. In doing so, it redefines the country's identity as one that was only made upon settler contact. Animal signs and imagery are, then, significant and historical role players in the cultural understanding and representation of contemporary Canadian nationhood.

Resisting the urge to recycle and revisit conversations such as the 'nature fakers' and 'victimhood' debates that have dominated reflections on animal writing in Canada, this book will demonstrate that the late twentieth century in Canada saw a development in the types of stories written about animals. By focusing on a number of texts written across the period of 1960–2000, this book will conduct the first systematic study of Canadian settler writing across this period to demonstrate that writing about animals in Canada in the last third of the twentieth century saw the emergence of more critically engaged representational strategies for depicting consciously pro-animal stories about reciprocated human-animal relationships. The novels in focus are *Never Cry Wolf* (1963) by Farley Mowat; *Surfacing* (1972) and *Life Before Man* (1979) by Margaret Atwood; *Bear* (1976) by Marian Engel; *The Wars* (1977) and *Not Wanted On the Voyage* (1984) by Timothy Findley; and *The Cure for Death by*

Lightning (1996) by Gail Anderson-Dargatz. Although it takes a chronological approach, this analysis does not simply survey the animal writing of the each of these decades and argue that each author is the most exemplary figure of that period. Rather the intention is to explore the forms of social identity-based, critical commentary on animal writing that takes shape across this period.

The point here is also not to argue for the persistent connection between Canadian identity and animals in literature as a genre in itself—the 'Canadian animal story' as it were—but rather to demonstrate that writing about animals in Canada across the period of the early 1960s into the late 1990s saw a move away from the idea that there is a single, homogenous Canadian identity or aspect of that identity that is or can be represented through animals, echoing the sentiments of Nicole Shukin's criticism of the beaver. As this book demonstrates, the idea of nation and national identity become increasingly fragmented and less of a focus as the period progresses, and the texts in this book begin to focus their representations instead on particular and nuanced aspects of personal identity, such as Indigenous identity, sexuality and gender, and the way in which these aspects fragment a fixed conception of Canadian settler identity as representable through animals.

Animal Writing in Canada

Although it is easy to identify an abundance of stories written by Canadian authors that are about or include animals (and not just settler authors), limited attention has been paid to the study of writing about animals in Canada, or why it is that so many Canadian authors have historically written, and continue to write novels about animals.

James Polk argued in 1972 that the motivation behind Canadian animal representation is a sense of 'victimhood' status inherent in the Canadian cultural psyche:

> As Canada's perennial questioning of its own national identity is increasingly coupled with a suspicion that a fanged America lurks in the bushes, poised for the kill, it is not surprising that Canadian writers should retain their interest in persecution and survival.[6]

Sharing this same theory, Margaret Atwood wrote in *Survival* also in 1972 that Canadian animal stories 'are about animals being killed, as felt emotionally from inside the fur and feathers.'[7] She explains: 'Canadians themselves feel threatened and nearly-extinct as a nation', meaning that these stories tap into a Canadian cultural fear and need for survival.[8] The prevalence of this victimhood/survival thesis is such that John Sandlos argues: 'subsequent criticism of the animal story in Canadian literature is, in many cases, a direct response to Atwood's and Polk's survival/victimhood thesis.'[9] Evidently, the cultural infamy of Polk's and Atwood's thesis, in addition to the lack of critical development in this area, means that criticism of Canadian animal fiction has been largely understood to be a nationalist subgenre. However, rather than buying into this connection between animals and the Canadian cultural psyche, Sandlos' states that Canadian animal writing has always been about understanding the relationship that Canadians have to the landscape and its animal inhabitants. Despite disagreeing with Atwood and Polk, then, Sandlos still continues to read the presence of animals in Canadian literature from a nationalist subgenre framework.

Sandlos determines that the biggest influence on Canadian animal writing is the work of nature writers Ernest Thompson Seton and Charles G. D. Roberts and their concerted effort to create a type of animal story that was not so concerned with binaries:

> The pervasive influence of Seton and Roberts ties the genre firmly to a natural history tradition, one that attempts to reconcile instinct with reason, biology with myth, human with animal, and physical fact with fictional narrative.[10]

He explains that their work 'was not intended to lament a "victimized nation" but rather to promote a sympathetic identification between the reader and the animal characters' by writing 'accurate natural history-stories that reflect the habits and behaviours of real animals within a fictional frame.'[11] The motivation behind this, he argues, is that in the 1970s in Canada a wider concern emerged regarding ecological destruction, such as lake pollution and species extinction. Writing about animals, then, served a new cultural concern:

> Literary animals who were shot, beaten, and unceremoniously killed may therefore have simply been creative "cannon fodder" in a larger effort to record destructive human behaviour toward the natural world.[12]

Sandlos' arguments are consistent with the environmental context of the 1970s, in which there were a number of ecological disasters and hardships experienced globally, such as famine in Bangladesh and the Sahel; inflation due to poor harvests in Europe and Asia, and sustained cold and water shortages in North America.[13]

Indeed the changing nature of the environment and the crises that were beginning to accumulate in this period sparked international concern and intervention. Three conferences titled 'Man and his Environment' were held in Banff, Canada, in 1968, 1974, and 1978, the purpose of which was specifically to bring politicians, professionals and researchers from countries around the world together to address what were seen as pressing environmental questions, including pollution, the relationship between ecology and economy, and interacting with the environment. Speaking at the opening of the Second International Banff Conference, the Director of the Environmental Science Centre at Kananaskis and Killam Memorial Professor at the University of Calgary, Dr J. B. Cragg said:

> Six years ago today many people did not accept the fact that man was in fact part of an all-embracing world problem. Today, the all-pervasive nature of the human environment is generally accepted, and that acceptance is shown in the plan of this conference.[14]

Although this speech and the framing of the conference in general reflects an anthropocentric perspective of environmentalism, it was evident that attitudes in Canada had shifted towards a focus on the idea of conservation. This change, Tina Loo points out, was reflected also in a number of policy changes in Canada. In 1962 Canada passed the federal Agricultural Rehabilitation and Development Act (ARDA), which 'encouraged the consolidation of small farms into larger and more efficient economic units and the reversion of marginal lands to their "natural state."'[15] Loo adds that these changes were systematic, indicating real, invested efforts:

> Government biologists were certainty aware of the importance of habitats in limiting factors in population growth, but it was not until the 1960s that they began to take the first concrete steps towards assessing and protecting them systematically.[16]

Despite this obvious period of change and concerted effort at prioritising environmental protection, little critical attention has been given to writing about animals and the environment across this period in Canada.

The only other literary study that engages with contemporary animal writing in Canada is Janice Fiamengo's edited collection, *Other Selves: Animals in the Canadian Literary Imagination* (2007). The collection is the first overarching study of animals in Canadian literature, bringing together contributions on poetry and fiction from a range of Canadian authors. Inhabiting the position staked by Atwood herself, in her introduction to the collection, Fiamengo argues that '"Speaking for" animals in Canadian literature and literary criticism has always been double-edged: both an exploration of the radical otherness of the animal and an intensely human, and human-centred endeavour.'[17] For Fiamengo, writing about animals in Canada hinges upon an ambivalently but residually anthropocentric framework that both acknowledges species difference but simultaneously reinscribes it. Although the collection endeavours to provide a systematic study, the literature in focus broadly spans from the eighteenth century, such as the inclusion of Thomas McIlwraith's *Birds of Ontario* (1894), through to contemporary works such as Yann Martel's *Life of Pi* (2002). Each chapter adopts a different thematic and methodological approach to the text, meaning that there is no overarching argument or definitive attempt to trace a particular concept throughout the collection. This suggests that Fiamengo, much like Polk, Atwood, and Sandlos, considers writing about animals in Canada to be an established nationalistic project or subgenre. As such, *Other Selves* is an extremely informative demonstration of the multitudinous ways in which Canadian authors have created stories about animals and the types of representational strategies they have adopted both historically and in some contemporary works, but it is not a critical project that is determined to prove something in particular about this mode of writing. There is, therefore, a gap in the critical field that this book aims to fill.

'Nature Fakers': Ernest Seton Thompson and Charles G. D. Roberts

Throughout this book, there are repeated references to the 'nature fakers', meaning the work of Ernest Thompson Seton and Charles G. D. Roberts. This is both in the novels themselves and in the secondary critical material mapping the historical context of writing about animals in Canada.

Although this book will not spend time regurgitating exhausted conversations about Seton and Roberts, it is important to know briefly the context of their work in order to understand how the contemporary writing in this book engages with it and the types of conversations that surrounded their work and continue to frame contemporary criticism.

Seton and Roberts were Canadian nature writers working in the late eighteenth and early nineteenth century. Their animal stories drew attention, both positive and critical because their work was considered overtly sentimental in its depiction of animals that were often being hunted and harmed. Their influence on contemporary Canadian writing has also been repeatedly emphasised. Polk and Sandlos consider Seton and Roberts to be the founders of an 'animal story tradition' in Canada. In particular, Seton's famous wolf, Lobo, who appears in the first of his short stories in *Wild Animals I have Known*, garnered legendary reputation in North America. His pelt is currently stored at the Ernest Thompson Seton Memorial Library and Museum in New Mexico and in 1962 Disney released *The Legend of Lobo*, an adventure film largely told from the point of view of a wolf named Lobo. That this was released just one year before *Never Cry Wolf*'s publication reinforces the continued receptive nature of the Canadian public to empathetic wolf narratives and the legacy of Seton, both as a Canadian writer and also as an animal advocate. Indeed Seton continued to lobby for the protection of wolves until his death in 1946.

So what has been the species politics at play within their work and in Canadian animals stories historically? Susan McHugh says of Seton and Roberts:

> These writers purportedly espoused a benevolent view of animal life that was anchored by strictly anthropomorphic storytelling techniques, and for this they were loved as well as reviled. Part of the reason that the nature fakers were assailed in public discussion was that they almost immediately proved so successful. Animal narratives dominated the literary marketplace at the turn of the twentieth century.[18]

It was for this anthropomorphic style that Seton and Roberts were determined to be 'nature fakers', criticised for straying from constructing biologically factual portrayals of animals. The success of these stories in Canada, McHugh argues, though, was due to a desire for animal stories to 'value nonutilitarian human-animal relationships.'[19] It is this notion of reciprocity, Sandlos similarly argues, that is a defining element of Seton's and Roberts' work and that marked the beginning of a Canadian animal story tradition.

For Sandlos, the 'nature fakers' criticism was/is misplaced because, he argues, their stories focus on representing a more active depiction of nature and animals, one that sought to capture the "real" sense of the world around us and those living in it, as opposed to either an imagined or basic, factual portrayals.

After *Never Cry Wolf*'s publication in 1963, much of the criticism echoed this same 'nature fakers' debate. As Karen Jones states, 'the controversy over *Never Cry Wolf* further encapsulates a crucial divide within modern environmentalism between professional science and amateur naturalism.'[20] Such criticism reiterates that contemporary animal stories in Canada are still being met with nineteenth-century arguments. In addition, Atwood recalls that when she was at school:

> Someone had given us Charles G. D. Roberts' Kings in Exile for Christmas, and I snivelled my way quickly through these heart-wrenching stories of animals caged, trapped and tormented. That was followed by Ernest Thompson Seton's Wild Animals I have Known, if anything more upsetting because the animals were more actual—they lived in forests, not circuses—and their deaths more mundane: the deaths, not of tigers, but of rabbits.[21]

Settler-Canadians then have been brought up reading Seton and Roberts, and in engaging with stories about animals, localised and full of tragedy. It is no surprise therefore, that critics such as Atwood, Polk and Sandlos have adopted the animal story as a marker of Canadian fiction.

Why Write About Animals?

The presence of animals in literature has been a historical constant. But the critical study of their presence, the field of literary animal studies, and the politics of representation, has developed significantly in the last twenty-five years. Marian Scholtmeijer takes Atwood's *Survival* thesis to task by detaching it from the nationalist framework and re-situating the presence of the animal in Canadian literature within a broader tradition of animal writing that she determines centres on the concept of victimisation. Amongst many writers, she argues, there is a perception that:

> Modern Western culture in general is under threat—and under threat specifically and directly as Atwood's remark suggests—from the animal. When modern culture reaches out to victimize the animal, it wounds itself. Each animal victim is a revelation. Each animal victim opens a path to modern culture's insecurity.[22]

This argument determines that animal representation, and the depiction of animal victims, is a decidedly human endeavour developed to reflect a modern sense of cultural insecurity. It simultaneously exposes and reinforces the marginality of animals and argues that literary animals are more nuanced than simply being a product of a unique national subgenre.

Critically engaging with this idea of the inseparability of human and animal narratives, McHugh argues:

> In certain historical and cultural moments, some literary and visual narrative forms become inseparable from shifts in the politics and sciences of species such that questions about animal narratives come to concern the formal and practical futures of all species life.'[23]

Literary animal representation here is a useful lens through which to examine the changing nature of wider species relations, particularly when it is approached through a critical lens that takes animals seriously as agents, capable of real reciprocated relations. The difficulty that lies within McHugh's argument is, as Mario Ortiz Robles argues, that the animal in literature is inherently tied to the politics of representation as a mode. In considering the animal in literature then, we might also consider the broader idea of a 'trope':

> The constant, if marginal, presence of animals in literature not only impels us to reconsider the significance of animal tropes, or, rather, of the animal-as-trope; it also pushes us to reassess the character, morphology, physiology, and force of tropes themselves, of the trope-as-animal.[24]

This entanglement of 'animal-as-trope' or 'trope-as-animal' suggests, he argues, that 'there is something literary about our relation to animals' and as such:

> Only by disentangling the various strands of the literary animal (of the literarity of the animal) at the place of its greatest visibility as figure (that is, in literature) that we can begin to understand the significance of animals "out there" in the place of greatest resistance to the figurality of the animal.[25]

The examination of literary animal representation is a vital part of understanding our wider relationship with the environment and species around us, and through such engagement, we might understand the politics that underlie the way in which these relationships are represented in literary narratives.

In *Writing Animals*, Timothy Baker posits that through the animal story, there is an 'understanding, and perhaps a dissolution, of the conventional binaries between human and nonhuman lives', which 'raises crucial questions about the nature of literary representation.'[26] Animal fiction has, then, a propensity to destabilise and bring into question both social and literary conventional norms. However, Baker, much like McHugh, emphasises that the 'extent to which nonhuman animals can destabilize narrative at the very same time they are bound by it' is only revealed when the 'representation of nonhuman animals in necessarily anthropocentric texts [is taken] seriously'.[27] It is precisely this notion of taking animals seriously that this book investigates within this particular set of novels. By placing these contemporary settler novels in conversation with one another this book examines the way in which the texts employ a variety of representational strategies to shed light on the politics of both settler relations and species representation across a specific period of time in Canada. It will demonstrate that these particular novels endeavour to engage in critical animal writing that destabilises hegemonic norms and binaries concerning human-animal relations as a tool for taking animals seriously as beings capable of placing demands back onto the human characters. This occurs through a self-conscious engagement with the historical and contemporary politics of species representation, their literary predecessors, and the kinds of ideas put forth by literary critics.

The Chapters

Within the triangular critical methodology that this book takes between Canadian nationhood, questions of species, and questions of personal identity, namely Indigeneity, gender, and sexuality, there are differences of emphasis demanded by each text and differences in critical approach. I have used particular secondary materials in particular chapters in order to best make sense of how that text responds to these set of questions regarding literature, animals and social identity. The structure and content of the chapters is as follows:

Following a chronological structure, Chap. 2 examines Farley Mowat's 1963 memoir *Never Cry Wolf*, which documents his experiences observing wolves in Churchill, Manitoba, as part of a government funded investigation into wolf behaviour. As a culturally visible piece of writing that is still continually drawn upon in conversations about wolves, opening with this text demonstrates the landscape of animal writing in the early 1960s and the reception of it. Engaging with ongoing conversations surrounding cultural conceptions of wolves in the work of Garry Marvin, Barry Lopez, and Philip Armstrong, Mowat's memoir dismantles a specific perception of wolves as dangerous, bloodthirsty hunters who are decimating caribou populations by instilling a sentimental depiction of wolves as anthropomorphic family units. The chapter identifies an irony surrounding this memoir in that the text is an aesthetic project aimed at debunking particular ideas about wolves, but in doing so, it produces another anthropocentric ideology about wolves and does so self-consciously. Through an exploration of Canadian parliamentary records and environmental history, the chapter demonstrates that *Never Cry Wolf* is a culturally visible piece of writing that influenced public opinions concerning wolves and blazed a trail in the 1960s between writing about animals in Canada and a more literary strategic type of writing.

Chapter 3 brings together two of Margaret Atwood's novels, *Surfacing* (1972) and *Life Before Man* (1979) to demonstrate that it is possible to pull Atwood's thinking together in a particular representational strategy that temporarily appears to be pro-animal, but that ultimately uses animals symbolically to represent human concerns and thereby abandons any attempt to handle animals as beings in their own right seriously. In both novels, the female protagonists enter what are determined to be pseudo-wildernesses—a log cabin by a lake in *Surfacing* and the Royal Ontario Museum in *Life Before Man*—and attempt to identify with the non-human animals they encounter as a means of escaping the stresses of their intimate relationships with overtly patriarchal men. What Atwood conveys, however, is that existence within these spaces is not sustainable; they are merely 'psuedo-spaces' from which the protagonists must ultimately emerge. Consequently, ethical identification with non-human animals cannot fully be realised, as it is abandoned in order to return to human society and to patriarchal order. The chapter develops existing criticism of the representational politics of animal display, such as museum spaces, to argue that the novels demonstrate a narrative use for animals through a configuration of encounters with the dead animal body as a subjectively transformative experience, allowing for temporary and symbolic refuge from victimisation felt in interpersonal relationships. The chapter focuses on moments in which dead animal bodies are put on display, such as in cruel acts of violence by hunters in Quebec in *Surfacing*, and the exhibition spaces and workrooms of the Royal Ontario Museum in *Life Before Man*. Such an analysis demonstrates that these types of anthropocentric techniques of representation are that which are actively resisted and re-worked in the novels of the authors that follow this chapter on Atwood, marking a critical turn in Canadian animal writing across this period.

Chapter 4 demonstrates that there is a significant turn in the 1970s towards a rejection of anthropocentric representations of animals, and that this is self-consciously engaged with in Marian Engel's novel *Bear*. It argues that *Bear* responds to dominant conversations in Canada concerning the symbolic use of animals in literature by self-consciously thematising animal writing to construct a story about a bear that refuses to conform to one such representation through an assertion of his material animality. To do so, the chapter focuses on a number of representational strategies that Engel employs to self-consciously engage with techniques that have frequented understandings of animals and writing stories about them. These include engaging with a range of literature on bears, from folklore stories to passages containing historical facts that litter the house the protagonist is staying in; to cultural ideas of bears; to the Canadian animal stories of Ernest Thompson Seton and Charles G D Roberts. Such an argument demonstrates that *Bear* is a text conscious of its literary predecessors and consciously situating itself within a developing tradition of writing about animals in Canada in the late 1970s. This focus on the critical turn evident in Engel's novel argues for its influence on the animal fiction that follows in this book. The novel's shift into more self-conscious animal writing reflects the development of representations that seek to take animals more seriously and become consciously pro-animal as the monograph develops.

Chapter 5 intersects the concepts of kinship and camp within two novels by Timothy Findley, *The Wars* (1977) and *Not Wanted on the Voyage* (1984). Defining camp as an aesthetic way of relating that seeks to work outside of dominant hegemonies, this chapter argues that there is a logic at play within Findley's work that is interested in dramatic, camp moments of defiance wherein the violent hierarchy and status quo of animal oppression are directly challenged by individual acts of care that are depicted in highly dramatized emotional camp moments. It contends that within these caring moments emerge relationships that are built on a more-than-human kinship. Both novels re-work well-known narratives within Canada, the biblical Flood and war narratives, as a method of demonstrating the power of stories in shaping cultural knowledge. They are also both self-consciously underpinned with patriarchal violence. By bringing these novels together, this chapter demonstrates that Findley's work conveys a development on the type of representation seen in Marian Engel's novel, *Bear*. Findley's novels build on the self-conscious and critically engaged type of writing about animals that reconfigures particular narratives to introduce a pro-animal message that comments on the ways in which we might establish more empathetic and caring human-animal relationships imagined through reconfigured versions of narratives of nation. Finally, the chapter highlights the value in utilising an intersectional approach of queer theory and animal studies to demonstrate that both are dedicated to a radically anti-hegemonic way of thinking, subverting particular narratives and opening up the possibility for a pro-animal ethics to emerge.

Lastly, Chap. 6 examines settler engagements with Indigenous stories and characterisations through a lens of species relations in Gail Anderson-Dargatz's *The Cure for Death by Lightning* (1996). The chapter builds on the concept of care established in Chap. 5 and argues that Anderson-Dargatz's novel encourages a re-evaluation of the way in which we engage with non-human animals, introducing an eco-sexual framework that encourages empathy and kinship with all beings. It does so by focusing on the polarising depictions of settler and Indigenous (Shuswap) characters in the novel, and drawing on Indigenous theories of eco-sexuality outlined by Kim TallBear (Sisseton Wahpeton Oyate) and Melissa K. Nelson (Anishinaabe/Métis) to push for the centring of Indigenous knowledge in building more sustainable relations with animals. The chapter acknowledges that despite a concerted effort to engage with Shuswap stories and characters, the novel ultimately still centres the settler experience in its narrative, encapsulating and enacting a form of displacement in its very construction. By treading this fine line between an attempted serious engagement with Shuswap culture and questions of cultural appropriation, the novel self-consciously demonstrates that it is imperative that settler literature must engage with and destabilise the types of oppressive hierarchies that underpin both species and settler-Indigenous relations, namely settler-sexuality and anthropocentrism, if settler culture is to follow. What does emerge successfully from the novel, however, are depictions of meaningful and caring relationships with animals that encourage us to radically rethink the epistemological understanding through which we approach both literary animal representation and material animal engagement.

It is important to note that not all of the novels in this thesis engage directly with Indigeneity, but it is a recurrent presence in the majority of them. Holding these works together highlights the recurring tendency by settler writers during this period to code Indigeneity in proximity to animals, and moreover, to represent Indigeneity as a state that can be temporarily adopted to gain closer identification with animals. Indigenous characters are thus largely marginalised and underdeveloped in representation, utilised only when characters seek specific knowledge. There is a move away from this way of thinking in the later works in this book. Findley does not attempt to engage or represent Indigeneity in *Not Wanted on the Voyage*, instead focusing on a settler creation story and the types of oppressions that have underpinned narratives such as these, ultimately as a means of considering alternative ways through which to construct empathy and kinship with animals and to play around with the types of narratives that have underpinned contemporary settler Canadian conceptions of national identity. Anderson-Dargatz does the opposite, and frames her entire novel with an engagement with the Indigenous story of Coyote in order to demonstrate the gap in knowledge in relation to species relations that could be filled by engagement with Indigenous epistemologies as legitimate and valuable knowledge sources. Thus, by holding Indigeneity in site throughout, this book demonstrates that advocating for identity with animals in Canada in the 1960s and 1970s is not something that is innocently done. There is a larger dynamic of species and postcolonial politics at work that in a process of developing more critically self-conscious writing that presents a counter-narrative of nation.

The term Indigenous used throughout this book refers exclusively to the First Nation Peoples of Canada. The book also refers to the specific First Nation locality in discussion where possible. In addition, the terms settler and settler literature broadly refer to the non-Indigenous, English-speaking population of Canada, excluding, in this case, Quebecois literature. This book therefore does not address all Canadian literary history, but a specific brand of it: a particular settler one. It acknowledges that this is not the 'normative' nor the more important Canadian literary history, nor does it try to imply this through such a specific focus. The decision to focus exclusively on settler fiction was motivated by a process of researching primary materials in which specific trends and characteristics of animal representation emerged that were being used by English-speaking settler writers in their configurations of writing about animals, and how these were often intersected with identity issues, such as gender, sexuality and Indigenous-settler relations. The book focuses specifically on the identification and development of particular representational strategies across what will henceforth be referred to throughout as settler stories about animals across this period in the late twentieth-century. It will show itself to be a development of an interest in Canadian literature that works across questions of species, nation (as understood in a settler context), and personal identity.[28]

It is also important to outline that not all of the authors advocate for a pro-animal ethics. Rather, by holding these novels in comparison with one another and tracing the development of animal representation across them, it is evident that the style of writing adopted for the animal story became more critically engaged and so too did a pro-animal ethics begin to emerge.

Looking across the chapters, the book demonstrates that Canadian settler writers have manipulated and put to use the figurative aspect of animal writing to reflect upon specifically settler-Canadian anxieties and concerns, which then become increasingly diverse and unstable as the period develops. Writing about animals in Canada has not only been influenced by nature writer giants Seton and Roberts, but also by specific novels and authors such Farley Mowat and Margaret Atwood, whose seminal narratives on animals in Canada have garnered sustained cultural fame. As such, there is evidently a developing self-reflexivity within the novels that this book examines. The texts actively engage with and critique writing about animals in the construction of their own narratives about human-animal relationships.

The novels that appear in this study are, then, stories about writing stories about animals. They play a self-conscious role in the changing nature of writing about animals in contemporary Canada during this period into more critically engaged writing about animals that attempts to take animals seriously as agents in reciprocated interspecies relationships. Animal fiction in late twentieth-century Canada, then, saw a development of a pro-animal message that sought to imagine and focus specifically on human-animal relationships that are built upon reciprocity, empathy, and care, and that are not grounded in a hegemonic nationalistic symbolism.

Notes

1. Leyland Cecco, "Indigenous input helps save wayward grizzly bear from summary killing," The Guardian, Sunday 19 April 2020, accessed 10 May 2020, https://www.theguardian.com/environment/2020/apr/19/grizzly-bear-canada-indigenous-conservation-british-columbia. [Subsequent references from Willie taken from this source].

2. Ibid.
3. Unfortunately, ten days after Mali was relocated, he was shot and killed thirty km from where he had been released after he reportedly swam onto a small island and came across a resident and his dog. The resident reported that he shot Mali in self-defence. The three local First Nations subsequently organised a series of town halls aimed at educating residents on using bear spray and safely securing their garbage. As for Mali, it was reported in late April 2020 that his remains were to be returned to the Mamalilikulla First Nation and that, following a ceremony, he would be buried on their traditional territories. Despite this, ministers promised First Nation representatives that Mali's case marked a "new-collaborative" approach to wildlife management processes.
4. Nicole Shukin (2009) *Animal Capital: Rendering Life in Biopolitical Times* (Minneapolis: University of Minnesota Press), p. 3.
5. Shukin, *Animal Capital*, p. 4.
6. James Polk (1972) 'The Lives of the Hunted' in *Of Heavenly Hounds and Earthly Men. Spec. issue of Canadian Literature*, 53, 51–59, p. 58.
7. Margaret Atwood (2012) *Survival* (Toronto: House of Anansi Press Inc.) p. 75.
8. Atwood, *Survival*, p. 81. I acknowledge that there are other reasons for this Canadian interest in animals, which are beyond the scope of this book, such as has been argued in Harold Innis' *The Fur Trade in Canada: An Introduction to Canadian Economic History* (1927), which ties the killing of animals in the fur trade to Canadian nationhood.
9. John Sandlos (2000) 'From within Fur and Feathers: Animals in Canadian Literature', *TOPIA: Canadian Journal of Cultural Studies*, 4, 73–91, p. 74.
10. Sandlos, 'From within Fur and Feathers', p. 82.
11. Sandlos, 'From within Fur and Feathers', p. 81 and 75 respectively.
12. Sandlos, 'From within Fur and Feathers', p. 85.
13. M. F. Mohtadi (1980) *Man and His Environment: Proceedings of the Third International Banff Conference on Man and his Environment* (Exeter: Pergamon Press Ltd) p. 53.
14. Quotation taken from M. F. Mohtadi, *Man and His Environment: Proceedings of the Third International Banff Conference on Man and his Environment* (Exeter: Pergamon Press Ltd, 1980) p. xiii.
15. Tina Loo (2006) *States of Nature: Conserving Canada's Wildlife in the Twentieth Century* (Vancouver: UBC Press) p. 183.
16. Tina Loo, *States of Nature*, p. 183.
17. Janice Fiamengo (2007) *Other Selves: Animals in the Canadian Literary Imagination* (Ottawa: University of Ottawa Press) p. 2.

18. Susan McHugh (2011) *Animal Stories: Narrating Across Species Lines* (Minneapolis: University of Minnesota Press) p. 213.
19. Susan McHugh, *Animal Stories*, p. 213.
20. Karen Jones (2003) 'Never Cry Wolf: Science, Sentiment, and the Literary Rehabilitation of Canis Lupus', *The Canadian Historical Review*, 84.1, 65–93, p. 65.
21. Atwood, *Survival*, p. 23.
22. Marian Scholtmeijer (1993) *Animal Victims in Modern Fiction: From Sanctity to Sacrifice* (Toronto: University of Toronto Press) p. 85.
23. Susan McHugh (2011) *Animal Stories: Narrating Across Species Lines* (Minneapolis: University of Minnesota Press) p. 4.
24. Mario Ortiz Robles (2016) *Literature and Animal Studies* (Abingdon: Routledge) p. 19.
25. Mario Ortiz Robles, *Literature and Animal Studies*, p. 9 and 25 respectively.
26. Timothy C. Baker (2019) *Writing Animals: Language, Suffering, and Animality in Twenty-First-Century Fiction* (Culemborg: Palgrave Macmillan) p. 4.
27. Baker, *Writing Animals*, p. 204.
28. In addition to issues of scope, there were core methodological challenges in engaging with First Nation literature and Quebecois literature in terms of accessing primary materials here in the UK. Certain lines of interpretative enquiry were excluded from focus. In my PhD thesis from which this monograph was developed, I attached a list of novels in the bibliography by settler writers, both English-Canadian and French-Canadian, and by First Nation authors, that were published between 1960–2000 and use animal representation. This was to provide an extensive demonstration of the background research that went into the primary materials used in this research, and to demonstrate the trajectory that the thesis and this book could have taken if it had been possible to access all of these resources or if I had focused on another specific cross-section of literature. There are also core issues surrounding language barriers that underpin the study of Quebecois literature and my ability to search for primary materials that have been translated.

CHAPTER 2

Reconfiguring Animal Narratives in Farley Mowat's *Never Cry Wolf* (1963)

The figure of the wolf has continued to occupy the Canadian and wider global literary imagination, and never more so than following the publication of Farley Mowat's 1963 bestselling memoir, *Never Cry Wolf*. The memoir, which documents Mowat's time observing wolves in the remote region of Churchill, Manitoba, was praised for playing a significant role in altering Canadian public opinion in favour of the wolf by countering the widely held narrative that wolves are an inherent risk to wildlife populations because they kill for sport. In contrast to these popular understandings, Mowat's wolves were depicted as a humorous anthropomorphised family unit, killing only the weak members of caribou herds. Such was its success in challenging dominant wolf narratives, environmental Historian Tina Loo credits Mowat's writing as having brought about a cultural 'rehabilitation' of the wolf.[1] Similarly, Karen Jones emphasises the text's place within a larger discourse of animal rights, stating that '*Never Cry Wolf* participated in the birth of a new environmental revolution.'[2] However, despite the public interest in the wolf that the book is said to have generated, closer critical engagement with the text recalls Barry Lopez's belief that 'the truth is we know little about the wolf. What we a good deal more about is what we imagine the wolf to be.'[3]

In constructing a narrative based around attempting to find out the "truth" about wolf involvement in the decline of caribou populations, *Never Cry Wolf* demonstrates that cultural imaginations of wolves in Canada have

© The Author(s), under exclusive license to Springer Nature Switzerland AG 2023
A. Higgs, *Animal Fiction in Late Twentieth-Century Canada*, Palgrave Studies in Animals and Literature,
https://doi.org/10.1007/978-3-031-42612-4_2

frequently been entangled with and understood in relation to the idea of protecting caribou. Indeed where populations of caribou in North America have declined, the culling of wolves has typically increased.[4] This has certainly been the case in British Columbia, where in 2019 plans were announced to eradicate up to 80% of the wolf population, and where it has been reported that the government spent almost two million dollars on culling wolves living in the same habitat as ten herds of endangered southern mountain caribou during the winter of 2019–2020 alone.[5] Unsurprisingly, this approach to managing the alleged predatory impact of wolves has divided opinion amongst researchers, politicians, activists, and ordinary citizens, and as a consequence, has drawn much attention to the plight of the wolf. Such conflict was also captured both in the construction and in the reception of *Never Cry Wolf*, a now seminal piece of writing about human-wolf relationships in Canada, which tapped into the complex relationship between humans, wolves, and caribou in 1960s Canada. More than this, however, the text is an example of the way in which literary narratives about animals are often formed as a direct response to cultural perceptions of animals and the environmental policies that shape our interactions with them.

Never Cry Wolf is a memoir with a particular narrative intention: that is, to counter the perception of wolves as dangerous predators by engaging in a number of representational techniques employed to evoke specific emotive and empathetic responses to wolves that endear them to the reader. In formulating such strategic writing, however, Mowat does not undermine the former dominant narrative by allowing the wolf to respond through a neutral reporting of their observed ecological behaviours, but rather Mowat constructs a new, emotive, and equally contrived narrative of a genteel, anthropomorphic family unit that incorporates the wolf into a nationalistic and anthropocentric framework. There is an irony surrounding the memoir, therefore, in that the text is an aesthetic project aimed at debunking wolf narratives, but in actuality, it produces another and does so self-consciously.

Much of the praise given to the novel, such as that by Loo and Jones, situates the memoir within an environmental movement that was garnering attention in the 1960s. Indeed, Edward A. Parson states that in the 1960s there was a shift in the 'broad character of major environmental stresses in Canada.'[6] A number of new environmental organisations were established, including The National and Provincial Parks Association of Canada (1963), World Wildlife Fund Canada (1967), the Canadian arm of the Sierra Club (1970) and the Canadian Nature Federation (1971) (now Nature Canada). In addition, much of the new attention being given to the environment was attributed to literary interventions in popular culture. The most prominent of which was Rachael Carson's *Silent Spring* (1962), which has been credited as the *Uncle Tom's Cabin* of the environmental movement, as Michelle Mart states:

> Rachel Carson…deserves credit for being the godmother of the Environmental Protection Agency, the ban on DDT and other pesticides, Earth Day, the 1972 Federal Insecticide, Fungicide, and Rodenticide Act, and indeed of "Environmentalism" as a philosophy and political movement.[7]

Similarly, Katrin MacPhee argues that there was a 'transnational sea-change in the 1960s, often associated with Rachel Carson's publication *Silent Spring* of 1962.'[8] The interest that Carson's narrative curated amongst the public in environmental affairs not only evidences that the public in the 1960s were primed to receive narratives that expressed concern for the degradation of the environment and its non-human animal inhabitants, but that literature as a medium was well positioned to carry out these exposés.

Notably, *Never Cry Wolf* makes no direct references to broader environmental issues; the memoir's sole focus is to influence public opinion in favour of the wolf by exposing alleged fallacies within representations that have been perpetuated by specific organisations, such as the Canadian Government and within some scientific textbooks. As such, there is no textual evidence that *Never Cry Wolf consciously* participated in this environmentalist movement. However, due to the cultural prevalence of environmental issues in the 1960s, evidently the memoir was able to feed into this dialogue and be successful in motivating public opinion in favour of the wolf. *Never Cry Wolf*'s success as a best seller, then, is likely a product of this cultural shift in attitudes towards more welfare-based conversations about animals in the 1960s and 1970s.

Such is the memoir's cultural visibility that it has been and still is repeatedly drawn upon in discussions of wolf culling policy across North America. Garry Marvin states:

> As a result of its publication the Canadian Wildlife Service received mail from all over the world condemning its programmes of intense wolf culling and supporting the man who was seen as a champion of these wild creatures in the face of an unfeeling wildlife bureaucracy.[9]

Similarly, in 1988, *The Associated Press* televised a section titled 'Wolves, Up Close and Personal' on "National Geographic Explorer", in which it was stated that:

> Anyone who has read Farley Mowat's best-selling "Never Cry Wolf", or just seen the Disney film adaptation, already knows wolves are not the slathering, indiscriminate killers of lore, but highly intelligent creatures with a well-developed social structure.[10]

In addition, the 2017 publication of the *New York Observer* titled 'Fear and Misinformation Fuel Government Killings of Wolves' references Mowat's text by directly quoting from the memoir.[11] That the text has repeatedly been drawn upon in human-wolf conversations testifies to the memoir's legacy as a culturally visible piece of writing that blazed a trail between Canadian animal writing and a more literary strategic type of writing about animals.

Taking note of this backdrop of a burgeoning environmentalist movement in Canada, this chapter will explore *Never Cry Wolf*'s strategic effort to influence public opinion in favour of the wolf in the 1960s by using a number of narrative techniques that focus on directly confronting specific negative wolf tropes and endearing the reader to Mowat's arctic mission to uncover what he presents to be the "truth" about wolves. The chapter will demonstrate that by using a humorous retrospective critical tone and by focusing on the representation of a number of specific behaviours, including the family pack, hunting practices and the wolf gaze, *Never Cry Wolf* seeks to undermine the common historical narrative that wolves are insatiable hunters. He does so by presenting the reader with a clash between the wolf narratives he has read before entering Churchill and the reality that he describes upon encounter with real, material wolves, which is the discovery of the animals living a life of peaceful, anthropomorphic domesticity.

The chapter will also examine the way in which Mowat draws the wolf into a Canadian nationalistic framework by introducing the idea that the wolf, caribou populations, and the wider northern wilderness space, are under threat from encroaching US interests. Protection for the wolf, then, the memoir posits, is in Canadian interests, inciting a nationalistic call to arms to defend the species. Furthermore, in carrying out his observations of the wolves, Mowat exploits the knowledge of the Indigenous characters that he meets, utilising them as guides, but invalidating their epistemologies of wolf-human relations as a means of better understanding the wolves. He therefore consolidates his narrative into a specifically pro-wolf, settler-Canadian story, producing his own form of curated knowledge about wolves that he criticised government officials and scientists for doing. The chapter will ultimately demonstrate that *Never Cry Wolf* is a text that reconfigures one contrived anthropocentric narrative for another, serving only to further cement the wolf's vague position in the Canadian literary imagination, denying the wolf recognition as a being that has its own needs and demands, and giving life to both Mowat's anthropomorphised narrative and his career as a storyteller.

A New Wolf Story

Throughout *Never Cry Wolf*, Mowat reiterates that prior to encountering wolves in Churchill, his knowledge of the species had been gained exclusively through reading scientific textbooks, hearing stories of alleged first-hand encounters, reading contemporary literary depictions, and through various pieces of information disseminated by his employers, the Canadian Dominion Wildlife Service (CDWS). By clashing the knowledge that he has gained from these sources, which is that wolves are single-handedly depleting caribou populations due to their bloodthirsty nature, with his encounter with an anthropomorphic family-centred wolf pack, Mowat employs a retrospective commentary that offers an often hyperbolised and humorous critique of his former ignorance. Such a strategy encourages the reader to take the same quizzical perspective and to express the same incredulity at having similarly fallen foul to the previous knowledge now deemed to be false. The text thus works in a self-reflective mode that is designed to allow Mowat to be critical and shed doubt on public attitudes to wolves, working to debunk these former narratives.

The humorous critique that Mowat employs to undercut this former knowledge begins when Mowat explains that prior to landing in the wilderness his employers, the CDWS, used a militarised rhetoric to describe the wolf and encouraged a military-style approach to his mission in the arctic, placing Mowat and the wolves into a conflict underpinned by an anthropocentric framework: that of soldier and enemy. This approach, he explains, stems from the rabies epidemic in Canada in the 1940s and 1950s, from which emerged a story regarding a dangerous and infected wolf that has continued to haunt cultural conceptions of the species. In Churchill in 1946, Mowat states that an infected wolf was said to have wandered into the town and attacked an Army Corporal. As a consequence, militant measures were employed to deal with the animal:

> Squads of grim-faced men armed with rifles, carbines and spotlights were soon scouring the surrounding country intent on dealing with a menace which, in a matter of hours, had grown into several packs of starving wolves.[12]

The description of the wolf as a 'menace' is a continuation of the intent that has been historically and anthropomorphically ascribed to wolves, positioning them as consciously villainous. Moreover, this story demonstrates that the alleged behaviour of one wolf has accumulated such narrative significance as to be taken as indicative of all wolves, and thus as justification for violently culling them from the area. Understanding wolves through this lens of villainy demonstrates that which Marvin has argued is the wolf's place within a 'complex system of crime, vengeance and punishment', confined only to be understood within these frameworks, even when it is revealed to be inaccurate and a grandiose version of events.[13]

By referencing this story, then, Mowat demonstrates that particular narratives about wolves have surpassed an interest in understanding real wolf ecology because the stories that exist about them are more exciting. He humorously reveals that the 'pack of starving wolves' was in fact a single 'cocker spaniel belonging to the Hudson's Bay Company manager', but that 'to this day there are residents of Churchill... who will, at the drop of a hat, describe the invasion of Churchill by wolves in 1946.[14] The wolves in Churchill in particular, then, are part of a species politics that codes them in particular narrative ways to create excitement around the history of the space and the human-animal interactions that have occurred within it. Furthermore, by drawing upon this specific narrative of a semi-fictional historical incident Mowat introduces an intertextual element to his memoir, layering narrative upon narrative to demonstrate the way in which particular stories have historically shaped national human-animal relations and have gone unquestioned because they feed into wider systems that benefit from particular conceptions of the species. (It is in this context that Mowat later reveals the Canadian government are gaining financially from wolf bounties.) This intertextuality reinforces the notion that the stories that have been told about wolves have accumulated a cultural wealth that is no longer interested in understanding and taking wolves seriously as a species that has a vast array of ecological behaviours and desires. Keeping the wolf within this framework of being a threat to humans has superseded the real and contextual facts surrounding their existence and relationships with humans and permits the CDWS to continue to militarise their interactions with them.

In addition, by layering this intertextual narrative against his encounter narrative, Mowat not only reinforces the hysteria around wolf stories, but it also allows him to expose and undermine the rabies story specifically. Rabies is a disease that when contracted by an animal causes a slow death and is often characterised by significant behavioural changes, such as foaming at the mouth and an increase in aggressive instinct. Wolves were one of the many animals infected with the disease during this period.[15] However, despite such knowledge of Rabies symptoms during the 1960s, Mowat states that the behaviour of infected wolves during this epidemic was not recognised to be an effect of Rabies contraction, but was attributed to typical aggressive behaviour associated with wolves. He says, 'the human reaction to them [was] usually one of unbridled terror—not of the disease, for it [was] seldom recognised as rabies, but of the wolves themselves.' (184) The use of 'unbridled' here evidences an excessive hysteria and also reflects an innate human preference for domesticated and tamed animals, specifically referencing a human-made tool for controlling domestic horses. Thus, Mowat demonstrates that the position the wolf occupied in the Canadian cultural imagination during this period, as a dangerous predator, is so solidified that even infected wolves were vilified as acting consciously and intently on harming humans, regardless of the knowledge concerning rabies and behavioural change.

The memoir's engagement with these unfavourable constructed narratives of wolves allows Mowat to make known to the reader the knowledge that he too entered the arctic space with prior to his encounters with the wolves. This works to explain the predetermined state of vulnerability that he adopts upon landing in Churchill and further reinforces the tension undercutting the dual level of narrative embodied by the memoir form, as his critical voice works retrospectively against his former self to narrate a story that capitalises on the cultural fear that surrounds wolves. The tension and fear that the memoir at first presents is perpetuated by the purpose of Mowat's journey into the arctic being to encounter wolves. This, he is informed by his military Chief advisor, is to investigate the 'carnage being wreaked upon the deer population by hordes of wolves.' (15) At this point in the text, this type of narrative that positions the wolves as wholly responsible for declining deer populations is further figured as undisputed when Mowat is informed of the fate of his Chief's predecessor:

> "My predecessor supplied the Minister with an explanation of this situation in which it was his contention that there were fewer deer because the hunters had increased to the point where they outnumbered the deer about five to one. The Minister, in all good faith, read this fallacious statement in the House of Commons, and he was promptly shouted down by Members howling 'liar!' and 'wolf-lover!'"[16]

Ironically, the aggressive behaviour attributed to the wolves is here subverted and embodied by the Commons Members. All notions of human culpability are wholly rejected as 'fallacious' because they do not fit into the dominant understanding of wolves as insatiable hunters. This is also the first indication in the novel that the attempt to change public perceptions of wolves might be met with opposition, particularly by those in power. As such, Mowat begins to introduce the species politics that his writing will engage with, which is examining why particular narratives regarding wolves have been perpetuated and which aspects of wolf ecology these narratives have honed in on.

Mowat's engagement with these vast negative representations of wolves serves to validate his reflexive narrative that it is easy to be drawn into these wolf stories. By detailing his own investment in these misconceptions, followed by his enlightenment through encounter, Mowat employs a particular literary strategy that does not target and criticise the reader and society more broadly for holding these negative views of wolves, but positions his writing as educational in its revelation of an alternative image of wolf life. He describes reading from the scientific guide given to him by the Wildlife Service that '"the wolf is a savage, powerful killer. It is one of the most feared and hated animals known to man, and with excellent reason."' (60) He adds, 'the reason was not given, but it would have been superfluous in any case.' (60) His blind acceptance of the 'superfluous' need for a reason suggests a retrospective critique of his willingness to unquestionably accept such officially sanctioned discourse. The evident fear that Mowat holds of the wolves is further reiterated when we are given a detailed description of his arms collection, which reflects his own engagement in the militarised dialogue surrounding the wolf and his mission. Mowat notes that it contained:

Two rifles, a revolver complete with holster and cartridge belt, two shotguns, and a case of teargas grenades with which I was expected to persuade reluctant wolves to leave their dens so that they could be shot. There were two large smoke generators prominently labelled DANGER, to be used for signalling to aircraft in case I got lost—perhaps—in case the wolves closed in. A case of "wolf getters"—fiendish devices which fire a charge of potassium cyanide into the mouth of any animal which investigates them—completed my arsenal. (18)

This is an example of Mowat's use of a retrospective, playful tone that is both ironic and critical in its use of 'persuade' and 'fiendish'. He deliberately employs this tone to poke humour at the type of relationship he is being conditioned to pursue with the wolves: that he might seek their compliance in their own assassination. Moreover, the description of an excessive collection of arms demonstrates the extent to which violence towards non-human animals has been normalised within specific cultural narratives. However, his description of the wolf as 'reluctant' marks a move away from his reliance on his former knowledge, which justifies and normalises such violence, towards a humorous critical consideration of the ludicrous nature of the techniques he has been told to practice. As such, this use of humour works to more broadly call into question both the practices adopted by the wildlife services, and the narratives that have perpetuated this militarised framework.

Howling: The Signal for Danger?

In addition to directly addressing the information about wolves he has been exposed to prior to his arrival in Churchill, Mowat builds on the literary strategy of using a retrospective humorous critical voice by using it to address a number of key ecological features of wolf behaviour that have taken on particular cultural significance. The next sections of this chapter will focus on these features, specifically depictions of howling, the wolf gaze, and the wolf pack.

Howling has long haunted cultural understandings of wolves because it has often been understood to signal an impending attack. Mowat exploits this understanding to dramatize his first experience with howling in Churchill, in which he describes feeling sheer panic, abandoning his arsenal of weapons and hiding beneath an upturned canoe. Such a depiction builds narrative tension, appearing at first to validate the fear that this understanding perpetuates, but is then rapidly undercut by the reality of the situation and the humour that follows. Mowat describes hearing the 'unmistakeable... howling of a wolf pack in full cry' (41), estimating that an enormous pack of at least four hundred wolves were heading in his direction. He adds, 'I therefore decided I should retire underneath the upturned canoe, so that the presence of a human being would not be readily apparent, with its consequent tendency to induce atypical behaviour in the beasts.' (42) His reaction and his exaggerated prediction of four hundred wolves is an intentional use of comedy as a narrative strategy for retrospectively criticising his behaviour and beliefs at the time. This is reinforced when the source of the sound is then revealed not to be wolves at all, but to be an Inuit man named Mike and his sled dogs.[17] His reference to the impending animals as 'beasts' and to their 'atypical behaviour' not only indicates the type of narrative that Mowat's knowledge of wolves previously hinged on, but it also provides further humour when juxtaposed with the arrival of domesticated dogs.

By choosing to hide rather than find his ammunition, Mowat demonstrates both a literal and figurative disarmament by the rapid presence of the animals and it is significant that he hides underneath an artificially made object, retreating back into that which is familiar, but revealing its inadequacy in this environment, the frozen lake. Mowat thus strategically leverages the comic consequences of his own belief in the dominant narratives surrounding the wolf in order to undermine them, as simply hearing the sound of howling induced a level of panic so immediate that he could only think to hide. Mowat's position here, then, without the desire to use ammunition, seemingly without accurate knowledge, and without an escape route, demonstrates his vulnerability within this space and the comedy that his narrator-self sees retrospectively in his condition. However, more than this, such a narrativisation is a move by Mowat to demonstrate that rather than his vulnerability stemming from the dangerous presence of wolves, it is rather a product of his lack of knowledge regarding the arctic space and its inhabitants—wolf, human, or other. This encounter makes clear that the dangerous, vast and empty subarctic supposedly inhabited by bloodthirsty wolves is also a place inhabited by Indigenous people and domesticated animals, undermining its haunting and negative conceptualisation. Mowat makes plain that his prior knowledge does not hold up with experience in this space and by reflecting upon this with humour, Mowat primes the reader for the continued undermining of particular behavioural tropes throughout his memoir.

WHO IS WATCHING WHOM? THE WOLF GAZE

Building upon this anticlimactic encounter with Mike's dogs and Mowat's ignorance surrounding howling, Mowat draws upon another feature that has garnered significance in the cultural imagination of wolves: the transformative experience of meeting the eyes of an animal, commonly referred to as the animal "gaze".

Philip Armstrong emphasises the symbolic weight that has been culturally attached to the gaze of animals and argues that the wolf's gaze in particular has historically been one of the most discussed of any animal species. This reinforces the type of hyperbolic speech and discourse that has surrounded the wolf and that Mowat seeks to work within:

> Conceived as a current, flame, fire, stream of particles, or corporeal ray, eyesight was not just an active force in itself but also a vehicle for other physical effects: poisons, contagions, influences of various kinds. Moreover this visual flux seemed especially menacing because it was observably strongest in the gaze of humanity's most feared animal predators: wolves and big cats.[18]

The significance of the wolf gaze then, hinges upon their status as 'feared predators', reinforcing the layered narratives through which the wolf is continually conceptualised, and how these amalgamate and develop to produce further narratives about them. Moreover, Armstrong's addition that 'the power of the animal gaze, whether natural or supernatural, is answered down the barrel of a gun'[19] is poignant way of conceptualising the complexity in being met by the animal gaze and the narrative desire to interpret it—one is aware of being looked at by something with agency, yet the consequences or the intention behind this gaze are unknown. In essence, one is rendered entirely vulnerable by being met with this inexplicable gaze, or this absent-presence.

Drawing on the conceptual significance of this trope, then, Mowat depicts an agency within the wolf gaze that permits the animal to both literally, during his encounter, and figuratively, on a broader narrative level, respond to the cultural depictions that have vilified it. As a consequence, rather than removing the narrative surrounding the wolf gaze entirely, Mowat reconfigures it through subversion. Indulging in equivalent strategies of narrativisation, rather than rejecting previous storytelling techniques surrounding the wolf, allows Mowat to present a more positive and empathetic depiction of wolf behaviour that still continues to operate within a dominant framework for understanding wolves, familiar through its appeal to established cultural configurations.

The language that Mowat uses to describe the transformative nature of the wolf gaze lends itself to the same type of speech that underpinned both the Rabies story and his own initial fear, in that it continues to enshroud the wolf with a sense of mystery and elusiveness that few are privileged to encounter. In contrast, however, to the fear and danger that he is expected to experience, upon encounter Mowat describes becoming paralyzed by the wolf gaze in a positive way. He states that he found himself 'peering straight into the amber gaze of a fully grown arctic wolf' and adds that 'for some seconds neither of us moved but continued to stare hypnotically into one another's eyes'. (54) The 'hypnotic' nature of the animal's gaze depicts such a moment between Mowat and the wolf as significant and transformative, positioning the gaze as capable of inspiring a nuanced state of self-reflection and transformation. The spatial suspension caused by the gaze of the animal that Mowat describes is another element belonging to dominant discourse surrounding wolves: that which has become known as 'fascination'. Armstrong discusses the history of this trope, denoting the seventeenth century author Edward Topsell's belief that 'the gaze of wolves causes muteness in humans.'[20] Mowat reinforces the significance of this trope through his contemplation regarding what it is about being seen by the wolf that creates such unease, and what the consequences of this unease are. This is demonstrated in his later description of being observed by a family of wolves:

> I was becoming prey to a small but nagging doubt as to just who was watching whom. I felt that I, because of my specific superiority as a member of Homo Sapiens, together with my intensive technical training, was entitled to pride of place. The sneaking suspicion that this pride had been denied and that, in point of fact, I was the one who was under observation, had an unsettling effect upon my ego. (72)

Mowat's identification as 'superior' juxtaposes with his description of himself as 'becoming prey' to doubt. In this instance, his 'intensive technical training' and species membership are rendered inconsequential as a means of securing his 'pride of place'. This means that Mowat's self-reflection occurs through a new perception of himself as vulnerable—an 'unsettling' concept.

The depiction of vulnerability produced through the animal gaze, as seen in this moment, has been famously discussed in Jacques Derrida's *The Animal that Therefore I Am*, which was first given as a speech in 1997 and is continually referred to by animal studies scholars as the seminal text on this concept. Such an engagement with the concept of experiencing vulnerability by being looked at by the wolf in *Never Cry Wolf*, then, emphasises the role and value in telling stories about animals, as they are able to engage with and critique particular cultural narratives and theories belonging to dominant conversations of human-animal relations. Mowat enters the space with a fixed perception of his relationship with wolves as being held within a militarised framework. However, on being observed by the wolves and meeting their gaze, Mowat represents that his knowledge and sense of understanding is being transformed and disarmed, leaving him with a new feeling of vulnerability that begs a deeper ideological engagement with the animals in question.

Not only does *Never Cry Wolf* tap into dominant conversations in animal studies surrounding the animal gaze in this moment, but Mowat's conception of his own vulnerability and the way in which he came to recognise it as a being a product of his own ignorance regarding wolf behaviour, rather than being an object of their prey, is an inversion of the typical trajectory of human-animal vulnerability narratives. There is, therefore, a dualistic element to the way in which the memoir engages in specific narrative strategies of utilising tension and retrospective critique to undermine and reconfigure his knowledge of wolves by demonstrating the misplacement of this concept of vulnerability. Mowat states that his 'pride of place' had 'been denied' by the effect of the wolf gaze. His use of Freudian vocabulary to discuss the consequences of such denial ('unsettling' his 'ego') implies a sense of vulnerability that has fractured his masculine core identity. His inversion from the observer to the vulnerable observed exposes the instability of his ideals regarding the influence and importance given to membership of 'Homo Sapiens'. Here, within this 'northern' space and in the eyes of these wolves, such constructs are rendered obsolete. Rather, the wolf emerges as an active being, gaining, through its' gaze, recognition as a species that experiences the world in much the same way as human-animals do, and is not the violent and dangerous creature understood by Mowat's previous engagement with discourse on the animal.

Such a depiction is an early inversion of the kind of human-animal encounter-produced vulnerability seen in the work of Val Plumwood, who also discusses a moment of emotional transformation after an animal encounter, describing her experience of being attacked by a crocodile whilst canoeing in Kakadu national park, Australia, as involving the realisation that she was in fact 'prey'. Much like Mowat becoming aware of the fallacy of the dynamics of his preconceived relationship with the wolves, Plumwood describes her experience as a state of recognition, stating that 'for the first time, it came to me fully that I was prey.'[21] She notes that it was only upon becoming aware of her own vulnerability in the face of a large predator that she realised the 'view of ourselves as rational masters of a malleable nature' was simply a 'delusion.'[22] Thus, by 'being prey' Plumwood became aware of the false dichotomy between 'human' and 'animal' and of the fragility upon which 'human mastery' has been constructed. However, whereas Plumwood enters the space unaware that she is the prey of a crocodile and consequently discovers her own vulnerability through being attacked, Mowat enters the subarctic believing that he is prey to wolves, only to realise that men are the bigger threat. Mowat's vulnerability, then, is produced through a recognition that he is in fact wrong about the wolves and the only thing that he is at threat of becoming prey to is his own ignorance.

The wolves do not attack, but rather they observe him. It is through being observed by the wolf, and caught in the animal gaze that Mowat 'sees' the wolf for the first time, and he recognises the ability of the wolf to 'see' him. This destroys the literal and figurative distance between himself and the wolf (and the reader through his narrative), revealing an individual agent that challenges the depersonalised narratives its species have been confined within. What unifies Plumwood's and Mowat's experiences, then, is an acknowledgment of animal agency that had previously been denied through a perception of oneself in Plumwood's case as a 'human' superior' and in Mowat's case, through the narratives surrounding 'dangerous' wolves he had engaged with prior to his encounter. Thus, this moment is a deliberate engagement with a culturally rooted wolf tale: the gaze as transformative. By playing on this trope and presenting a scene that challenges dominant discourse, Mowat subverts the wolf trope from within; still playing into socially accepted knowledges of wolf characteristics—for example, that there is something unique about their gaze—but altering them to present a positive depiction of wolves that grants them a new narrative in favour of their character and reconfigures this concept of vulnerability as being a product of displaced knowledge rather than animal aggression.

Wolfish Anthropomorphism

By rupturing and reconfiguring wolf narratives by using this retrospective critical voice to comment on established tropes, Mowat invites the reader into a dynamic in which, through the doubts raised about their former knowledge, they remain open to the new knowledge that Mowat will put forth. Mowat then turns his attention and narrative strategy towards the construction of a new story regarding wolf behaviour that is employed to depict an overtly positive and empathetic image of the animals. This purpose of this narrativisation is to challenge one specific type of narrative that has framed wolves as dangerous, bloodthirsty hunters and to ask, who might benefit from depicting wolves in this way?

In order to endear his audience to the wolves and stir up feelings of empathy, Mowat focuses on his representation of the pack, depicting a nuclear family of wolves, playing with and raising their children. Marvin has said of Mowat's depiction that: 'in terms of the descriptions of the lives of wolves this was more an intensely anthropomorphic soap opera than an account of the social ecology of a wolf pack.'[23] Whilst there may be some weight in Marvin's statement regarding the accuracy of Mowat's representation, it is evident that Mowat employs a sentimental form of anthropomorphism because he is invested in challenging the former narratives surrounding the species and in implementing an alternative narrative that isn't necessarily ethnologically accurate, but is a strategy for convincing the reader that the wolf is worthy of moral consideration and protection. In addition to his use of anthropomorphism, Mowat's use of familial and domestic imagery is also framed by descriptions of a genteel and colonial nature. This places the wolves within a settler-colonial cultural understanding, and draws upon an idealisation of masculinity and Canadian colonial history, whilst simultaneously centring the family unit within this nationalistic imagery.

The pack consists of a mother and father, whom Mowat affectionately names George and Angeline, an uncle, named Albert, and three young pups. Notably, these names are English and French by source, which is a reflection of Mowat's humanisation of these wolves within a specifically Canadian settler cultural conception. He describes George as, 'the kind of father whose idealized image appears in many wistful books of human family reminiscences' (91) and moreover, he adds that 'he reminded me irresistibly of a Royal Gentleman for whom I worked as a simple soldier during the war.' (91) Mowat's reference to the wolf as a

'Royal Gentleman' under which he had previously served is likely a reference to George VI, thus bringing the wolves back into a militarised rhetoric but subverting it by using the military lexicon to represent the wolves in a positive and almost heroic, admirable way. Through this imagery, Mowat reconfigures the position of the wolves from the enemy into an ally and settler-colonial war hero that must be protected and not vilified.

In addition, by depicting George in this way Mowat deliberately invites the reader to familiarise themselves with George as a kind of 'father figure' and in doing so, he demonstrates that the kinds of familial relationships and the construction of gender roles present in human communities extend to wolves. The focus that he places on the representation of the family unit emphasises the playful nature of the wolves, and he does so by again using the memoir's form of double temporality to retrospectively criticise his ignorance regarding wolf behaviour. He states that prior to his encounters with the wolves he was 'still labouring under the delusion that complex communications among animals other than man did not exist.' (95) However, on one occasion when observing the unfamiliar behaviour of the adult wolves, he became concerned for Albert, wondering if he 'had somehow transgressed the wolfish code, and was he about to be made to pay for his transgressions with his blood? It looked that way.' (169) But when continuing to observe he realised that the animals appeared to have been enjoying themselves. He states that 'the three wolves separated, shook themselves, sniffed noses, wagged their tails hard, and trotted back to the den with every indication that a good time had been had by all.' (171) His choice of 'labouring' and 'delusion' to describe his commitment to his former knowledge reinforces the change in his opinions and affirms the secondary level of self-critique inherent in his narrative that encourages a similar critical engagement from the reader. The particular use of these words implies a criticism of those still committed to the type of knowledge that Mowat is undermining, indicating that they too are 'labouring' to consolidate an image of the wolf that is 'delusional' in its conception.

Building on this image of the wolf as an anthropomorphised genteel nationalistic war hero, Mowat turns the narrative towards counteracting the rhetoric surrounding the wolves' hunting practises in a radical move that positions them as an ecologically responsible species. This strategically draws the wolf further into the nationalist realm by implying that rather than decimating the Canadian wilderness, the wolf plays an integral role in maintaining it.

When observing the wolves hunting, Mowat describes that rather than stalking and attacking vast numbers of the deer, the wolves do not attack at all. Rather, he describes witnessing a technique in which they make sudden bursts of movement to frighten the caribou, and then, when the caribou move away, they appear to observe them and look for weaknesses in movement or pace that would make for an easier kill. Mowat's incredulity at this clash with his former understanding leads him to exclaim that 'the scene was all wrong.' (191) He adds:

> These were novel concepts to one who had been taught to believe that wolves were not only capable of catching almost anything but, actuated by an insatiable blood lust, would slaughter everything that came within their range. (200)

Mowat's use of 'novel concepts', 'taught to believe' and 'insatiable blood lust' are examples of his strategic use of retrospective critical voice applied throughout the memoir to convey an almost humorous ignorance surrounding his prior knowledge. There has been dispute amongst scientists, animal behaviourists, and literary authors regarding this idea that wolves only target the weakest members of herds. Barry Lopez argues that 'wolves do not just kill the old, the weak, and the injured. They also kill animals in the prime of health. And they don't always kill just what they need; they sometimes kill in excess.'[24] However, Marvin, writing in 2012, argues that 'wolf biologists seem to agree that, wherever possible, wolves target and then test potentially weak and vulnerable individuals as part of their strategy.'[25] The accuracy of Mowat's narrative, however, is not the focus of this chapter; it is to demonstrate the way in which narratives about animals are developed and maintained to suit particular human needs. Through this description of witnessing their hunting practices, then, Mowat not only undermines the notion that wolves kill vast numbers for pleasure, but Mowat is also able to carve a new story in which he depicts wolves as necessary and valuable protectors of the ecosystem through a representation of their hunting practices as involving carefully targeted attacks on weak herd members.

By combining these narratives of wolves as anthropomorphised family units and as both nationalistic and ecological heroes, Mowat rallies concern and empathy for the wolf, compounding in a newfound sense of desire to protect them. This allows Mowat to turn the narrative towards the question of who has been peddling the rhetoric of the wolves as dangerous hunters. This, controversially, he reveals, is the Canadian government.

Mowat informs the reader that the government are making considerable economic income through deer and wolf bounties. By revealing this after he has presented an alternative narrative to the reader, Mowat is able to strengthen his depiction of wolves by implying that the former narratives he is challenging have been perpetuated by a government that has a financial interest in upholding them. Furthermore, such a revelation demonstrates that wolf-human relationships in the region, and human-animal relations more broadly speaking, are commonly underpinned and influenced by a species politics that serves human interests. As Lisa Johnson argues, when confronting knowledge about animals, 'the important inquiry is not, what is true? Rather, the question is what are the politics of truth that allows truth claims to be made and authenticated?'[26] Mowat's memoir contends, then, that financial investment in the wolf has provided a purpose for perpetuating the stereotype of the wolf as dangerous and that this has been a strategy for demonising the wolf to provide a method of deflection from Governmental interests:

> Wherever men have engaged in the mindless slaughter of animals (including other men), they have often attempted to justify their acts by attributing the most vicious or revolting qualities to those they would destroy. (235)

This is a poignant moment of social commentary from Mowat, emphasised through his use of 'mindless' and addition of 'including other men', which serves to point out that the alleged brutality of wolves is an attribute that in actuality belongs to human culture.

In exposing this alleged government interest, Mowat returns to a nationalistic framework and attempts to appeal to nationalist sensibilities through the addition that the vast number of the hunters being permitted access to Churchill and engaging in the slaughter of wolves are from the United States. Mowat states that 'the tourist bureau of the Provincial Government concerned had decided that Barren Land caribou would make an irresistible bait with which to lure rich trophy hunters up from the United States.' (237) He adds that 'parties of sportsmen' were being flown into the subarctic space 'for a thousand dollars each', enticed by the promise of 'a first-rate set of caribou antlers'. (237) Thus, by suggesting that there is a threat to wildlife populations coming from the United States, Mowat introduces another element to his narrative: that of the threat of US expansion. Protecting the wolf, then, becomes synonymous in Mowat's narrative with protecting Canada. Brian Johnson argues that:

> Mowat's representations of the North as a neglected resource throughout the 1960s and 1970s remain intensely nationalist, even flagrantly imperialist, calling for a greater northern settlement to protect Canada's resources from American predation.[27]

The strategy employed in the memoir, then, is not only to focus on the reconfiguration of particular narrative traits, but in doing so replace the source of the threat from the dangerous wolf 'predator' to American 'predation'. This rapidly launches the wolf from the role of perpetrator to victim. It is important to note though, that by inciting a settler-nationalistic claim to the protection of the wolf, Mowat diminishes Indigenous land claims through an emphasis on the need for a stronger claim to wilderness spaces in Canada. Stephen Henighan has stated that 'the 1960s was also marked by a buoyant Canadian nationalism, which peaked with the celebration of the hundredth anniversary of Canadian nationhood at Expo 67 in Montreal.'[28] Such a context means that Mowat was able to indulge in his anthropomorphic depiction of wrongly accused wolves because of rising nationalist sensibilities and to incorporate the wolf into the Canadian imaginary as an important configuration of this Canadian settler identity, inevitably bringing with it a new set of politics to untangle.

The sentimental narrative that Mowat constructs is therefore self-consciously underpinned by an appeal to familiarity and to nationalism. He admits himself that scientific objectivity, as an approach does not allow for the subjective experience of individual wolves and their dynamic idiosyncrasies, stating that 'no matter how hard I tried to regard them with scientific objectivity, I could not resist the impact of their individual personalities.' (91) This individualisation of the wolves, and indeed the entire familiarisation with the wolf pack throughout the text, serves, according to Tina Loo:

> Only to underscore the wickedness of the poisoning campaign carried out against them and the corruption of humans who were so alienated from the natural world that they could orchestrate such a thing.[29]

Loo's reference to the 'poisoning campaign' works as a double entendre—the reputation of the wolf is being poisoned through objectifying discourse such as that seen in Mowat's textbook, but also the wolf is literally being poisoned by the government's culling programme.[30] Thus, Mowat's narrative operates at a dual level, on the one hand constructing a new representation of wolves that anthropomorphically emphasises particular characteristics of wolves that would elicit empathy and challenge former dominant understandings of them as violent and dangerous animals, but it also re-directs this violence towards the government, exposing them as responsible for violence against both wolves and caribou and exposing their economic interest in the region. Mowat's narrative becomes less about constructing a true representation of wolf ecology, then, but rather it is testament to the power of narrative and the way in which particular strategies of representation produce specific dynamics of species relations, and how these dynamics might be informed by contextual factors, such as nationalistic settler anxieties regarding land claims.

SETTLER STORIES AND INDIGENOUS ERASURE

Underneath *Never Cry Wolf's* attempt to close the figurative gap between humans and wolves is a narrative erasure of the Indigenous people who Mowat encounters in his memoir. Despite relying on his Indigenous guides, Mike and Ootek, to help him navigate the space and whom both willingly share their knowledge of wolves with him, Mowat frequently undermines their position as reputable knowledge sources by refusing to believe their claims about wolves until he either witnesses it for himself or he reads it in one of his own scientific textbooks. In addition, he repeatedly finds humour in the fear that the Indigenous characters' have of his presence in Churchill, failing to acknowledge the fear of displacement that underpins this.

Indeed Mowat's memoir gives little attention to the Indigenous-settler conflict that occurred in the region historically, informing his relationship with the Indigenous persons he encounters. Governmental policies, such as the introduction of animal bounties or 'conservationist' restrictions on the hunting of particular species have significantly limited the rights of First Nation Peoples to hunt, even in the contemporary era. This impacted not only Indigenous basic legal rights to their own lands (protected by treaties), but it impacted their ways-of-being in that they could no longer practice traditional methods of relating to the environment that they called home. Hunting was often a source of livelihood for many Indigenous Nations, but it was also a food resource. Daniel Heath Justice (Cherokee

Nation) summarises that 'through force, coercion, trickery, or other non-consensual means, Indigenous peoples lost lives, lands, and livelihoods as a result of non-Indigenous appropriations of lands and territories.'[31] In addition, Loo explains that this displacement specifically targeted Indigenous local knowledge:

> Wildlife conservation marginalized, dispossessed, and displaced rural people by imposing and legitimating one kind of relationship with nature over others, it was an instrument of colonization. But conservation was not just a way of managing the marginal, disciplining them to use resources properly: it was also an attack on local knowledge.[32]

Historically, Indigenous populations hunted animal species sustainably, in part because they had their own environmental knowledge systems in place that emphasised concepts such as stewardship and kinship. The decision to place restrictions upon the hunting practices of the Indigenous Nations across North America under the guise of conservation was, then, transparently and systemically violent. It was evident that the economic and social erasure of Indigenous Nations and knowledge in constructing environmental policy and practises ensured that settler interests remained privileged and protected, and in doing so, Native communities continued to suffer depredation and displacement.

Mowat does refer to the disenfranchisement of the First Nation people after discovering the carcasses of 'twenty-three' caribou that had been slaughtered by gunfire from an overhead plane. He states that:

> The Cree who accompanied me had observed this sequence of events for himself the previous winter while acting as a guide. He did not like it; but he knew enough of the status of the Indian in the white man's world to realise he might as well keep his indignation to himself. (239)

It is evident from this account that these events have been occurring for a significant period of time, unnoticed by those who do not inhabit or visit the land. By noting that his guide has been forced to keep his 'indignation to himself' Mowat acknowledges his colonial cynicism and cultural silencing. It does appear that, through his documentation of this indignation, Mowat is being critical of the settler-Indigenous colonial power dynamic by repeating the guide's awareness of the 'white man's world' and thereby highlighting the systemic oppression of Indigenous peoples, however, this aspect of his critical tone within the memoir remains largely underdeveloped. Rather than then giving further attention to this vein of enquiry, Mowat positions the guide, and Indigenous identity more broadly, as being so in proximity to non-human animals that Indigenous cultures become unfortunate casualties in the destructive management of the environment and its non-human animal inhabitants.

The depiction of Indigenous people as 'closer' to nature is a frequent stereotype employed by settler cultures. Johnson explains:

> Confronted by an indigeneity that is desired but out of reach, the settler-invader produces compensatory narratives of indigenization founded on the production of stereotypes that associate the indigene with nature and the land.[33]

This trope is a strategy of erasure. It permits the blending of the Native character into the background and forces them into a constructed binary of nature/culture and Indigenous/settler, dismissing them as legitimate sources of knowledge by rendering them as wholly symbolic figures. As is the case in Mowat's memoir, Indigenous people were often employed to operate as guides for settler explorers or tourists in the more remote wilderness areas of North America and were expected to share their knowledge of the region, but were not consulted by authorities when making environmental management decisions. As such, Mowat's depiction of his interactions with Indigenous characters read as little more than a literary device intended to validate the claims that he makes in the text by providing his narrative with a 'Native authenticity' that is desired by settler subjects in narratives about the environment.

Such characterisation of the Indigenous characters exposes an irony in Mowat's own narrative. He is critical of the blind acceptance of the knowledge regarding wolves that has been disseminated throughout Canadian settler culture and that has demonised wolves. However, he simultaneously denies credence to Indigenous knowledge and ways of relating, and privileges his own education despite his reliance on such knowledge to survive on his expedition. This is evident in his treatment of Ootek and the alternative understanding of wolves that he offers Mowat. Ootek tells Mowat that he has a particular interest in wolves because 'his personal totem, or helping spirit, was Amarok, the Wolf Being.' (119) Ootek's familial and thus intimate relationship with the animal presents a striking alternative epistemological understanding of human-animal relationships to that represented by Mowat. Heath Justice confirms that it is integral to 'keep in mind that Indigenous traditions generally don't limit the category of *person* solely to the *human*' and that 'multiplicity is inherent in kinship; good relations require acknowledgement and, importantly, mindful accommodation of difference'.[34] Indigenous relations with the more-than-human world, then, are integrated into a practise of kinship, wherein humans have a duty to form good relations with all beings, without drawing lines between species. To relate to the wolf through a spiritual and familial lineage is to remove anthropocentric boundaries and move beyond dominant settler understandings of animals. Such boundaries, this chapter has demonstrated, motivated prior representations and stories of wolves within settler scientific discourse and have subsequently influenced government culling policy.

Ootek's attempt to draw Mowat into the knowledge of Indigenous kinship and to explain his relationship with wolves falls on deaf ears. This is confirmed when he later tells Mowat a story from Inuit folklore, detailing the intricate relationship between wolves and caribou, and the way in which the wolves keep the caribou strong through the process of natural selection, again affirming this context of interrelations between species. Mowat is sceptical of this tale, stating that:

> Although I had already been disabused of the truth of a good many scientifically established beliefs about wolves by my own recent experiences, I could hardly believe that the all-powerful and intelligent wolf would limit his predation on the caribou herd to culling the sick and the infirm. (126)

Mowat's response works on multiple levels. He accepts that his encounters have undermined previous knowledge that he once held regarding wolves, but he is reluctant to accept Ootek's tale because it does not fit into settler epistemologies of knowledge production. As Thomas King states:

> Among the many things that Europeans had to deal with upon their arrival in the North American wilderness were Live Indians. Live Indians, from an Old World point of view, where an intriguing, perplexing, and annoying part of life in the New World.[35]

Part of the humour Mowat attempts to construct in his narrative is his navigation of these encounters with Indigenous characters who present vastly different relations with the wolves than his own framework of understanding can comprehend. By seemingly affirming the dichotomy between Indigenous knowledge and westernised scientific knowledge, Mowat undermines the validity of Ootek by presenting his stories as little more than entertaining anecdotes that Mowat can only legitimise through his own observations. This is evident when Ootek informs Mowat that wolves have been known to adopt the orphaned pups of another deceased wolf. This Mowat says, is a 'touching story' but not one to which he could give 'due credence'. (147) It is only later when Mowat hears this same discourse from another source, that of a 'white naturalist of such repute' that he 'could hardly doubt his word.' (147) Such blatant hierarchisation of knowledge sources demonstrates that the perpetuation of the narrative of wolves as aggressive and cunning hunters serves not only to justify a systemic power dynamic between humans and wolves, privileging the human, but it is also colonially motivated. This colonial species politics serves to perpetuate and consolidate the authority of the Canadian settler government and the settler population as the only reputable sources of knowledge, whilst disregarding, exploiting, and harming Indigenous and non-human animal populations for economic and political benefit.

The text itself, then, *Never Cry Wolf*, capitalises on this dynamic, utilising Indigeneity and Indigenous characters as fictional strategies for gaining proximity to animals and for gaining knowledge about particular animal species. This is, according to Margaret Atwood, a trope that appears commonly in Canadian literature:

> This use of the Indian—as a mediator between the whites and a Nature which is life-giving rather than death-dealing—is paralleled by attempts to find in Indian legends mythological material which would function for Canadian writers much as the Greek myths and the Bible long functioned for Europeans.[36]

Ootek and Mike are, for Mowat, characters that form part of his literary strategy, anchoring his narrative in specifically Canadian sources that appear to legitimise his experiences. However, this is used to establish the framework of a settler-centred narrative and not give any real credence to the Indigenous persons as legitimate sources of knowledge about wolves. Rather, Ootek and Mike are depicted as sources of 'mystical' entertainment, providing Mowat with what he sees merely as humorous and unbelievable anecdotal stories about relationships with wolves.

Never Cry Wolf: A Culturally Visible Text

Despite the memoir's disregard of Indigenous characters and knowledge, dominant criticism of the text concerns its alleged move away from scientific objectivity towards the use of anthropomorphism to make claims about wolf ecology. However, it is by daring to challenge previous understanding of wolves in his depiction of his anthropomorphised wolf family that *Never Cry Wolf* became a culturally famous text, credited by many as radically repositioning the wolf in the Canadian cultural imagination.

Tina Loo demonstrates this cultural infamy in her documentation of a number of letters that were sent to the Canadian Wildlife Service after the text's publication. The content of the letters varies, from those complaining about the "wasted" use of their tax money on "unnecessary" environmental policies, to those expressing outrage and confessing their support for the wolf. One such example is a particularly tragicomic letter from a small child named Shawn:

> My name is Shawn. I love wolfs. I want to like you but I cannot because I saw one of you kill a wolf. Are you listening I hope so. You can stop killing them I know you can for me! So stop. Love, Shawn.[37]

It is evident that *Never Cry Wolf* appealed emotionally to public empathy, evoking a strong reception in favour of the wolf, and that such reception demonstrates, as Marvin denotes, that when writing about animals 'scientific ideas can never fully be separated from cultural ones.'[38] So strong was *Never Cry Wolf*'s appeal to culture through what appeared to be scientific observation but that was in fact sentimental anthropomorphic writing, the memoir has taken on a cultural value of its own, popularised and fetishized as a canonical source of knowledge about wolves.

However, despite such apparent pro-wolf momentum, it is difficult to find evidence of any specific wolf policy changes in the Canadian parliamentary records immediately after the text's publication that make reference to or that can be attributed directly to the text. There is, though, a general consensus across contemporary Canadian (and more broadly North American) environmental criticism, such as in the work of Loo and Jones, and visible in the publication of so-called "controversial" environmental texts, such as *Silent Spring*, that the 1960s and 1970s saw a cultural move in attitudes away from support for culling towards environmental conservation. *Never Cry Wolf*, Loo argues, was a significant factor in aiding in this change:

Three years after *Never Cry Wolf* was published, British Columbia reorganized its Department of Recreation and Conservation. After nearly sixty years, the government got out of the "game" business, replacing its "Fish and Game" division with one responsible for the Province's "Fish and Wildlife". According to the man who headed it, this small semantic change altered more than the branch's letterhead, and the explanation for it was rooted in the same shift in attitude that had made Farley Mowat's book a best-seller.[39]

Whilst policy may have not immediately changed, then, it is significant that the attitudes of both the public and a minority of those in power during this period did. The move away from "game" to an emphasis on "wildlife" in British Columbia marks a shift away from animals as objects worth monetary value towards an acknowledgement of their subjectivity, and towards conservation rather than domination. This indicated grassroots beginnings of a new conservationist framework that would go on to develop further in the 1970s when the government eventually set up its own environmental agencies, rather than simply supporting private organisations.[40] Understanding *Never Cry Wolf*'s place in the Canadian literary canon, then, is to acknowledge that it is irrevocably tied to a sense of North American environmental pride that flowered in the 1960s.

Conclusion: A New Kind of Story about Animals

It is evident that *Never Cry Wolf* is credited with having an instrumental role in shaping conceptions of wolves both during and post the 1960s era in an almost culturally fetishistic kind of way. Much like its literary predecessor, Seton's *Lobo, the King of Currumpaw*, in 1983, the memoir was also adapted into a film of the memoir's same name by Disney and directed by Carroll Ballard. Garnering much greater success than the adaptation of Seton's story, it grossed over $27 million at the box-office and received an Academy Award nomination. Undoubtedly, therefore, the memoir gained a cultural reputation that has continued to hold, cementing its place as a culturally visible piece of Canadian writing about animals that demonstrates that particular strategies of narrativisation (namely anthropomorphism) can mobilise perspectives of animals and the consequent relations that humans construct with them.

Mowat's use of a narrative that appeals to cultural sentiment through the anthropomorphic wolf family shares a consistency with the work of

Mowat's Canadian animal story predecessors, Seton and Roberts, but it also marks a move away from their work through its retrospective, critical memoir form and also through its positive cultural reception. Evidently, public outcry outweighed criticism of the memoir's accuracy, as a new level of concern was garnered for wolves that had not existed previously. *Never Cry Wolf*, through both its narrative strategy of depicting humanised wolves worthy of empathy and its timing, tapped into a growing concern for the environment in North America and successfully broke away from the critical confines of the 'nature fakers' argument. In doing so, the core of the memoir remains ironic: on the one hand, it is an aesthetic project aimed at debunking wolf narratives, but on the other, it simply produces another and does so self-consciously, consolidating the wolf's position within an anthropocentric cultural and fictional framework.

Notes

1. Tina Loo (2006) *States of Nature: Conserving Canada's Wildlife in the Twentieth Century* (Vancouver: UBC Press) p. 173.
2. Karen Jones (2003), 'Never Cry Wolf: Science, Sentiment, and the Literary Rehabilitation of Canis Lupus', *The Canadian Historical Review*, 84.1, 65–93, p. 86.
3. Barry Lopez (1979) *Of Wolves and Men* (New York: Simon & Schuster; Rev Ed edition) p. 3.
4. As of March 2022, all subspecies of caribou now appear on the Canadian 'List of Wildlife Species at Risk', ranging in categories from 'threatened' to 'endangered https://species-registry.canada.ca/index-en.html#/species?sortBy=commonNameSort&sortDirection=asc&pageSize=10&keywords=caribou [Accessed 3.3.2022].
5. https://vancouversun.com/news/local-news/b-c-predator-cull-would-target-80-per-cent-of-wolves-in-caribou-recovery-areas and https://thenarwhal.ca/bc-caribou-habitat-fossil-fuel-subsidies/ [Accessed 12.1.2022].
6. Edward A. Parson (2000) 'Environmental Trends and Environmental Governance in Canada' in *Canadian Public Policy / Analyse de Politiques*. 26, 123–143, p. 124.
7. Michelle Mart (2009) 'Rhetoric and Response: The Cultural Impact of Rachel Carson's Silent Spring' in *Left History*, 14:2, 31–57, p. 31.
8. Katrin MacPhee (2014) Canadian Working-Class Environmentalism, 1965–1985' in *Labour / Le Travail*, fall: 74, 123–149, p. 128.
9. Garry Marvin (2012) *Wolf* (London: Reaktion Books Ltd) p. 146.
10. Katherine Baker (1988) *The Associated Press*, December 13, Entertainment Byline PM cycle.

11. Michael Sainnago and Chelsea Skojec (2017) *The New York Observer*, Byline, January 5.
12. Farley Mowat (1963) *Never Cry Wolf* (New York City: Back Bay Books/ Little, Brown and Company) p. 184. [All subsequent quotations are taken from this edition].
13. Marvin, *Wolf*, p. 89.
14. It has proven difficult to find any historical record of this event other than Mowat's reference.
15. George Colpitts (2017) 'Howl: The 1952–56 Rabies Crisis and the Creation of the Urban Wild at Banff', in *Animal Metropolis: Histories of Human-Animal Relations in Urban Canada*, ed. by Joanna Dean, Darcy Ingram and Christabelle Sethna (Calgary: University of Calgary Press) pp. 219–253, p. 219.
16. I cannot find record of this discussion happening in Canadian Parliament despite searching through archives from 1950–1970. I have found one record of the discussion of wolves and predator control in the House of Commons in 1950, raised by a Mr Adamson, which appears to be in line with the anti-wolf Parliamentary mentality depicted by Mowat in the 1960s. Mr Adamson describes wolves as 'ferocious killer[s]' and states that 'more destruction is caused to wildlife by protecting the predators than has ever been caused by even the greatest extent of hunting by man'. He asks that wardens be allowed to shoot wolves or indeed any predators (such as Grizzly bears). The item concludes 'item agreed'. This is in 'House of Commons Debates', 21st Parliament, 2nd Session, Volume 3, p.1016 http://parl.canadiana.ca/view/oop.debates_HOC2102_03/1016?r=0&s=1 [Accessed 15 November 2017]. Mowat, *Never Cry Wolf*, p. 15.
17. Mowat refers to Mike throughout *Never Cry Wolf* as an Eskimo. The name Eskimo was given by non-Inuit people and is considered derogatory in its conception. It is said to mean "eater of raw meat". The Alaska Native Language Centre notes that the people of Canada prefer the term Inuit, which means "people". I have therefore chosen to use the word Inuit when discussing Mike. Source: https://www.uaf.edu/anlc/resources/inuit-eskimo/ [Accessed 28 March 2017].
18. Philip Armstrong (2011) 'The Gaze Called Animal' in *Theorizing Animals: Re-thinking Humanimal Relations*, ed. by Nik Taylor and Tania Signal (Leiden: Brill) pp. 176–199, p. 181.
19. Armstrong, 'The Gaze Called Animal', p. 185.
20. Armstrong, 'The Gaze Called Animal', p. 181.
21. Val Plumwood (1995) 'Human Vulnerability and the Experience of Being Prey', *Quadrant*, 39.3, 29–34, p. 30.
22. Plumwood, 'Human Vulnerability and the Experience of Being Prey', p. 34.
23. Armstrong, 'The Gaze Called Animal', p. 145.

24. Barry Lopez (1979) *Of Wolves and Men* (New York: Simon & Schuster; Rev Ed edition) p. 4.
25. Armstrong, 'The Gaze Called Animal', p. 27.
26. Lisa Johnson (2012) *Power, Knowledge, Animals* (Basingstoke: Palgrave Macmillan) p. 21.
27. Brian Johnson (2009) 'Viking Graves Revisited: Pre-Colonial Primitivism in Farley Mowat's Northern Gothic' in Unsettled Remains: *Canadian Literature and the Postcolonial Gothic*, Ed by Cynthia Sugars and Gerry Turcotte (Waterloo: Wilfred Laurier University Press) 23–50, p. 28.
28. Stephen Heninghan (2002) *When Words Deny the World: The Reshaping of Canadian Writing* (Erin: The Porcupine's Quill) p. 34.
29. Loo, *States of Nature*, p. 174.
30. Mass poisoning has historically been a popular form of culling in North America (and elsewhere) through the dispersion of chemicals such as Strychnine across vast areas, which are then ingested by the animals. This strategy is still in use. Sources: http://westernwildlife.org/gray-wolf-outreach-project/biology-behavior-4/ [Accessed 6 November 2017] https://www.raincoast.org/2015/01/alberta-wolf-slaughter/ [Accessed 30 November 2017].
31. Daniel Heath Justice (2018) *Why Indigenous Literatures Matter* (Waterloo, Ontario: Wilfred Laurier University Press) p. 11.
32. Loo, *States of Nature*, pp. 49–50.
33. Johnson, 'Viking Graves Revisited', p. 26.
34. Daniel Heath Justice, *Why Indigenous Literatures Matter*, p. 37 and p. 38.
35. Thomas King (2012) *The Inconvenient Indian: A Curious Account of Native People in North America* (Minneapolis: University of Minnesota Press) p. 59.
36. Margaret Atwood (2012) *Survival: A Thematic Guide to Canadian Literature* (Toronto: House of Anansi Press Inc) p. 110.
37. Loo, *States of Nature*, p. 176.
38. Marvin, *Wolf*, p. 34.
39. Loo, *States of Nature*, p. 210.
40. Source: Tina Loo, *States of Nature*, p. 210.

CHAPTER 3

Trauma on Display: Women's Wilderness Writing and Animal Ciphers in Margaret Atwood's *Surfacing* (1972) and *Life Before Man* (1979)

In 1986 Heather Murray wrote, 'wilderness in Canada is where you make it, or where you imagine it to be. It is not a place, but a category.'[1] For women writers in Canada, Murray argues, this category is often a 'pseudo-wilderness': a space that might only exist as an imaginative possibility or a site that is only to be visited briefly. Within these pseudo-wildernesses the female narrative is fraught with a double-voice, in that by entering the typically masculinised space of the wilderness, the women are both pioneering and resisting; they are 'the muted and the dominant.'[2] In Margaret Atwood's 1972 novel *Surfacing*, the protagonist returns to the place where she grew up in rural French Canada to search for her father who has gone missing. As she spends more time in the wilderness space of her childhood, she confronts past trauma, including the trauma of an abortion she was forced to have by a previous partner, disconnecting her emotionally from her friends and partner who have journeyed with her and pushing her further into the wilderness space. Similarly, *Life Before Man* (1797) follows three characters: married couple Nate and Elizabeth, and Lesje, Elizabeth's colleague at the Royal Ontario Museum and Nate's lover. Like the narrator of *Surfacing*, Lesje seeks refuge from the stress of being involved in domestic affairs in the realm of the non-human, indulging in

© The Author(s), under exclusive license to Springer Nature
Switzerland AG 2023
A. Higgs, *Animal Fiction in Late Twentieth-Century Canada*,
Palgrave Studies in Animals and Literature,
https://doi.org/10.1007/978-3-031-42612-4_3

imaginative fantasies of the museum displays coming to life around her and submerging her in a "life before man".

This chapter will utilise Murray's conception of pseudo-wildernesses in Canadian women's writing as a context for exploring *Surfacing* (1972) and *Life Before Man* (1797). It will demonstrate that there is a representational logic that underpins both novels in which the female protagonists enter pseudo-wildernesses—a log cabin by a lake in *Surfacing* and the Royal Ontario Museum in *Life Before Man*—and attempt to identify with the non-human animals they encounter as a means of escaping the stresses of their intimate relationships. Existence within these spaces is not sustainable, however; they are merely 'pseudo-spaces' from which the protagonists must ultimately emerge. Consequently, ethical identification with non-human animals cannot fully be realised within these spaces, as it must be abandoned in order to return to human society and to patriarchal order.

In 1972, Atwood wrote in her seminal text on Canadian fiction, *Survival*, that a distinctively recognisable feature of Canadian writing is the presence of 'animal victims.' These animals, she argued, symbolise a deep-rooted Canadian psyche of vulnerability, produced by a settler-colonial mentality that feared displacement by US expansion and reflected growing environmental concern:

> Canadians themselves feel threatened and nearly-extinct as a nation, and suffer also from life-denying experience as individuals—the culture threatens the "animal" within them—and that their identification with animals is the expression of a deep-seated cultural fear. The animals, as Seton says, are us. And for the Canadian animal, bare survival is the main aim in life, failure as an individual is inevitable, and extinction as a species is a distinct possibility.[3]

Atwood is, then, invested in a similar representational use of animals to that of Mowat, utilising them symbolically to reflect specifically Canadian/human anxieties. However, she does not subscribe to the technique of anthropomorphism that underpins Mowat's story-telling. Rather, the animals in *Surfacing* and *Life Before Man* are utilised as fictional tools to evoke human subjective contemplation of this sense of victimhood and are not endowed with elaborate narratives of their own. To demonstrate this, this chapter will focus on moments within the novels in which dead animal bodies are put on display, such as in cruel acts of violence by hunters in *Surfacing*, and the exhibition spaces and workrooms of the museum in

Life Before Man. These moments expose the normalisation of violence towards non-human animals and the way in which the female protagonists temporarily identify with the animals through a shared sense of victimhood that they identify as stemming from male violence.

Adam Dodd, Karen A. Rader and Liv Emma Thorsen write that 'real animals have become inseparable from a variety of human modes and practices of display: museums, illustrated books, even the internet' and that 'these animals become ironically visible only through occupying multiple and contradictory cultural and temporal spaces.'[4] The kinds of interactions that occur within these spaces are often the only interactions that some humans have with non-human animals, making them key spaces for animal visibility and human-animal interactions. As Dodd, Rader and Thorsen state, 'it becomes evident that what is ultimately presented are representations of animals as they really are for the producers of the representations themselves', meaning that the way in which animals are represented, both textually and in temporal spaces like museums, is anthropocentrically constructed.[5] Thus, as Samuel J. M. M. Alberti argues: 'to understand the afterlives of animals, we therefore address here their consumption as well as their production.'[6] Atwood's novels engage with this relationship between producing and consuming animals in practises including hunting, fishing, and taxidermy displays. In the novels, the production of animal bodies for display enables the animal to continue being consumed in its afterlife by the human observers in a way that is motivated by a recognition of their own victimhood and unhappiness within their own relationships. The animals thus provide an imaginative escape for the protagonists, acting as ciphers for indulging in fantasies outside of human society but never being fully realised as individuals themselves.

Although the bodies of dead animals litter both of Atwood's novels, there is a change between the way in which these dead animals and the relationships formed with them by the human characters are figured. This development is one that moves the scope of representation from the popular, local scale in *Surfacing* to a national scale in *Life Before Man*. *Surfacing* depicts particular representational strategies that focus on establishing the right to hunt and own Indigenous land, such as the killing and displaying of a heron by a group of hunters, a family of taxidermy moose put on display outside a hunting post shop and a desire to immerse oneself in the wilderness in a problematic process of 'Indigenising'. In *Life Before Man* however, this use, display and engagement with animal bodies is elevated to an institutional level: the museum space. In this space, animal bodies are employed alongside educational material, escalating and intellectualising the use of animal bodies as a means of contextualising a particular human history (a settler one). Both of these spaces are sites that are fraught with colonial history, forcing the protagonists to reflect upon their own sense of Canadian identity and their relationship to Canadian land through engagement with the non-human body.

Violence, Displacement and Patriarchal Objectivity in *Surfacing*

Janice Fiamengo says of *Surfacing* that the novel engages with complicating the concept of nationalism, stating that 'the narrative some critics have made of *Surfacing* reveals a nostalgia for an idealized 1960s Canadian nationalism' but determining that 'what Atwood's novel reveals, on the contrary, is that such a position never existed'.[7] The narrative that she identifies instead is one that Diana Brydon shares, that 'the fundamental repression in *Surfacing* may well not be the abortion but "genocide of First Nations peoples,"' determining the novel as an exploration into the narrator's confrontation with and acceptance of her complicity in colonial violence through her settler status.[8] In contrast, Robert McKay focuses on the novel's engagement with animal suffering, arguing that the narrator carries out an 'identification with the animal on the level of the body' in an attempt to reject human society.[9] McKay argues that such identification fails because the narrator must return to human society and abandons her 'bodily connection' to animals, determining that 'the exclusion of the animal, as a figure of the "inhuman", is constitutive of the human community.'[10] Whereas McKay recognises this identification with animals as situated in the body and in a search for the maternal, this chapter will argue that the narrator in *Surfacing's* attempt to reject the human society that she has recognised as her oppressor is also fraught with colonial connotations. In confronting violence against the non-human animal, the narrator is forced to accept Canadian complicity in a system of violence that she determined to be American.[11] Thus, by bringing together Brydon and McKay's criticism, this analysis of *Surfacing* will demonstrate that reading along the intersection of colonial history and ethical identification with non-human animals reconstitutes the narrator's conception of her own victimhood as a distinctly Canadian characteristic into an imagined state that she desires as a means of grieving her feelings of displacement in the pseudo-wilderness of her childhood home.

The narrator's ethical identification with the non-human hinges on her disconnection from human society as a result of feeling displaced within the childhood space that she nostalgically idealises. This first materialises when she is on the journey back into the wilderness in which she grew up and she finds that it is no longer the untouched, idyllic, and peaceful location she remembers. It is now overrun with commercial businesses and is a popular spot for tourists and hunting enthusiasts. Many scholars have traced a relationship between hunting and masculinity, also noting its common framing by colonial legacies. Karen Jones states: 'contours of masculinity, conquest, and renewal shaped the hunting experience and, in turn, the environmental history of the West.'[12] This convoluted dynamic is still evident in *Surfacing*, signified through the display of three anthropomorphised moose statues outside of a shop at which the narrator and her party stop. The statues are described as 'a father moose with a trench-coat and pipe in his mouth, a mother moose in a print dress and flowered hat and a little boy moose in short pants, a striped jersey and a baseball cap, waving an American flag'.[13] The presence of the American flag signifies on a surface level that the shop's intended purpose is as a stopping post for American tourists visiting the area for hunting holidays. However, to the narrator it signifies a growing encroachment of American interests in her Canadian space, and a commercial encouragement of this.

The anthropomorphic nature of the statues incites hunters into the store by conveying a friendly, comedic, and whimsical representation of moose that plays on a conventional mode of representing animals as "willing to be slaughtered." These moose statues greet the same humans that will later go on to kill real members of the species that they represent, operating as dead-yet-living representations of living-but-soon-to-be-dead real animals, and signifiers of ecological domination. The narrator's engagement with this reality means that the idealised conception she holds of the space as a peaceful refuge from the violence of the city, and as the place she associates with an innocent childhood, is punctured by her unfamiliarity with the space, her confrontation with the violence of the large-scale commercial hunting that now operates in the area, and the inevitable deaths of its non-human inhabitants.

The emotional difficulty *Surfacing*'s narrator experiences when confronted with the violence that has overtaken her childhood town pervades her interactions with the male characters in the novel, including in her close personal relationships. David and her partner Joe begin a film project at the lake-house in which they film scenes of the narrator and Anna in their swimwear, and then later invasively films the innards of a dying animal. Their footage is underpinned by an objectifying male gaze that aligns the women and the animal through a shared sense of objectification, one that recalls Carol J Adam's statement that 'women and animals are similarly positioned in a patriarchal world as objects rather than subjects.'[14] Through the construction of this footage, then, the narrator enforces the trope of vulnerability that Atwood defined as stereotypical to Canadian writing in *Survival* by representing this vulnerability as gendered.

Joe and David direct Anna to remove her bikini and ignore her protests, telling her to '"look sexy now, move it; give us a little dance"' (130) to which the narrator notices that 'Anna stood for a moment, brown-red with yellow fur and white markings like underwear, glaring at them.' (130) Anna is exposed, dehumanised, and likened to a frightened animal through the description of her skin and body hair as her 'fur'; the animal imagery both highlighting and enhancing the sense of vulnerability the film is capturing and simultaneously producing. The focus the film has on exposed bodies is further demonstrated in their later filming of a dead fish. They 'solemnly film the fish innards, collapsed bladders and tubes and soft ropes, rearranging them between takes for better angles.' (63) This invasive image, denoting 'innards' and 'ropes' being re-arranged to suit the male gaze demonstrates their nonchalance towards the bodies of their subjects. Much like Anna, the fish is subjected to visual (and in this case physical) exploitation and objectification for the purpose of male entertainment. Such behaviour evokes a specific traumatic memory for the narrator of the dehumanisation she felt when having an abortion:

> You might as well be a dead pig, your legs are up in a metal frame, they bend over you, technicians, mechanics, butchers, students clumsy or sniggering practising on your body, they take the baby out with a fork like a pickle out of a pickle jar. (74)

The narrator's description reads akin to a vivisection scene, describing herself as a 'dead pig' and noting that the doctors were 'practising on [her] body'. Moreover, a sinister tone is set through the uncomfortably blasé description of the 'baby' being removed 'with a fork like a pickle out of a pickle jar', again dehumanising the narrator and mirroring the bodily re-arrangement demonstrated earlier by David and Joe. By referring to herself as a jar she implies that she has been left empty after having her contents removed, reinforcing further the emotional trauma of this experience. The powerlessness that she felt is evidenced when she states that they 'tie your hands down' and that 'they don't want you to understand', which introduces an abusive power dynamic to the memory that is heightened further through her continual reference to the medical professionals as 'they', homogenising and refuting any familiarity with them. Finally, her rule of three list—'technicians, mechanics, butchers'—reinforces again her feelings of dehumanisation under their care, each word escalating the level of separation and brutality, suggesting that she felt like an object for repair or a non-human body about to be sliced up for consumption, much like the fish.

The narrator's identification with an animal and use of imagery akin to a pig in the slaughterhouse taps into a particular strategy of conceptualising her objectification. Evidently, the narrator feels her human status should spare her of such treatment, but empathy and autonomy are denied to her because she is a woman. By conceptualising her suffering through an animalistic lens the narrator evidently recognises a common experience of violence, however, such a comparison is motivated by a desire to conceptualise her trauma and propel her subjective transformation away from human society and patriarchy towards an affiliation with nature. Such identification allows Atwood to shed a light on the workings of patriarchy by centring the female perspective in a new type of Canadian wilderness pioneer story that narrativises resistance to violence and a desire to overcome anxieties of displacement.

Visualising Victimhood in Hunting Displays

The narrator's descent into a rejection of patriarchy and embracing of her own victimhood culminates in a climactic encounter with a dead heron that has been killed and hung up by a group of male hunters. The display of the heron, strung up in an exhibition of conquest enables it to be read as a continuation of the colonial practice of hunting for masculine pursuit (frequently referred to as trophy hunting). However, the function of the heron is that it serves not only as a physical sacrifice at the hands of the hunters, but it is also sacrificed narratively. The heron's death and displayed dead body marks a turning point in the novel in which the narrator is triggered into a new level of subjective contemplation of herself as a victim. She thus decides to run away to the woods in a literal and figurative rejection of a society that enables such violence. Whilst this suggests that empathy for the animal is conveyed, ultimately, the animal body is configured as a literary device for the narrator's emotional journey, and the novel lacks real and sustained engagement with the heron as a subjective victim that places its own demands back onto the narrator.

McKay pinpoints the discovery of the dead heron as the most significant moment in the development of the text's animal ethics. His analysis focuses on the bodily response of the narrator to such an encounter, reinforcing the narrator's attempted connection to the non-human through a rejection of language and search for the maternal. However, the pro-animal turn in the novel is neither consistent nor developed, and it collapses before the possibility of ethical politics can be produced seriously. Rather, what emerges from this encounter is a recognition that the same violence that harmed the heron is that which the narrator feels is harming her: it is a conceptual embodiment of her own suffering:

> It was behind me, I smelled it before I saw it; then I heard the flies. The smell was like decaying fish. I turned around and it was hanging upside down by a thin blue nylon rope tied round its feet and looped over a tree branch, its wings fallen open. It looked at me with its mashed eye. (109)

The sensory descriptions force an uncomfortably intimate and invasive engagement with the scene's gruesome nature. The heron has been manipulated into a position that deliberately marks the intention of the hunters to dominate and deny the animal the freedom of movement that marks its own species' idiosyncrasy. Its large wings are no longer spread by the liberated movement of flight but hang loose and spread open by its side, its legs bound by rope. The distortion of the heron's agency is reinforced by the narrator's statement 'it looked at me'. This is reminiscent of Farley Mowat's transformative encounter with the wolf gaze, but it is subverted and rendered tragic because this transformation occurs upon encounter with a dead animal, offering a different type of communication through its 'mashed' gaze.

Although the narrator acknowledges a system of violence that enabled this treatment of the heron, she is unable to accept Canadian complicity within this system:

> Why had they strung it up like a lynch victim, why didn't they just throw it away like the trash? To prove they could do it, they had the power to kill.

Otherwise it was valueless: beautiful from a distance but it couldn't be tamed or cooked or trained to talk, the only relation they could have to a thing like that was to destroy it. Food, slave or corpse, limited choices; horned and fanged heads sawed off and mounted on the billiard room wall, stuffed fish, trophies. It must have been the Americans. (110–111)

That 'relation' to the heron can only be met through 'destroying' it is an emotive critique of hunting, the same activity which now governs the primary human-animal relations in the area. The narrator's sarcastic addition of 'limited choices' followed by her reference to the many forms in which animal bodies are turned into ornaments further evidences the narrator's understanding of the heron's death being the result of a system that normalises violence to the extent that it is a form of entertainment that can be repeatedly re-enjoyed through the memorialisation of the animal's death in display. Notably though, the narrator's conclusion that those responsible must be "American" works to destabilise the sense of enlightenment that McKay and Aguila-Way give to the narrator. The narrator denies Canadian complicity within these systems of violence by believing this system of violence to be an exclusively US ideology, something that also ignorantly bleeds into her conception of anti-blackness and slavery in this passage. The narrator's recognition of the violence against the heron is therefore situated in an anthropocentric and inaccurate nationalistic anxiety about protecting the Canadian environment from foreign (American) material and ideological expansion, when in reality, these systems of violence are also inherently Canadian.

Fictionalising Canadian Complicity in Violence Against Non-Human Animals

The binary that the narrator creates between America and Canada allows her to take comfort in what she perceives as her own "Canadian innocence" in a system of violence. Her dislike for a group of hunters that she encounters is made apparent when one asks her which part of America she is from. She takes offence at this presumption, and tells him she is Canadian, to which she notes that 'his face lit up, he'd seen a real native.' (122) Her use of the word 'native' is not only an indication of her own delusion regarding her relationship to the space, but it is undercut by the humorous revelation that the hunter is himself from Toronto. Whilst the narrator presumed his apparent happiness was because they were unlike, it was in fact spurred by a sense of familiarity and recognition. The narrator states: 'I was furious with them, they'd disguised themselves', (122) exposing her own embarrassment at having made this mistake, but also indicating the emotional vulnerability that is produced as a result of no longer being able to take comfort in the binaries of American-Canadian, violent-non-violent, and perpetrator-victim that she has constructed. She is forced to confront normalised violence as a Canadian issue, and to contend with the reality that her perception of herself as a victim is in fact an imagined, and even desired, state.

Atwood acknowledges this in *Survival*, stating that although the trope of being a victim pervades Canadian literature, it is not necessarily a reality but more a cultivated perception. She states that 'perhaps our condition is that of "exploited victim," but by now our *real* condition may be "those who *need* to be exploited victims."'[15] In this context, the empathy that the narrator expressed towards the heron, recognising in it her shared experience of victimhood at the hands of American men encroaching on the space she calls home, collapses, and is replaced by the narrator's contemplation of her Canadian identity in this new context. Ruptured from her identification as a victim, the narrator's nationalism is complicated; what does Canadian identity look like if, rather than being defined by victimhood, it is underpinned by a continuing history of violence?

Notably, Atwood stated in *Survival* that Canadian literature's focus on '"where is here?" has been replaced by "who are we?"'[16] Similarly, Dennis Lee, to whom Atwood dedicated *Survival*, argues that settler Canadian identity hinges on the problem of being 'not-yet-Canadian' and a language 'drenched with our non-belonging'.[17] He emphatically states, 'try to speak the words of your home and you will discover—if you are a colonial—that you do not know them.'[18] This sense of conflict over national identity, then, is inherently tied to settler colonialism and a desire to belong. This is certainly true for the late 1960s and early 1970s, in which there was a notable tension in Indigenous-settler relations following the election of Pierre Trudeau in 1968 and the introduction of *The White Paper* in 1969 by the Minister of Indian and Northern Affairs, Jean Chrétien. This paper proposed to end the legal relationship between Indigenous persons and the Canadian state by dismantling the Indian Act and eliminating *Indian* as a distinct legal status. This was met with strong opposition from Indigenous leaders and communities across the country and a new era of Indigenous political organisation emerged.

In 1969, Cree writer and activist Harold Cardinal published *The Unjust Society*. This landmark book was written as a direct response to *The White*

Paper and called for radical change in Indigenous rights, education, and policy, satirically noting that the MacDonald-Chrétien 'doctrine' could be interpreted as "the only good Indian is a non-Indian".[19] In addition, Cardinal pointed out the irony in Canadian public empathy directed towards the US and the horrors of the Vietnam War when a blind eye was being turned to the 'cultural genocide' being committed in their own country:

> We do question how sincere or how deep such concern may be when Canadians ignore the plight of the Indian or Métis or Eskimo in their own country. There is little knowledge of native circumstances in Canada and even less interest. To the native one fact is apparent—the average Canadian does not give a damn.[20]

This vocalisation of Indigenous-settler tension and the desire to challenge the government's White Paper culminated in The Indian Association of Alberta's production of *The Red Paper*, formally known as *Citizens Plus*. Under the leadership of Cardinal and supported by the National Indian Brotherhood, the Red Paper was presented to Pierre Trudeau and Cabinet members in a momentous confrontation on Parliament Hill. Tension and fear emanating from the US, therefore, became less of a Canadian concern in this period when it was evident that there were internal disputes happening within Canada itself, fragmenting the idealised nationalistic image spewed by PM Trudeau and his liberal supporters.

Considering this context, *Surfacing* engages with the cultural tension of the early 1970s by toying with the concept of Canadian ignorance and self-realised constructions of victimhood. The narrator's mistake is reflective of a common tendency in settler Canada to look to place blame and criticism elsewhere, when in reality self-criticism and reflection are crucial if the settler population of Canada are to come to terms with their own sense of self and of national identity in a postcolonial society fraught with its own conflicts. Turning this back to Atwood's Canadian victimhood complex, such a confrontation with the violence that underpins settler society arguably holds the propensity for radically destabilising contemporary understandings of Canadian identity. Moreover, if settler Canadians are no longer the victims but in fact benefit from their perpetrator ancestors, how does that change how they relate to animals?

Indigeneity, Animality and Proximity to the Land

Atwood's narrator holds fast to the need to identify as a victim. Once her binary understanding of American/Canadian, man/woman, perpetrator/victim is shattered, rather than dismantling this oppositional way of thinking and coming to terms with an identity that is not anchored in victimhood, the narrator seeks to resituate her victimhood in a different binary. In the novel's climax, she rejects human settler society by choosing to hide in the wilderness in a problematic process of 'Indigenising' to reassert her attachment to the land and render herself innocent of complicity in the violence that operates within the space. She therefore constructs a new binary that pushes away from the concepts of settler/human/culture/men towards Indigenous/non-human/nature/women because they allow her to avoid complicity in Canadian settler colonial violence.

The connection that the narrator makes between Indigeneity and proximity to nature and animals is one that has long flourished in Canada. Fenn Stewart explains that there is a historical perception amongst the settler population that 'the "Indian" is said to exist in a "state of nature", not fully human, incapable of law, unburdened by property ownership or other rights', and so settlers have attempted to adopt an 'Imaginary Indian' status to replicate this 'state' and claim the land as their own.[21] This is also a concept that Atwood herself has theorised in her work as 'Grey Owl syndrome', denoting a 'white Canadian desire' to achieve 'Indian' status and thereby claim a spiritual and ancestral relationship with the land.[22] 'Grey Owl syndrome', was coined after the famously fraudulent conservationist Archibald Belaney, who adopted a false Indigenous identity, naming himself Grey Owl, in the belief that this would legitimise and/or authenticate his work and message. Archibald worked closely with the Canadian National Park organisations and publicly documented his adoption of a family of beavers. His relationship with the beavers provided the Canadian public with a new perspective of an animal that had once played a significant part in the history of the country as a popular pelt: the beaver was now an affectionate and charismatic pet. Tina Loo denotes that 'just as the beaver had to become human to be saved, Grey Owl argued that humans had to become Aboriginal in order to be conservationists.'[23] Archibald's relationship with the beavers, then, projected a connection between Indigeneity and the ability to form meaningful human-animal relationships, and it reflected a wider context of settler anxiety surrounding displacement:

Grey Owl's significance also reflects what Indigenous cultures and literary theorists have identified as the ambivalent settler desire to achieve "cultural fusion [through] violent appropriation"—to embody and to "destroy [the land-scape's] original inhabitants."²⁴

It is this move towards 'embodying' that Atwood's narrator, fearing her own displacement in a space that she no longer recognises, engages in.

Complicating the narrator's sense of displacement, however, is the English and French territorial dispute that was growing in tension in the 1960s and 70s. She states:

> My country, sold or drowned, a reservoir; the people were sold along with the land and the animals, a bargain sale, solde. Les soldes they called them, sellouts, the flood would depend on who got elected, not here but somewhere else.' (126)

The narrator switches between French and English, whilst simultaneously conveying her sense of displacement through her lamentation of 'my country.' She utilises biblical-style flood imagery to suggest that the outcome of an impending election could be catastrophic for certain demographics of Canadians living in this area. Notably, 1960s Quebec saw what is known as the Quiet Revolution, a period of significant change in Quebec in which there was a fight for greater control over the region's economic resources and their distribution. In the 1970s the Parti Québécois was elected, who advocated for Quebec's Independence and so began a decided move to redefine francophone society and consider Quebec's place in Canada.²⁵ Such a reference by Atwood's narrator therefore evidences the narrator's grandiose feelings of displacement and makes clear her perception of the changing nature of her home space to be akin to a tale of destruction and genocide. In attempting to come to terms with her status as a displaced person, forced from the space by both hunters and Anglo-French settler territorial disputes, the narrator retreats from human society, away from her peers, and into the woods in an attempt to position herself as a displaced Native figure; a 'role' that allows her to identify as a victim of settler culture and of territorial development whilst simultaneously reclaiming an imagined relationship to the land.

In light of the fracture of her conception of Canadian identity through being confronted with the Canadian nationality of the hunters, the narrator conceptualises a broad understanding of Indigeneity as an identity that is not underpinned by violence or the suppression of violent histories, stating that 'the Indians did not own salvation but they had once known where it lived and their signs marked the sacred places, the places where you could learn the truth.' (139) It is evident that she associates the homogenous figure of the 'Indian' or Indigenous culture more broadly with sources of authentic connection to nature, or 'truthful' and 'sacred' relations to the land. She therefore positions Indigeneity as an identity that can be adopted for resisting 'culture' and reasserting her relationship to the space.

This is most evidently reinforced in the scene in which she returns to society, enacted by a problematic fantasy of herself as a Native experiencing their first encounter with a settler. She performs her own imaginative conception of re-entering the world afresh, drawing upon the biblical flood myth she previously referenced. Noting that Joe is looking for her, she states, 'what's important is that he's here, a mediator, an ambassador, offering me something: captivity in any of its forms, a new freedom?' (186) The oxymoronic link she creates between 'captivity' and a 'new freedom' demonstrates the fragmented and irrational nature of the narrator's conscience, but reaffirms the comfort she finds in structure, society, and routine. For her, the notion of being looked after by this 'ambassador' in a 'captive' space brings with it the possibility of a new start. This romanticised and insensitive idealisation of an Indigenous-Settler first encounter overlooks the reality of the genocide brought by the arrival of the Europeans for the First Nations People of the Americas by suggesting it brought a favourable new beginning for them, but it permits the narrator a means through which to re-enter her former 'human' life. This serves to reaffirm the failure of the narrator to understand the history of the space that she is in, the foundations of her identity as a settler, and her failure to put into practice the sympathy and rejection of violence she previously recognised through her encounters with non-human animal victims. Such a return to the human community requires an abandonment of the ethical identification with non-human animals because Atwood makes such a union between the two impossible. This is reinforced by the final line of the novel, 'the lake is quiet, the trees surround me, asking and giving nothing.' (186) Whereas previous identification with the non-human through a rejection of the human brought a sense of communication, such as being seen in the eyes of the heron, now that she has made her choice to return to Joe and the human, settler society that he represents, the trees and lake remain silent, refusing to engage.

Surfacing, then, encapsulates the depth and complexity of the conflict of identities occurring in Canada during the 1970s. In addition, the novel conceptualises female trauma through the narrator's recognition of her own oppression and experience of violence at the hands of men. This subjective transformation, first into a recognition of such violence and then an attempt to overcome this violence, is brought about through a recognition of suffering in animals at the hands of men and then is rejected through a process of Indigenisation and embracing of the nonhuman, perceived as a binary to oppressive settler culture. Atwood's novel demonstrates a use of both animals and Indigeneity as symbolic fictional devices that are utilised to construct, define, and detail settler anxieties and feelings of displacement, whilst also being used as a means through which the female experience of trauma can be imagined and represented. The animals remain static devices of Atwood's understanding of Canadian cultural imagination, objects of temporary ethical engagement, but ultimately overlooked and confined to this anthropocentric representation as ciphers of human victimisation.

THE PSEUDO-WILDERNESS OF THE MUSEUM IN *LIFE BEFORE MAN*

Similar to its literary predecessor *Surfacing*, there is a significant dearth of criticism written on *Life Before Man*. Much of what there is has focused its attention on the scientific strands of the novel and its engagement with ideas of extinction. Little attention has been paid, therefore, to the nonhuman animals in the novel or to the colonial and environmental politics that underpin the museum setting. In the late 1990s Marilyn French argued that *Life Before Man*'s publication during a culture of increasing environmental concern in the 1970s and its engagement with the Palaeolithic world offers the perspective that 'humans are a mere dot on the graph of time: we may become extinct, our stories frozen like fossils; we may only be the beginning.'[26] This configuration of science and narrative is similarly picked up on by Fiona Tolan, who, writing from a more contemporary perspective in 2007, argues that through the character of Lesje, a young Canadian-Ukrainian Palaeontologist, the novel begins to confront the conflict between Feminism and science that was plaguing gender conversations during this period:

> *Life Before Man* touches upon issues that feminism was beginning to encounter, but would only take up much later. Its recognition of the masculine rationalism implicit in science connects this novel to many of the issues

raised in Atwood's earlier works, and suggests that they are not as far removed as might be first thought.[27]

Tolan explores the application of various scientific theories within the novel, such as Darwinism, and argues that Atwood's novel pre-empted a period of later discussion in Feminist conversation surrounding gender roles and biological determinist theories. Carol L. Beran however, approaches the novel through a more localised, domestic lens, and emphasises instead that the vast intertexts in the novel 'define the cultural context each of the three main characters absorbed in childhood that influences their vision of reality.'[28]

Noting this gap in the literary criticism on this novel, therefore, the second half of this chapter will focus on *Life Before Man*'s engagement with human-animal relations by focusing on the museum setting of the novel and how it functions in a similar way to the setting of *Surfacing*—as a pseudo-wilderness that the female protagonists enter temporarily in an attempt to imaginatively escape into the realm of the non-human. Such a comparison of these settings, moving from the popular and local scale of vacationers and hunters in *Surfacing* to the national scale of a physical bricks and mortar institution in *Life Before Man* opens up conversations around settler institutions and species relations more broadly, demonstrating that dead animal bodies can be used to convey narratives of national history through their arrangement in museums.

In *Life Before Man*, the human characters' imaginative indulgences in the display rooms, bringing the dinosaurs to life in mythic fantasies, permits them an escape from their domestic stresses. For Lesje in particular, the museum space allows her to construct her own connection to Canadian identity, shedding her Ukrainian identity and sense of alienation by anchoring herself to a site of Canadian history and forming imagined relationships with the iconographies of extinct Canadian beings that litter the museum walls. The museum operates on a dual level, then, in that, in it, particular narratives are constructed by displaying both human and non-human animal bodies in particularised ways, and new narratives are constructed by the observer in their engagement with such displays. As occurs in *Surfacing*, the non-human animals in *Life Before Man* remain confined to the realm of the symbolic—hunted and displayed in both the real wilderness and in the museum's artificial representation of the wilderness—and the women return to their relationships.

Socially Politicised Spaces of Interaction with Animal Bodies

Alberti writes that 'for those beasts destined to become museum specimens, biological death is only one moment, one narrative hinge of many.'[29] For the non-human animals that litter museums their biological lives may have ended when they died, but their museum and display lives begin and continue to be re-cycled and re-narrativised in contemporary displays. To enable such precise construction, the private workrooms of museums hold stocks of deconstructed non-human animal bodies, skin, and bones. *Life Before Man* contains numerous engagements with the museum's private construction rooms, which are notably coded as androcentric spaces that nurture masculinity and female bodily objectification. In contrast, the public exhibition spaces are coded as liberating subjective spaces in which protagonists can imaginatively escape the narratives of their everyday lives and submerge themselves within a fictional wilderness and narrative represented and brought to life by the bodies on display.

The novel's representation of the spaces in which the physical manipulation of animal bodies occurs links male violence to the destruction and display of animals in a similar logic to that of *Surfacing*:

> They have a freezer full of dead carcasses, camels, moose, bats, and when they're ready to assemble the skeleton they strip most of the meat off and put the bones into the Bug Room, where carnivorous insects eat the shreds of flesh remaining. The Bug Room smells of rotting meat. Outside the door, several pictures of naked women are Scotch-taped to filing cabinets. The technicians in that department work to rock and country music from the radio.[30]

Lesje's description of the atmosphere within the laboratory depicts the space as like a butcher's shop, detailing the violent processes through which the non-human bodies are dismembered and stored. There is a distinct focus on descriptors related to death and decay in terms such as 'carcasses', 'skeleton', 'flesh', 'shred' and 'rotting meat', the latter additionally inciting an uncomfortable visceral engagement with the space. This creates a sense of irony given that it is in this space that specimens are constructed for display to represent a living mammal, but the design process itself is fraught with violence and underpinned by death. In addition, the work process is set against a backdrop of 'pictures of naked women' and 'rock and country music', reflecting the androcentric nature of the space and its workers.

The insidious nature of this scene is not the blatant critique of the objectification of women's bodies by Atwood, but her depiction of this objectification as being woven into the environment in which these men are working. Second Wave feminist Andrea Dworkin wrote in 1980:

> The power of sex is ultimately defined as the power of conquest' and that 'the power of sex, in male terms, is also funeral. Death permeates it. The male erotic trinity—sex, violence, and death—reigns supreme.[31]

Life Before Man appears contemporaneous with this argument, particularly given the 1970s feminist ideological context, and it is certainly possible to read this scene through this lens: the stripping and re-constructing of non-human bodies stems from the same masculine desire for 'conquest' that enjoys and produces the manipulation of human female bodies in pornography. Similarly to *Surfacing*, then, both non-human and women's bodies are consumed as objects for visual objectification through a process of male domination that denies them autonomy and subjectivity. However, in contrast to the blatant feelings of unease that appear in *Surfacing* when Anna is forced to remove her clothes for David's video, Lesje appears de-sensitised in her nonchalant description of the work room because the misogynistic framework in *Life Before Man* embeds misogyny and objectification subtly into the very frameworks of the everyday working environment. Furthermore, in the knowledge that these laboratories are the spaces in which specimens are kept private before being manipulated and prepared for display, the presence of the pornographic posters indicates towards a grassroots patriarchal system that underpins the very fabric of the museum and the displays curated.

It is unsurprising that Lesje finds comfort and refuge in the public display galleries, amongst the finished specimens and away from the objectifying masculinity of the laboratories. Her imaginative interactions with the display pieces temporarily give the non-human bodies a subjective narrative of her choosing that restores that which was literally and figuratively stripped from them in the private work rooms. Lesje undergoes much trauma and stress throughout the novel; her ex-partner William rapes her, and she is burdened with the responsibility of being a stepmother rapidly after beginning an affair with Nate, despite being largely uncomfortable with the thought of motherhood. Thus, by imagining that the non-human animals come to life around her, Lesje is able to mentally escape from the reality of her trauma and to fantasize about existing within another world, absent of men and the need to navigate domestic relationships.

The display rooms operate through Lesje's interactions as spaces that distinctly contrast with the laboratory spaces in the novel, resulting in a dichotomy that is spatialised as public/private, dependent entirely on the nature of the interaction with, and the relationship between, the non-human body and the human observer:

> Looking up at the immense skulls towering above her in the dim light, the gigantic spines and claws, she almost expects these creatures of hers to reach down their fingers in friendly greeting. Though if they were really alive they'd run away or tear her apart. Bears, however, dance to music; so do snakes. What if she were to press the buttons on the filmstrips and, instead of the usual speeches or the cries of walruses and seals used to simulate the underwater voices of the marine reptiles, some unknown song were to emerge? Indian music, droning, hypnotic. Try to imagine, says the brochure she wrote, a guide for parents and teachers, what it would be like if suddenly the dinosaurs came to life. (302)

Lesje refers to the display specimens as 'hers' implying a special type of relationship with the display beyond simply curator-specimen. Dodd writes of museum taxidermy that 'what is ultimately presented are representations of animals as they really are for the producers of the representations themselves.'[32] By interacting with these display figures Lesje is able to construct a narrative of her own choosing, reclaiming a sense of autonomy that has been lost in her personal life. The specimens are physically 'immense' in size, but they are also figures of her imagination, 'reach[ing] down their fingers in friendly greeting', rendered more bizarre by the use of 'fingers'. Atwood appears here to be recognising that there is a necessary gap between fantasy and ideals, and that whilst fantasies are valuable, so too are displacement activities that condition the relationship of the human self to the world. The practice of building these dinosaur displays, then, has multiple purposes: to literally build and portray Palaeolithic life, but also to symbolically open up a comfort and sanctuary in imagining oneself in a "life before man".

Lesje does recognise the limited and temporary nature of her imaginative interactions with the dinosaurs, however, when she ponders, 'though if they were really alive they'd run away or tear her apart.' (302) She evidently acknowledges the behavioural norms of the non-human animals she wishes to interact with, but this acknowledgement is rapidly disregarded by her following reference to 'bears and snakes that dance.' The knowledge of these 'dancing animals' comforts her desire to imagine a reciprocated relationship with the display specimens by recalling two non-human species that have been used to provide entertainment, and in the process problematically bypasses the violent means with which this is made possible. Her contemplation of human-animal relationships consolidates the notion that to conceive of non-human animals in a way that suits one's imaginative enjoyment enacts a similar form of objectification to that seen in the private workspace. It means that the way in which the animals operate as display pieces is entirely subjective to the viewer and can have little to do with the knowledge we have of that individual or the species more largely.

Stephen Asma states:

> The odd thing about a specimen is that it's a kind of cipher when considered in isolation. Specimens are a lot like words: they don't mean anything unless they're in the context of a sentence or a system, and their meanings are extremely promiscuous.[33]

To refer to the meaning of a specimen as 'promiscuous' reinforces the notion that the animals on display lose something of their own animality and individual identity in the process of becoming museum specimens. Alone they are cryptic 'ciphers' but collectively they are exactly as the viewer interprets them to be: essentially 'real' but 'not real' representations of the spectator's perception of non-human animals, promiscuously changing with each new spectator. In the novel then, the dinosaurs on display provide a source through which Lesje can escape the domestic pressures she is experiencing by imaginatively transporting herself into a fictional world and interaction with that specimen and its fantasy world correlatives. The imaginative capacity of the dinosaurs stems from the fact that they are iconographies of extinct beings. They are a reminder of an 'other world' that is different to the one that we and other non-human animals currently occupy. Thus, their display in the museum demonstrates what scientific knowledge about historic animals can allow us to see, but also to imagine on a narrative level. The enjoyment that is gained through interacting with extinct beings is drawn from the notion that we are permitted to imagine and create a level of fictional narrative surrounding them by the very nature of their current existence as creatures from an unknown past.

Forging Personal Identity through Interaction with Museum Display

Throughout the novel and compounding with the trauma of an oppressive heteronormative patriarchy, Lesje struggles with her identity as a Ukrainian and feelings of disconnection from Canadian culture. She therefore attempts to immerse herself within the historical displays of the museum in an effort to situate herself within a Canadian historical identity that echoes the 'Indigenising' carried out by the narrator of *Surfacing*. In depicting protagonists that attempt to appropriate someone else's narrative in order to feel connected to the space which they inhabit, Atwood's novels contemplate the complexity of contemporary Canadian settler identity by implying that much of what underpins settler identity is the search for it. *Life Before Man* therefore begs the question: how do settlers both document and interact with the history of their nation in a postcolonial context? And what role do non-human animals play in this?

In both the museum in *Life Before Man* and in museums around the world more broadly, displays of extinct animal species are positioned alongside Indigenous artefacts and temporalities. Notably, one of the display pieces described in the novel is a totem pole, an item that still holds significant importance in many Indigenous communities. Displaying the totem pole in the museum, however, forges a systemically violent connection between Indigeneity and history, freezing Indigenous cultures in the past and contributing to the denial of present-day Indigenous autonomy. Pauline Wakeman has commented on the politics of displaying Indigenous artefacts alongside taxidermy, arguing that it contributes to a narrative of a 'lost past'. She states that 'the stuffed animal and the plastic Indian are rendered interimbricated figures of extinction, the lost corpses of an atavistic past' and that there is a 'colonial logic embedded in the structure of dioramic display' which 'fetishizes the supposed lost objects of a primitive wildness.'[34] Museum displays such as that described in the novel, then, contribute to difficult and skewed perceptions of Indigenous-settler relations and deny de-colonial progress by retaining an attachment to an imagined history. In addition, placing animals alongside Indigenous figures not only 'racializes' them, but it also aligns them with the non-human and contributes to a wider narrative of both colonial and ecological oppression. Much like in the mind of the narrator in *Surfacing*, in the museum setting the Indigenous individual is more closely aligned with the non-human animal in a display that not only 'fetishizes the lost objects of a primitive wildness' but also re-invents the narrative that this 'wildness' is the reason for their 'extinction'. Evidently, the role of animal taxidermy as a cipher means that animal taxidermy specimens are employed in displays to render and signify Indigenous bodies on display as 'less-than-human', and as a less 'civilised or developed' population.

That museum displays can reinvent national and personal narratives underpins Lesje's idealisation of the museum. For Lesje, the museum is an institution that allows her refuge from the conflict that she feels exists between her Ukrainian and Jewish heritage, reinforced through her statement that 'instead of synagogue Lesje attended the museum'. (87) Through interaction with the various displays, therefore, Lesje comforts her feelings of displacement by imagining herself into these narratives of Canadian space and identity, unknowingly feeding into a settler Canadian anxiety that yearns to prove a historical connection to the space. She identifies an opportunity for her 'foreign' identity to be shed by submerging herself within an environment that hinges on subjective narrative construction and is a producer of a multiplicity of stories:

> Sometimes she thinks of the Museum as a repository of knowledge, the resort of scholars, a palace built in the pursuit of truth, with inadequate air conditioning but still a palace. At other times it's a bandits' cave: the past has been vandalized and this is where the loot is stored. Whole chunks of time lie here, golden and frozen; she is one of the guardians, the only guardian, without her the whole office would melt like a jellyfish on the beach, there would be no past. She knows it's really the other way around, that without the past she would not exist. Still, she must hold on somehow to her own importance. She's threatened, she's greedy. If she has to she'll lock herself into one of these cases, hairy mask on her face, she'll stow away, they'll never get her out.' (300)

Lesje's description reiterates the museum's colonial foundations. The juxtaposition of 'repository of knowledge' and 'built in the pursuit of truth', with her description of a 'bandits' cave' ironically exposes the fallacy of the former denotations. Her choice of 'bandits', 'loot' and 'vandalized' confirms that she is aware of the conditions under which much of the items have been acquired and the politics of their display. Her statement, 'built in the pursuit of truth', then, exposes an ironic notion that truths are subjectively manipulated, and in the context of a museum institution, contemporary conceptions of nation are moulded. Animal bodies are also often utilised in the process of this. In addition, much like the pseudo-wilderness of the log cabin space in *Surfacing*, the pseudo-wilderness of the museum space means that her presence there is temporary, and she cannot, in reality, 'stow herself away'.

Women's Wilderness Writing and the Representational failure of a Pro-Animal Ethics

This chapter has built upon Heather Murray's statement that much of Canadian women's wilderness writing takes place in pseudo-wildernesses by using *Surfacing* and *Life Before Man* to demonstrate that the pseudo nature of these wildernesses results in a failure to establish a sustained and developed pro-animal ethics. Throughout both novels, the female protagonists interact with non-human animals as a means of imaginatively escaping their own trauma at the hands of the men around them. Furthermore, this trauma is wrapped up in colonial connotations throughout, forcing the protagonists to revisit their conception of their own identity in relation to contemporary Canadian culture.

By bringing together a comparative analysis of *Surfacing* and *Life Before Man*, this chapter has demonstrated that it is possible to pull Atwood's thinking together in a particular representational strategy that sees animals employed symbolically to contemplate human concerns. In *Surfacing*, the narrator's identification with animal suffering and consequent attempted rejection of human society through a process of Indigenisation is reflective of her own subjective sufferings, including a sense of victimisation in her relationships and an encroaching feeling of displacement. In *Life Before Man*, however, human-animal interaction is coded as a creative process. Animal bodies and the stories attached to them are manipulated purposefully to reflect particular narratives of mastery and historical identity, and also act as sites through which to imaginatively escape into. Atwood's representation of non-human animals, therefore, is situated within the symbolic realm as it denies individual animals a sustained and material engagement that considers the demands that they place upon the human characters. Rather, Atwood uses animal bodies throughout the novels to construct human narratives that reflect upon questions of identity, both national and personal in 1970s and 1980s Canada.

Notes

1. Heather Murray (2013) 'Women in the Wilderness (1986)' in *Greening the Maple: Canadian Ecocriticism in Context*, edited by Ella Soper and Nicholas Bradley (Calgary: University of Calgary Press) 61–85, p. 62.
2. Ibid., p. 76.
3. Margaret Atwood (2012) *Survival* (Toronto: House of Anansi Press Inc.) p. 81.
4. Adam Dodd, Karen A. Rader and Liv Emma Thorsen (2013) *Animals on Display: The creaturely in Museums, Zoos, and Natural History* (Philadelphia: The Pennsylvania State University Press) p. 3 and p. 5 respectively.
5. Dodd, Rader, Thorsen, *Animals on Display*, p. 5.
6. Samuel J. M. M. Alberti (2011) *The Afterlives of Animals* (Charlottesville: University of Virginia Press) p. 8.
7. Janice Fiamengo (1999) 'Postcolonial guilt in Margaret Atwood's *Surfacing*', The *American Review of Canadian Studies*, 29.1, 141–163, p. 159.
8. Taken from Fiamengo 'Postcolonial guilt in Margaret Atwood's Surfacing', p. 145.
9. Robert McKay (2005) '"Identifying with the animals": Language, Subjectivity, and the Animal Politics of Margaret Atwood's Surfacing' in *Figuring Animals*, ed. by Mary Sanders Pollock and Catherine Rainwater (London: Palgrave Macmillan) pp. 207–227, p. 222.
10. Robert McKay, '"Identifying with the animals": Language, Subjectivity, and the Animal Politics of Margaret Atwood's Surfacing', p. 225.
11. This chapter will utilise the term "American" to refer to the United States of America simply because the narrator of *Surfacing* does so. I acknowledge that America is not synonymous with the USA and that the Americas refers to North and South America.
12. Karen Jones (2015) *Epiphany in the wilderness: hunting, nature, and performance in the nineteenth-century American West* (Boulder: University Press of Colorado) p. 34.
13. Margaret Atwood (1979) *Surfacing* (London: Virago Press) p. 7. [All subsequent quotations taken from this edition].
14. Carol J. Adams (1990) *The Sexual Politics of Meat: A Feminist Vegetarian Theory* (Bloomsbury Academic Publishing) p. 157.
15. Atwood, *Survival*, p. 86.

16. Margaret Atwood (2012) *Survival: A Thematic Guide to Canadian Literature* (Toronto: House of Anansi Press Inc.) p. xxii.
17. Dennis Lee (1974) 'Cadence, Country, Silence: Writing in Colonial Space', *Boundary 2*, 3.1, 151–168, p. 162 & 163 respectively.
18. Dennis Lee, 'Cadence, Country, Silence: Writing in Colonial Space', p. 163.
19. Cardinal, Howard (1969) *The Unjust Society* (Vancouver: Douglas & McIntyre) p. 1.
20. Cardinal, *The Unjust Society*, p. 3.
21. Fenn Stewart (2014) 'Grey Owl in the White Settler Wilderness: "Imaginary Indians", Canadian Culture and Law' in *Law, Culture and the Humanities*, 1.1, 1–21, p. 3.
22. Margaret Atwood (1995) *Strange Things : The Malevolent North in Canadian Literature* (Oxford: Oxford University Press).
23. Tina Loo (2006) *States of Nature: Conserving Canada's Wildlife in the Twentieth Century* (Ottawa: UBC Press) p. 116.
24. Stewart, 'Grey Owl in the White Settler Wilderness', p. 7.
25. In 1980 the Parti Québécois (a social democrat party, elected in 1976) held a referendum for Quebec's independence. The proposal to seek succession from the Canadian Government was defeated. Sources: John A. Dickinson and Brian J. Young, *A Short History of Quebec* (McGill-Queen University Press, 2002) and https://www.thecanadianencyclopedia.ca/en/article/quiet-revolution [Accessed 23 February 2020].
26. Marilyn French (1980) 'Spouses and Lovers, *Life Before Man* by Margaret Atwood', *The New York Times*, February 3, p. BR1.
27. Fiona Tolan (2007) *Margaret Atwood: Feminism and Fiction* (Leiden: Brill) p. 94.
28. Carol L. Beran (2009) 'Intertexts of Margaret Atwood's Life before Man', *American Review of Canadian Studies*, 22.2, 199–214, p. 200.
29. Alberti, *The Afterlives of Animals*, p. 6.
30. Margaret Atwood (2002) *Life Before Man* (Great Britain: Penguin Random House, Vintage Classics) p. 212.
31. Andrea Dworkin (1980) 'Beaver and Male Power in Pornography', *New Political Science*, 1.4, 37–41, p. 41.
32. Dodd, Rader, Thorsen, *Animals on Display*, p. 5.
33. Asma, *Stuffed Animals and Pickled Heads*, p. xiii.
34. Pauline Wakeman (2008) *Taxidermic Signs: Reconstructing Aboriginality* (Minneapolis: University of Minnesota Press) p. 5.

CHAPTER 4

Writing Bear(s): Thematising the Canadian Animal Story in Marian Engel's *Bear* (1976)

"What the actual fuck, Canada?" wrote one Imgur user in an online post in July 2014.[1] Attached to this exclamation were three images of a thread on Tumblr in which a user had seemingly stumbled across Marian Engel's 1967 novel, *Bear*, a novel about an archivist who tries to enter into a physical relationship with a bear. '*It is a literal bear*' [his italics], the poster states, 'it sounds like the most fucked up romance novel in existence'. Other Reddit users flocked to respond, with one stating:

> You guys don't understand. Screw it being a bestseller, 50 Shades of Grey is a bestseller, this book won the *Governor General's Award*. That's the highest literary award in Canada. That's the Pulitzer Prize of Canadian literature. *Bear* is a part of Canadian literary history.[2]

The common source of shock that threaded throughout the discussion wasn't the explicit nature of the novel specifically, but rather the astonishment that the bear protagonist isn't a metaphorical bear. Another user stated that when studying the novel in High School, his entire class had expected to find out that the female protagonist was just fantasising about her sexual awakening in an animalistic metaphor. However, he stated that a classmate who read ahead announced to them all with horror: 'guys, no, she *literally* fucks the bear.'

© The Author(s), under exclusive license to Springer Nature
Switzerland AG 2023
A. Higgs, *Animal Fiction in Late Twentieth-Century Canada*,
Palgrave Studies in Animals and Literature,
https://doi.org/10.1007/978-3-031-42612-4_4

The cultural controversy that *still* surrounds the novel, then, stems from the novel's rejection of metaphor and symbolism in its depiction of a real bear. The novel follows the narrative of an archivist, Lou, who is sent to a large house on an isolated island in northern Ontario to document the vast contents of the property's library. Upon arriving on the island, Lou discovers that there is also a bear living there, chained to a small doghouse on the grounds. Thus begins a story of fascination and intrigue, as Lou becomes enamoured with the bear and attempts to draw him into a relationship with herself, but she is continually met with the indifference of a smelly, disinterested bear. It is surprising therefore, that despite the novel's realist animal protagonist, Engel's novel has continually been discussed in academic criticism from within the context of Margaret Atwood's 1972 *Survival* thesis, which, as Chap. 3 demonstrates, determines that the animals within Canadian literature are often employed as representatives of Canadians themselves.

John Sandlos argues that Engel's novel sits on the same 'boundary between physical reality and myth' that is visible in the work of her literary predecessors, Ernest Thompson Seton and Charles G D Roberts.[3] However, Sandlos also believes that Engel's protagonist is marginally less 'biological' and more 'enigmatic' than the animals in the work of Seton and Roberts. Helen Tiffin argues that the bear 'disappear[s] from his own narrative', referring to him as both an 'avatar' of the wilderness and a 'catalyst' for Lou's sexual awakening.[4] Similarly, Margery Fee argues that Lou uses the bear 'as the kind of mirror … a surface onto which to project fantasy',[5] which Paul Barrett acknowledges 'analyses Bear's presence only in respect to his meaning for Lou.'[6] Gwendolyn Guth pinpoints what she determines is a departure from animal symbolism in the form of the novel, specifically honing in on Engel's layering of mythic texts against a realist narrative: 'Engel scrutinizes the dilemma of animal representation by couching the almost fabular story of a woman's sexual tryst with a bear within the framework of a novel that critic after critic praises for its believability, its realism.'[7] Such a form then, Guth contends, aids in capturing and attempting to handle the complexity involved in fictional animal representation. Tania Aguila-Way takes this line of enquiry further to argue that Engel's novel:

> Seems to anticipate Wolfe and Haraway's shared insistence that relating ethically to animal others demands, first and foremost, that we conceive of human-animal interactions as material-semiotic encounters.[8]

Such praise for the novel specifically rests on its realism and refusal to confine the bear within a symbolic framework. Aguila-Way's analysis confirms that Engel's novel marks a divergence from dominant understandings of Canadian animal writing, arguing that it 'tear[s] at the limits of the semiotic field constructed by nationalist discourses of the 1970s and reinforced by Atwood's own theorisation of the animal in *Survival*.'[9] Given the ground-breaking nature of the novel, then, in its 'tearing' up of the symbolic framework of Canadian animal writing, it is no surprise that, as the accounts on Tumblr have noted, *Bear* is culturally acknowledged as a significant placeholder in the history of Canadian literature and indeed in the wider field of contemporary animal writing more broadly. In constructing an animal protagonist that is indecipherable in his rejection of symbolic understanding, Engel's novel proves that it is possible to deliver nuanced animal representation that offers constructive ways of thinking about human-animal relationships outside of a symbolic framework.

In addition to the limited criticism of the novel praising the text's development of a new type of writing about animals, little attention has been paid to the self-conscious nature of *Bear*, in both narrative and form. This chapter will address this gap in the literary criticism of the novel by exploring the way in which Engel's novel thematises the complexity involved in writing about animals by drawing upon the components that have previously marked writing about animals in Canada, such as Atwood's symbolic animal rhetoric, and then demonstrates their failure to equip Lou with any knowledge of how to relate to the bear. The chapter will show that the novel holds these strategies within sight, self-consciously centring them as the very structure of the narrative as a way of acknowledging the literary-historic representational pitfalls in depicting the material animal. This fictional strategy positions *Bear* as a text that is both made of and situated within a literary tradition of writing about animals in 1970s Canada.

The bear in Engel's novel is not one that conforms to the protagonist's (Lou's) fantasy narratives, but rather he remains steadfast in his indifference: he is smelly and he looks nothing like the teddy bears Lou has encountered in popular culture. Despite this purposeful denial of symbolic characterisation and understanding of the bear, Mary K. Kirtz argues that Engel's novel is an example of an 'intramodernist' text and states that the novel is 'without any self-reflexive acknowledgement of the artificiality of its constructs or a total dissolution of its form.'[10] However, she adds that it does 'serve[s] as a meditation on how we read, interpret, and shape both texts and objects to satisfy our own perceptions of the world.'[11] These ideas do appear to contradict one another; *Bear* is a novel full of 'self-reflexive acknowledgment' precisely because it is a 'meditation on how we read'—specifically on how we read the animal story when the animal is denied a symbolic characterisation that allows us to project our own meaning onto it (like we do the museum animals).

In order to examine the novel's self-conscious and intertextual construction, this chapter will examine Engel's engagement with representational techniques that are employed as a strategy to enact and critique ways of writing about animals that have tended to represent the animal symbolically as a means of reflecting human concerns. This includes the novel's heavily stylized engagement with the practise of storytelling, as throughout the novel, Lou repeatedly fails to relate to the bear because she attempts to understand him using her knowledge of fictional narratives, cultural depictions, and small historical notes left around the house by former owner Colonel Carey. By holding these specific representational techniques in sight through Lou's attempted indulgence in them, Engel both critiques and undermines them as tools for developing a reciprocal relationship with the bear by reinforcing his materiality and the demands that he places upon Lou through his indifference.

Taking on board the idea of a move towards taking animals seriously, this chapter will contend that *Bear* offers no viable resolution to the question of human-animal relations, but that it does reflect on the construction of animal writing and interrogate the boundary that exists between the symbolic and the material animal. Such an emphasis on the biological reality of the bear reinforces the novels engagement with the work of Engel's predecessors Seton and Roberts, and the authors preceding her in this book, a connection that reinforces Engel's text as consciously made of literature. However, *Bear* marks a move away from the work of these former animal texts by choosing to interrogate the material reality of approaching animals using anthropomorphic and symbolic understandings. As such, *Bear* attempts to establish a foundation for interrogating writing about animals in Canada by taking to task the political motivation to use animal representation for anthropocentric means. The significance of *Bear* to the development of writing about animals in Canada during the late 1970s therefore, cannot be understated. *Bear* imagines Canadian identity as able to operate with and alongside animality, not only from within it, thus restoring and emphasising Engel's novel as a deliberately self-conscious fictional story about the border between the symbolic and the material animal.

Framing Narrative 'Failure' as Narrative

Throughout *Bear*, Lou frequently refers to different discourses surrounding bears a means of finding a way to relate the animal she is confronted with. These sources permit her to indulge in an imagined relationship and understanding of the bear that is then consistently ruptured by his indifference to her and his failure to behave in correspondence to these discourses. The narrative of the novel, then, becomes a story of Lou's failure and the bear's constant defiance of her understanding. He remains steadfast in his materiality.

Lou learns that old literary tales once informed the bear's former owners' relationship with him through the various notes that she finds littered around the house. These contain a mixture of scientific information and folklore on bears that span a vast geographical range. One note states that 'in the lore of Ireland … there was a god who was a bear' and another that, 'the Norwegians say, "the bear has the strength of ten men, and the sense of twelve" … they refer to it as … the old man with a fur cloak.'[12] Amongst the notes are also historical sources detailing the geographical location of bears across the world, demonstrating that the occupants of the house once actively sought to uncover historical literary narratives of bears that might also assist them in understanding how to develop a relationship with the real bear on the island. More importantly though, the notes provide a more reflexive purpose in the novel's narrative. These notes consistently insert themselves into the narrative at random moments as and when Lou discovers them in a deliberate method that reflects the continued temptation and tendency to revert back to literary and cultural discourse when attempting to construct relations with animals.

Building on this reflexive purpose to the notes in terms of disrupting the narrative, the contents of the notes and the narratives that Lou indulges in throughout the novel also serve a critical purpose. The inclusion of various historical and literary narratives surrounding bears enables Engel to hold in plain sight the discourses that have tended to dominate understandings of them, so that they can then be critiqued and undermined. This is evident in particular when Lou begins to indulge in a fantasy of having a romantic and/or sexual relationship with the bear:

> She lay naked, panting, wanting to be near her lover, wanting to offer him her two breasts and her womb, almost believing that he could impregnate her with the twin heroes that would save her tribe. (143)

This imaginative indulgence is particularly poignant given that there is a 'long cross-cultural obsession with women and bears' that Robert E. Bieder says 'continues to this day.'[13] The inclusion of this common narrative, therefore, not only allows Engel to demonstrate that there are a number of narratives that have tended to underpin human-bear relationships, but that these narratives are anthropocentric in that they serve human imaginative purposes. By indulging in this narrative, Lou is able to escape from the reality of the island and into a fantasy in which the bear reciprocates her affections. Further to this, the reference she makes to 'her tribe' appears to signify that she is indulging in a settler fantasy of securing an attachment to the land through a relationship with the bear. In addition, her description of their children as 'twin heroes' functions as a reference to the founding twins of Rome, Romulus and Remus, who, according to stories, were raised by a she-wolf. Such a reference is a move by Lou to draw on another narrative of an interspecies relationship as a means of validating her fantasy. This feeds into the wider self-reflexive narrative of demonstrating the way in which this historical narrative feeds into the contemporary one being enacted by Lou. The addition of 'almost believing' indicates Lou's awareness of the fine line between her imagination and reality, but it also indicates the hope in her statement. As such, the threat of reality is rapidly and temporarily dismissed as the narrative shifts towards a surrealist, fetishist tone, as Lou begins to fully submerge herself within an imagined romanticised relationship with the bear.

Such is Lou's indulgence that her subjectivity and the coherence of the narrative begin to break down. She embarks on a sustained chorus-like drawn-out sexualised poetic address to the bear, including statements such as, 'Bear, make me comfortable in the world at last. Give me your skin', 'Oh, thank you, bear. I will keep you safe from strangers and peering eyes, forever. And more explicitly, 'what I want is for you to continue to be, and to be something to me. No more, Bear.' (132) Lou's poetic statements depict her engagement with a sustained and elaborate fantasy surrounding her relationship with the animal. The stylistic effect of repeatedly referring to him as 'Bear' reflects a desire to claim his presence, which she has otherwise failed to capture elsewhere. It is also a denotation of his species, which complicates the subjectivity of the address. He becomes then, within her fantasy, an imagined lover forced to bear the confines of his own species. Her request, 'give me your skin' in order to feel 'comfortable in the world' indicates Lou's feelings of alienation from human society and the consequent desire she has to be closer to the bear, perceiving his animality as a refuge to the society she left behind when she entered the island. Evidently, if she can have his skin then she can escape into the fantasy narrative of their relationship. However, her next statement: 'I will keep you safe', re-asserts her species difference and the potential threat posed by humans to animals, further convoluting the address.

Such a contradiction of being protected and also offering protection reflects the non-linear level of symbolic and surrealist engagement that Lou is attempting with the bear, as she rapidly passes in and out of her imagination and reality. Her reference to 'strangers and peering eyes' not only encapsulates a desire to protect the bear from literal strangers but the meta nature of the narrative extends this protection to a desire to shield him from literary eyes and being captured within a representation, including within the novel itself. Lou's attempts to draw the bear into a dialogue are repeatedly ruptured by the realisation that 'Bear did not reply.' (35) Whereas Lou perceives his 'bear-ness' as permitting a fictional relocation of their relationship and a cross-species understanding, Engel's construction of a bear that remains steadfast in his indifference reinforces the representational critique that Engel is enacting. Through this clash of realism and surrealism within the novel, Engel reinforces the undercutting of Lou's *imaginative* conceptions by Bear's *real* indifference. Such narrative fantasy will not permit Lou a relationship with this bear, as he literally ignores her 'narrative'.

The failure of this narrative of a woman-bear relationship in providing Lou with access to the bear is just one of the representational strategies Engel employs in demonstrating the bear's narrative elusiveness. Guth says of the 'bear's shifting and sliding identities':

> These renderings signal the clash between Lou's heuristic use of metaphor/anthropomorphism and the kind of courteous (not quite contemplative) seeing that allows the bear to be rigorously (even realistically) his inscrutable self.[14]

Guth thus identifies an agency within this clash between Lou's language for the bear and his material presence, which this chapter identifies as a deliberate strategy designed to remove power from the human subject and place it with the animal subject: subverting traditional literary representational power dynamics in which the human protagonist and author usually determine and dictate the animal. Engel's bear asserts himself materially through his very refusal to be projected onto representationally.

Popular Culture as a Representational Reference

In addition to the novel's undermining of historical and literary narratives as a basis for encounter, the novel also demonstrates that more common and popular cultural understandings of bears are similarly unhelpful for forming relations with material animals.

Lou has to remind herself that the bear is a real bear, and is surprised when his appearance falls short of her expectations both in his physicality and behaviour, stating that 'this is a bear. Not a toy bear, not a Pooh bear, not an airlines Koala bear. A real bear' (32) and noting that 'its nose was more pointed than she had expected—years of corruption by teddy bears, she supposed—and its eyes were genuinely piggish and ugly.' (34) Lou's acknowledgement here that her expectation of bear's appearance has been 'corrupted' by 'teddy bears' narratively frames and identifies the pitfalls in approaching the animal through popular culture and discourse, as these are fictional narratives that are providing no real knowledge that is useful here in this encounter. Moreover, the reference she makes to an 'airlines Koala bear' alludes to an advertising campaign for the Australian airline Qantas, created in 1969 by advertising agency Cunningham and Walsh (Fig. 4.1).

This campaign utilises the cute, cuddly appearance of the koala in its imagery to draw tourists to the airline, centring the animal in various poses and costumes as a representational icon for Australia. Such a reference in the novel reiterates the layering of intertextual references that underpin both her interaction with bears and the novel's form more broadly, and how far these are from the material animal she is attempting to understand—koalas, of course, aren't even bears. It also serves as a reminder of the symbolic power that can be found within animal representation; the Koala was effectively leveraged to stand in as a symbol of Australia and as such, the airlines koala reinforces the way in which these narratives are anthropocentrically incorporated into the national consciousness.

In a reflective moment of contemplation, Lou acknowledges that there is a disconnection between the material bear that she has encountered and the dominant cultural narratives that underpinned her prior understanding of them. She states, 'you have these ideas about bears: they are toys, or something fierce and ogreish in the woods, following you at a distance, snuffling you out to snuff you out. But this bear is a lump.' (33) This quotation functions as an animal story within itself, in that it retells a narrative of bears as monstrous hunters lurking within the woods which is then contrasted with the indifferent 'lump' that she has encountered. As

Fig. 4.1 Qantas advert, 1982. (Used with permission)[15]

such, Lou's acknowledgement of the failure of her 'ideas about bears' serves as a specific and purposeful reminder of the way in which particular narratives have shaped and can still shape our conceptions of animals. By creating a smaller narrative within a narrative that is then undermined, Engel's plot mirrors her wider narrative purpose: to construct an intertextually self-conscious novel whose purpose is to critique and undermine the way in which we develop stories about animals.

Despite Lou's acknowledgement of her narrative failures, her reference to Bear as a 'lump' not only refers to his unruly and unknown physicality, but it symbolically indicates her commitment to moulding him like a 'lump' of clay into a characterisation of her preference. Throughout the novel she continually changes her descriptions of him, denoting that he appears to present himself to her each time in a different guise: 'Yesterday he stood there staring at me like a fur coat, she thought, and today he looked like some kind of racoon.' (50) His rapid change from a 'fur coat' to a 'racoon' encapsulates the bear's elusive representational nature; his appearance ranging from an item of clothing made from animal skin to an animal of an entirely different species. This representation is not only indicative of Lou's confusion regarding the material nature of the bear and her desire to inflict an image onto him that she can comprehend him with, but it is also indicative of an elusive agency that belongs to the bear through Engel's strategy of refusing one fixed description for her animal protagonist.

Barrett has determined Lou's changing descriptions of bear as a 'language failure', stating, 'Lou's approximations and descriptions of Bear as a strange object-subject indicate his enigmatic quality and the failure of Lou's language to fully account for his animal presence.'[16] This rightly acknowledges that Engel's protagonist fails to grasp the bear's materiality or his 'animal presence', and continually approaches him through comparison to another object. However, rather than a 'language failure', this chapter contends that *Bear* deliberately avoids capturing the animal through language. Thus, this is not a language *failure*, but a language *rejection*. It is a deliberate contemplation on the type of language that surrounds animal representation within literature, and a consequent rejection of the language of symbolic characterisation. No one type of language or mode of comprehending the bear will suffice, as *Bear* is specifically interested in exposing and representing the multitude of ways in which animals are approached in representation, utilising this as its central narrative.

The incomprehension that occurs within Lou's language surrounding the bear, and her temporary acknowledgement of it, does not encourage her to abandon her search for a characterisation for him. Rather, she looks elsewhere and draws on fictional narratives, such as *Robinson Crusoe* (1917), *Oroonoko* (1688) and *Atala* (1801),in an attempt to find someone else's language that she can submerge herself in as a means of relating to bear. This further reiterates the self-conscious nature of the narrative layering occurring in the novel and functions as an attempt to incorporate her relationship with the bear into a settler-colonial, settler-subject dynamic. Lou's arrival on the island is a product of Engel's imagined literary world, which is then layered by Lou's own perception of the island as a literary world in which she can inhabit the role of a fictional character and thereby engage in a narrative with her fellow bear character.

Inhabiting these narratives, whilst gazing out of the window onto the island, Lou imagines herself into the role of an explorer who has discovered it for the first time: 'for a moment she was Cary advancing boldly on the new world, Atala under one arm, Oroonoko and the handbooks of Capability Brown under the other.' (57). *Atala* was written by a French author after his travels in North America, and predictably centres upon the 'savagery' of the Natives in contrast to the 'saintly' European settlers; *Oroonoko* follows an African prince who is tricked and sold into the British slave trade; and finally, Capability Brown was an English landscape architect. Tiffin has commented on these textual choices, stating that '*Robinson Crusoe* was written at the time of European territorial and capitalist expansion, and it has been almost commonplace to read it as paradigmatic of colonial encounter.'[17] Lou is then, placing herself in the role of the coloniser, encountering the island space and its bear inhabitant for the first time. Applicable to Lou's purpose behind adopting this role is Aguila-Way's discussion of Cary's notes, stating that they 'can be read as an ironic commentary on the ethical pitfalls of the settler—invader impulse to incorporate the animal other.'[18] Thus, through indulging in this literary fantasy and positioning herself as this settler-invader figure, Lou attempts to enter into a recognisable relationship dynamic which is upheld by the fictional worlds she is inspired by and operates alongside the animal or colonised 'other' represented by the bear.

Bear Asserts His Materiality through Violence

The novel's self-conscious warning about the fallacies of approaching the material animal using imagined cultural and literary narratives is brought to a climax through Bear's attack of Lou when she attempts to entice him into engaging in sexual activity.

In this moment, Lou's comprehension of what is real and what is imagined in her relationship with the bear breaks down to the extent that she attempts to position herself in a way that she understands 'animalises' her and attracts the bear. Since her 'human' methods of relating have not worked, this reads like a desperate final attempt to find a means of provoking reciprocity: 'she took her sweater off and went down on all fours in front of him, in the animal posture.' (113) Whereas she adopts this pose in the hopeful belief that it might finally be a means of communicating to him her desires in a way that he understands and reciprocates through intimacy, the bear reacts with violence: 'he reached out with one great paw and ripped the skin on her back.' (156) There is a significance placed here on the point of physical contact as the means through which the bear's materiality is asserted. It is however, still a story, and not any more or less real simply because it draws attention to specific physical aspects of the animal rather than just semiotic descriptions. Rather, this moment ruptures Lou's fantasy of imagining an intimate relationship with the bear, which has been conceived of through her symbolic characterisation of him.

In addition, this moment of physical contact serves to confirm that although Lou might have the imaginative upper hand with regards to her armoury of representational strategies, the bear's materiality is what matters in this moment of interaction and, indeed, is the more assertive in the dynamic of their relationship (or lack thereof). This moment of rejection is the point in the novel that the bear is the most active, marking a definitive change from his former passivity and disinterest. Ironically, however, this clawing of Lou's back re-asserts the bear's right to be passive. The animal protagonist makes a definitive, explicit refusal to play a part in the narrative that the human characters (and readers) desire for him. Bear's rejection of both Lou's 'animal pose' and invitation into her narrative leaves her in total confusion, noting with a double emphasis on 'nothing' when she says that 'she could see nothing, nothing in his face to tell her what to do.' (156) Despite Lou's attempts to indulge in her own fantasy narrative of a relationship with a bear, her relationship with him is in reality entirely empty of symbolic meaning.

Lou's acceptance of this is realised at the end of the novel when the bear is taken away to be looked after elsewhere and he does not appear to show Lou any indication of a goodbye:

> She was left standing, watching the bear recede down the channel, a fat dignified old woman with his nose to the wind in the bow of the boat. He did not look back. She did not expect him to. (164)

In this quotation, Lou is still not able to capture the bear through representation, noting that he appears like an 'old woman.' However, she does now expect and accept his indifference to her, indicating a level of progression in her understanding of *not* understanding him. Despite this acknowledgement however, this moment seems to contribute towards a new narrative surrounding the bear—one that represents him as an elusive figure that will predictably remain steadfast in his indifference: indefinable and impenetrable. Such a narrative serves to indicate a remaining desire to read significance into the events that have transpired on the island and to seek meaning within their relationship through the ability to predict his indifference.

'Animal Tracks in the Margin': Meta-Narrative Engagement with Canadian Animal Writing

The conflict that Engel represents between the imagined and the material animal extends beyond a focus just on the animal within *Bear*. The intertextual and Meta engagement that the novel makes with the Canadian authors of animal stories that have preceded her novel thematises animal writing to situate *Bear* within a literary-historical tradition of animal writing in Canada. Although the novel does not offer a resolution to the lack of animal knowledge offered in animal stories, it is interested in its relationship with literature and how we might interact with animals through writing, centring the question of representation at its core.

The role of Engel's protagonist, Lou, within this analysis of the novel's intertextual mediation on animal stories has been touched upon by Kirtz, who identifies Lou as a character that 'serves the text both as realism's fictive character and as postmodernism's model reader, constructing worlds out of the words she finds.'[19] As such, Kirtz argues, *Bear* 'serves as a meditation on how we read, interpret, and shape both texts and objects to satisfy our own perceptions of the world.'[20] However, as mentioned previously in this chapter, Kirtz also described *Bear* as a novel 'without any self-reflexive acknowledgement', which fails to acknowledge the novel's ability to serve as a mediation on reading and representation using a 'model reader' precisely because the novel is self-reflexive. The meditative characterisation of Lou serves to unify the narrative of the novel itself and the wider questions that the novel contends with concerning the construction of narratives.

This is visible in particular when Lou identifies a number of authors of animal writing, including both British and Canadian authors, of whom she is now critical of in their techniques of representing animals:

> She had read many books about animals as a child. Grown up on the merry mewlings of Beatrix Potter, A. A. Milne, and Thornton W. Burgess; passed on to Jack London, Thompson Seton or was it Seton Thompson, with the animal tracks in the margin? Grey Owl and Sir Charles God Damn Roberts that her grandmother was so fond of. Wild ways and furtive feet had preoccupied that generation, and animals clothed in anthropomorphic uniforms of tyrants, heroes, sufferers, good little children, gossipy housewives. At one time it had seemed impossible that the world of parents and librarians had been inhabited by creatures other than animals and elves. (65–66)

Lou's reference to Beatrix Potter emphasises the animal story as a tradition of her childhood that carries over into adulthood as she progresses to the Canadian authors. The temporality of this indication, in addition to her reference to 'pass[ing] on to Jack London', suggests a kind of cultural colonial relation, since the Canadian writers were often writing earlier than the Anglo-American ones. Furthermore, Lou's emphasis on her grandmother's 'fondness' for Charles G. D. Roberts, whose middle name she mockingly states as 'God Dam' exposes exasperation at having heard his name so often. This, combined with her comment that these stories 'preoccupied that generation', further ties stories about animal representation into questions of national identity, but it emphasises that this relationship, built upon these types of animal stories, is out-dated and specifically popular with the older generation. Lou's exasperation therefore indicates a desire for a departure from these out-dated and over-referenced animal stories, reflecting the opening up of a new kind of animal narrative that *Bear* attempts to represent through Lou as the figure of the contemplative reader.

Lou's scrutiny of animal writing more broadly appears to take to task Atwood's thesis in *Survival* regarding the Canadian pre-occupation with using animals to represent Canadians themselves. Lou states that the animals in the work of these names authors were 'clothed in anthropomorphic uniforms', implicating them in parable-like stories that are absent of the material animal. Consequently, Lou questions the role that these types of narratives might play in informing popular understandings of material animals that might be encountered in real life:

> She had no feeling at all that either the writers or the purchasers of these books knew what animals were about. She had no idea what animals were about. They were creatures. They were not human. (66)

The self-reflexivity inherent in this quotation implicates Engel herself within this category of writers contending with representing animals. Such a positioning does not equate her novel as the antithesis to its predecessors by presenting an alternative to such 'anthropomorphic uniforms', but rather it critiques particular methods of representation such as anthropomorphism that have characterised the animal story up until this point. This puts forth a new kind of animal story that tries to avoid such symbolic characterisation, is conscious of its representational techniques, and holds these concepts in explicit sight. Lou emphasises again the fallacy of approaching the animal through an anthropocentric lens by separating humans and animals through her labelling of animals as 'creatures' and as 'not human', which is a direct resistance to the anthropomorphism that littered the texts she named previously.

In these self-consciously intertextual moments in which Lou engages with animal writing there is evidence of the beginning of a pro-animal thought that considers the kinds of questions that both authors and society more broadly might ask about animals. Although there is no explicit evidence of pro-animal ethical arguments put forth in the novel, Lou's interest in the bear and in the complexities of animal representation does reflect the type of questions that inform such arguments. As such, *Bear*'s contemplation of literature that attempts to represent human-animal relations lays bare that it is itself made of literature. After coming to terms with her ignorance, Lou begins to scale back the types of questions she asks about the bear, and rebukes the anthropocentrism that underpins her curiosity: 'How come he knows his way upstairs? No, back to the beginning: how and what does he think?' (67) Furthermore, when observing the bear, she notices no specific aspects in his behaviour that indicate a particular thought process or personality trait:

> He, she saw, lay in the weak sun with his head on his paws. This did not lead her to presume that he suffered or did not suffer. That he would like striped or spotted pyjamas. Or that he would ever write a book about humans clothed in ursomorphic thoughts. A bear is more an island than a man, she thought. To a human. (66)

The reference that Lou makes to the writing of a book 'about humans clothed in ursomorphic thoughts' is a deliberate engagement with the novel's status as a human written book about a bear clothed in humanist thoughts, and the bizarre nature of this type of narrative construction. The notion that a bear might try to write about a human using 'ursomorphic thoughts' is intended to demonstrate the seeming idiocy of applying characteristics specific to one particular species to another and the inevitable absence this language would provide. This passage therefore reflects on the limitations of human language to construct fictional narratives about other animal species because of the desire to ascribe meaning to these stories from within an anthropomorphic framework.

Further to this, the question of the bear's suffering evokes reference to Jeremy Bentham's seminal statement in the literature of animal rights. The novel's engagement with such ideas adds yet another layer of narrative self-reflexivity, honing in on the kinds of questions and theories that have historically shaped human-animal relations and ethics. Lou's statement that 'a bear is more an island than a man' followed by the addition 'to a human' has been read by Guth as 'closer to indicating the bear's affinity with the non-human physicality of the natural world then to suggesting a symbolic neo-human isolation.'[21] Guth thus resists centring the human experience within this reference, and so reinforces the novel's determination to undermine the symbolic use of animals. And indeed such a statement by Lou is an explicit affirmation that attempting to approach the animal through symbolic and representational techniques is flawed because the anthropocentrism that underpins these textual moves does not consider the animal within its own species framework. The novel, then, through Lou's musings, works to expose and undermine the type of animal narratives that favour symbolic or anthropomorphic representation by creating a story that attempts to narrate the complex process of representing animals, exposing representation to be politically motivated for anthropocentric purposes. Not only does this mean that the material animal will always inevitably fall short of our literary expectations, but it also threatens our ability to take the animal seriously as an individual capable of placing demands back onto human characters.

A Story about Writing a Story about a Bear

Bear is a self-conscious, intertextual, and highly thematised engagement with representing animals in literature. It centres its critique on a number of representational tropes surrounding bears, including teddy bears and folklore tales of woman-bear relationships that fail to hold up upon encounter with the material bear living on the island. On leaving the island, the novel's protagonist, Lou, has developed no further understanding of how to relate the bear than she had on her arrival. Such a failure to comprehend the bear within a framework of her understanding serves as a metafictional device for shedding light on the way in which animals in literature are often represented within anthropocentric and/or symbolic frameworks that serve human meanings and purposes and do not attempt to understand the animal as an individual capable of placing demands back onto the human characters.

Engel's novel draws this contemplation of resisting one way of representing the bear, characterising a bear by his evasion of a characterisation, out into a wider critique of Canadian animal writing more broadly through Lou's reminiscence of the work of authors such as Seton and Roberts. Such an engagement marks the novel's deliberate situating of itself within a Canadian animal writing tradition, whilst simultaneously symbolising a decided move away from the representational techniques that have frequented this former literature, and indeed have come before this chapter in the work of Mowat and Atwood. *Bear* is, then, a novel about writing about animals. It asks the reader to consider what it might look like to consider the animal in its materiality, even if it is mundane and smelly, like Bear. Though it is not explicit in putting forth a pro-animal ethical message, the novel is underpinned by the realisation that the process of making animals into symbolic characterisations in writing is politically motivated for anthropocentric purposes, such as normalising the keeping of a bear as a pet by imagining him as a reciprocal lover. The genius of Engel's writing lies in its intertextual and self-conscious storytelling of telling stories, laying bare its presence in a literary animal tradition in Canada.

Notes

1. https://imgur.com/gallery/uf3YE [Accessed July 2022].
2. User wordsofdiana www.dirtyriver.tumblr.com.
3. John Sandlos (2000) 'From Within Fur and Feathers: Animals in Canadian Literature' in *TOPIA: Canadian Journal of Cultural Studies*, 4, 73–91, p. 88.

4. Graham Huggan and Helen Tiffin (2010) *Postcolonial Ecocriticism* (London: Routledge) pp. 197–198.
5. Margery Fee (2014) 'Articulating the Female Subject: The Example of Marian Engel's Bear', *Atlantis: Critical Studies in Gender, Culture & Social Justice* (1986) in Paul Barrett, '"Animal Tracks in the Margin": Tracing the Absent Referent in Marian Engel's *Bear* and J. M. Coetzee's *The Lives of Animals*', *Ariel: a review of international English literature*, 45.3, 123–149, p. 24.
6. Paul Barrett (2014) '"Animal Tracks in the Margin": Tracing the Absent Referent in *Marian Engel's Bear and J. M. Coetzee's The Lives of Animals*', *Ariel: a review of international English literature*, 45.3, 123–149, p. 125.
7. Gwendolyn Guth (2007) '(B)othering the Theory: Approaching the Unapproachable in *Bear* and Other Realistic Animal Narratives' in *Other Selves: Animals in the Canadian Literary Imagination*, ed. by Janice Fiamengo (Ottawa: University of Ottawa Press) pp. 29–50, p. 31.
8. Tania Aguila-Way (2016) 'Beyond the Logic of Solidarity as Sameness: The Critique of Animal Instrumentalization in Margaret Atwood's *Surfacing* and Marian Engel's *Bear*', ISLE: *Interdisciplinary Studies in Literature and Environment*, 23.1, 5–29, p. 21.
9. Aguila-Way, 'Beyond the Logic of Solidarity as Sameness', (p. 16).
10. Mary K. Kirtz (2009) 'Facts Become Art Through Love': Narrative Structure in Marian Engel's *Bear*', *American Review of Canadian Studies*, 22.3, 351–362, p. 354.
11. Kirtz, 'Facts Become Art Through Love', p. 354.
12. Marian Engel (2021) *Bear* (London: Daunt Books) p. 82 and p. 117 respectively. [All subsequent quotations are taken from this edition.]
13. Robert E. Bieder (2005) *Bear* (London: Reaktion Books Ltd) p. 64.
14. Guth, '(B)othering the Theory: Approaching the Unapproachable in *Bear* and Other Realistic Animal Narratives', p. 41.
15. An example from Qantas's advertising campaign (1982) Used with Permission from Qantas. Taken from: http://www.vintageadbrowser.com/airlines-and-aircraft-ads-1980s/8 [accessed 10 March 2020].
16. Barrett, '"Animal Tracks in the Margin", p. 140.
17. Tiffin, *Postcolonial Ecocriticism*, p. 169.
18. Aguila-Way, 'Beyond the Logic of Solidarity as Sameness', p.15.
19. Mary K. Kirtz, 'Facts Become Art Through Love': Narrative Structure in Marian Engel's *Bear*', p. 354.
20. Ibid., p. 354.
21. Guth, '(B)othering the Theory: Approaching the Unapproachable in *Bear* and Other Realistic Animal Narratives', p. 38.

CHAPTER 5

Queership, Kinship, Careship: Adopting An Ethics of Care in Timothy Findley's *The Wars* (1977) and *Not Wanted on the Voyage* (1984)

"Oh God, Findley—*not more rabbits!*"[1]

In 1984 Timothy Findley humorously recalled his agent moaning the above aloud as she read through the pages of a television script he had just delivered to her. Indeed, his affection for animals and authorial fascination with writing stories about them infiltrates his vast catalogue of writing. The world that Findley imagines in his writing is one in which interspecies interactions are not governed by oppression, but instead demonstrate a deep level of care: there is no "us" and "them" in Findley's world, only "we". Although much critical attention has been paid to Findley, little focus has been given to the intersection in his work between his depiction of caring interspecies relationships and the queer elements of his writing. Reading across this intersection recognises the emphatic coding in Findley's writing that these oppressive and violent patriarchal regimes are both heteronormative and anthropocentric in construction.

This vein of critique is particularly evident in two of his novels, *The Wars* (1977) and *Not Wanted on the Voyage* (1984), both of which are set within the context of two larger, famous narratives of nationhood: the First World War and the story of Noah's Ark in *Genesis*. The context of these narratives is overwhelmingly patriarchal—Findley's protagonist in *The Wars* must navigate the realm of soldierly life and the masculinist ideals that uphold this, including bedding prostitutes and euthanizing wounded horses, and in *Not Wanted on the Voyage*, both God (Yaweh) and Noah (Dr Noyes) are depicted as oppressive patriarchs that cast aside those 'not wanted' in pursuit of their ideal society, enacting grandiose violence against women and animals both on and off the ark.

Rather than focusing explicitly on this violence, however, this chapter will focus on the moments in Findley's novel in which his characters are depicted as challenging this type of domineering relationship and instead forming caring and meaningful relationships with non-human animals, recognising their individuality and ability to place demands back onto the human characters. In doing so, Findley's characters become outcasted, seen as existing outside of the normative violent structures operating around them and actively defying the orders of their superiors in order to protect non-human animals in grandiose acts of care. It is these hyperbolised and, what this chapter will determine as 'camp', moments of defiance that bring together the queer and caring elements of Findley's writing, demonstrating the value of utilising a queer framework in destabilising dominant hegemonies.

Using J. R. Ackerley's novel *My Dog Tulip* (1956) as her critical focus, Susan McHugh has commented on the possibilities that are opened up by working across an intersection of queer theory and animal studies. She argues that literature that focuses on relationships between gay men and animals in particular contributes to a:

> notion of sodomite culture that I formulate along the lines of what Warner and Lauren Berlant term a "queer counterpublic," that is, queer culture formulated as a subordinate (and explicitly not separate) sphere founded on "nonstandard intimacies."[2]

As such, the applicable nature of queer studies and queer narratives to animal writing is a product of this shared sense of camaraderie in navigating the heteronormative world and the regulation of particular sexual practices that pervades even dog owning. McHugh calls this relationship 'pack sexualities', explaining that it is a 'triangulation of gay men, bitches, and their usually "mongrel" (whether human bisexual or canine mixed-breed) sex partners.'[3] Unlike Ackerley, however, Findley uses relationships with animals in his novels not as an avenue through which to express frustration related to sexuality, but rather to represent the difficulties that arise for particular characters—those both overtly queer in their sexuality and those figuratively queer in their refusal to conform to heteronormative behaviours—in navigating the hegemonic heteronormativity of particular spheres. Findley's 'pack sexualities' are therefore underpinned by an empathy that emerges as a product of a shared experience of oppression.

That we see these moments of empathy in camp moments of defiance in the work of Findley is because camp as a concept and aesthetic actively seeks to frustrate hegemonic norms from within a queer framework. Esther Newton states:

> Camp is not a thing. Most broadly it signifies a relationship between things, people, and activities or qualities, and homosexuality.[4]

Richard Dyer concurs, stating that 'identity and togetherness, fun and wit, self-protection and thorns in the flesh of straight society—those are the pluses of camp.'[5] He adds that camp is a 'way of being human ... without conforming to the drabness and rigidity of the hetero male role.'[6] Thus, using this understanding of the concept, the camp sensibility at work in Findley's novels operates as a framework for reconfiguring the narratives that Findley's novels are set within (war and Genesis) and to offer instead a depiction of human behaviour that demonstrates deep and sustained care for non-human animals. As Dyer states, 'Camp sensibility is very much a product of our oppression,'[7] reinforcing that it is a sensibility well positioned to expose and reconfigure oppression into a narrative that is more ethically engaged than the animal writing seen previously in Canada in the 1970s.

Defining an Ethics of Care

In Findley's novels, to choose to show care to animals in defiance of orders that dictate otherwise is a political move that not only exposes a system of inequality that is patriarchal and heteronormative, but it also attempts to represent relationships between humans and animals that are built on responsibility and reciprocity: that which this chapter will refer to heretofore as *kinship*. In *Making Kin not Population* and *Staying With the Trouble* Donna Haraway makes a 'plea for other-than-biogenetic kindred.'[8] She explains that 'people become kin largely by sharing experiences and generating a sense of belonging 'and that 'the recomposition of kin acknowledges that all earthlings are relatives with affines, and it is past time to practice better care of kinds-of-assemblages (not species one at a time)'.⁹ The significance of constructing non-biological kinship, she argues, is that 'such belonging—such kinship—can not only be across species but blur such boundaries.'¹⁰ In fostering kinship relations across species boundaries through caring, then, we destabilise the types of divides that have normalised the speciesist maltreatment of animals.

The overwhelming message within Findley's novels is that in order to work against the oppressive experience of living under a domineering patriarchal hegemony, one must actively show care towards all those around you, including animals. This situates his ethics within a wider criticism of a political system. This system is aptly named by Donovan a 'sex-species system' because, she argues, there is significant overlap in the inequality of sexual and species relationships.¹¹ By acknowledging the intersections between the oppressive experience of being queer in Findley's novels and the experience of non-human animals, this chapter gives value to the political ethics at work in *The Wars* and *Not wanted on the Voyage*, reinforcing them both as novels interested in emphasising the importance of caring and kinship as a means of combatting patriarchy. Although the references that this chapter will make to the concepts of caring and empathy are underpinned by this framework set out by Haraway, Adams, and Donovan, its interest in the elements of Findley's work, and in the queer/species intersection, moves beyond their focus on a feminist gender logic. In both *The Wars* and *Not Wanted on the Voyage*, Findley manipulates famous narratives by focusing on characters that queer the status quo by challenging an authority that he codes as androcentric and heteronormative. By aligning patriarchy, hierarchy, and masculinity with oppression and violence, and femininity, non-heteronormative queer identity and non-human animals with sympathy, care, and affection, Findley forges a symbiotic relationship between queering and caring that appears simplistic in its binary form, but is in fact a deliberate camp and stylised engagement with such binaries.

Re-imagining Heroic Duty through an Ethics of Care in *The Wars* (1977)

The Wars follows nineteen-year-old protagonist Robert Ross, who enlists in the Canadian army during the First World War after the death of his disabled sister, who fell from her wheelchair when Robert was 'making love to his pillows.'[12] Feeling responsible, Robert's enlistment becomes a concerted effort to make reparations for what he felt was his inability to protect someone vulnerable. However, Robert struggles with the experience of deployment, including the conditions of the trenches, the treatment of horses on the front line and navigating the masculinist sphere of soldierly life, which do not seem to match up with the heroic, protective image he'd imagined.

In a diversion from stereotypical war narratives of overtly masculine heroes but still lending itself to the tradition of realist war fiction, Findley characterises Robert as someone who struggles to engage with the 'rules' of war, recoiling from killing and from the activities the other soldiers like, such as visiting local brothels, and ultimately refusing to conform to the military system of authority that dictates the orders he must unquestionably follow. Robert is instead presented as steadfastly sensitive and protective of those he deems to be vulnerable—previously his sister, now the horses that are also deployed to the front line—and queer in his sexuality, uncomfortable when pressured to engage in sexual activity with a sex worker and preferring the close companionship of his fellow soldiers Harris and Rodwell. Whilst not the explicit focus of this chapter, the queer nature of *The Wars* has been previously discussed by Shane Rhodes, who states that the novel 'explores the queer erotics, both loving and violent, inherent in male-male bonds especially heightened in the greatest of "homosocial" events, war.'[13] Findley's decision to inhabit the military fictional world and to characterise Robert as queer, then, is deliberate attempt to draw upon this homosocial context and to reimagine a different kind of war novel in which the idea of heroism is repurposed.

This chapter will focus on how this is achieved through a camp aesthetic that applies melodrama and conscious exaggerated stylisation to meet the cultural logic of the military hero on the same pitch, but to subvert and reconfigure it. In the climax of the novel, Robert abandons his military duty in a desperate act to save a large number of horses from certain death on the front line. Such a depiction, of an act of defiance that requires the abandonment of military duty in favour of an act of care towards non-human animals, resituates the concept of duty within an ethical tradition and challenges historical and national narratives of heroism by imagining a heroic act as one in which the importance of protecting the marginalised and abandoning the principles that oppress them is realised.

Horses as Victims: Military Coded Violence Towards Horses

Woven throughout Robert's experience on the front line is the experience of the horses that are transported with him and his military company. It is clear that, like Robert and his colleagues, horses are also victims of the military code of violence that Robert is confined by. They are described as being transported in dangerous conditions to Europe, where they are subjected to carrying soldiers and heavy goods through the muddy conditions of the frontline, and where thousands of them consequently died.[14] Amongst the normalisation of these violent conditions, however, Findley's protagonist stands alone as seemingly the only soldier who is distressed by the harm that comes to the horses. As a consequence, Robert resists integrating himself with the human soldiers he is serving with and instead takes every opportunity he can find to seek solace in the company of non-human animals.

Horses become the main recipients of Robert's care and affection, seeming to comfort that protective instinct he let slip when his beloved sister Rowena fell from her wheelchair. The horses, it seems, permit him to build bonds outside of the code of violence that dominates life on the front line. Unfortunately for Robert, his interactions with horses are also often emotionally traumatising events, as he finds himself caught between the way he is ordered to interact with the animals in his military duty and his empathetic desire to care for them.

Robert's love for horses begins on board the ship that first transports him to the battlefront in Europe. Such was his enjoyment in caring for the horses that he is described as being 'disengaged from the other life on the upper decks' (53) and opting to visit the horses even when he is off duty. The symbolic division of decks marks the figurative divide that Robert draws, disengaging himself from soldierly life above and immersing himself in the lower world of the horses, where he can practice care. This practice of kinship, as aforementioned and conceived by Haraway, speaks to Robert's desire to form close relationships across species boundaries that are built upon intimacy and care, rather than the violent hierarchies that have put his own species at war. As Haraway argues, 'meetings make us who and what we are in the avid contact zones that are the world. Once we have met, we can never be "the same" again.'[15] As such, it is this notion of contact and interaction that forms the establishment of a new kind of relationship with the world and the non-human beings in it.

The clashing of Robert's practice of kinship with the military world he inhabits is focalised when he is asked to shoot a horse that is injured on the boat. Acutely aware of what is expected of him, Robert notes that he 'could barely move in his panic but he knew that he had to show his nerve and his ability as an officer.' (66) This dichotomy between his real 'panic' and his desire to show 'nerve' conceptualises the hypermasculinity underpinning the officer role, as a necessary component of the role is evidently the abandonment of emotion (temporarily at least). Robert consolidates this notion by reciting what he imagines will be recorded of him following this incident, capturing the fragile boundary of success as defined by his ability to 'control' the situation or 'show decisiveness' (67) and not by his ability to show empathy or to acknowledge the distressing nature of euthanizing a struggling animal. Robert, however, demonstrates his distance from these characteristics by figuratively recognising the horse as an individual by describing emotional turmoil in its eyes: 'the horse's gaze was turned in their direction—white with alarm in the lantern light.' (66) There is an ethical war raging in Robert's conscience; he must fulfil his military duty and prove that he is capable of fulfilling the stoic, hyperbolised masculine role of an officer, but at odds with this are his feelings of an ethical duty of care towards those he perceives as vulnerable—in this moment, the horse. The irony of this scene is that despite Robert's role as the horse's executioner, he shares the animal's panic.

That Robert is a figurative alien in this violent space is further conceptualised through his ignorance surrounding the taking of life. Robert recalls that 'he'd seen a picture of a cowboy shooting his horse behind the ear. The image rose in his mind—black and white and clumsily drawn—a child's world picture of exactly what to do.' (67) This troubling intrusion of violence into a childhood memory reflects the shattering of Robert's innocence in this moment. Such ignorance compounded with the fact that Robert is taught no real method of shooting the horse implies that there is no method of 'teaching' killing within the military; it is less a learnt behaviour rather than an adoption of a new code of ethics in which killing is permitted, normalised, and expected.

This connection between a masculine arena and the justification certain codes within this grant towards killing animals (and humans) is discussed by Donovan and Adams. They determine in a steadfast binary that the masculine approach to animal rights is disconnected from individual beings and is concerned with policing who can and can't be killed, whereas a feminist ethics of care concerns itself more particularly with specific animals and sympathetic concern for the well-being of all species:

> Whereas the masculine concern with rights, rules, and an abstract ideal of justice tends often to seem like "a math problem with humans" (28), the feminine approach offers a more flexible, situational, and particularized ethic.[16]

Robert's failure to conform to the traditional image of a masculinised war hero through his ignorance and emotional affectation in shooting the horse evidences Findley's particular positioning of him as a protagonist that is more in line with the principles of feminist care.

Such is the depth of his desire to care that the sound of the gunshot immediately transports him back into his last traumatic memory, the loss of his sister:

> He fired.
> A chair fell over in his mind.' (68)

Robert's ethical framework shifts in this moment to incorporate horses. In following his military duty, Robert recognises that he once again neglects the internal ethical duty he feels towards those he deems vulnerable—first Rowena, and now the horse. His inadequacy in this space is further highlighted by his numerous unsuccessful attempts to shoot the horse. Afterwards he notes that 'he didn't want to meet the other man's eyes just yet—though he didn't know why.' (69) Such confusion evidences his conflict of duty, stemming from both his inability to effectively shoot the horse, failing to effectively carry out his duty, but also the shame of having killed another being. Peter Webb argues that 'this scene marks the point at which Robert leaves behind the last vestiges of domestic innocence and enters a world of horrific experience.'[17] Such is decisively the case: the journey on board the ship becomes both a literal and figurative move away from his innocent, domestic home-life represented by Rowena and her rabbits, towards the front line, a site of a coded violence in which he'll go on to witness and partake in normalised mass killing.

Whereas this chapter locates in this scene a focus on the particular intimate relationship between Robert and horses as a depiction of an ethical departure from dominant hierarchies of behaviour that underpin specific spheres of human culture, Webb argues that Findley's novel pays homage to the role of horses in the First World War. He states:

> The scene acknowledges the horses as sentient beings and the forgotten victims of human conflict. Captured and broken in the Canadian wilderness, herded onto the ship, then marginalized by the military system, the horses provide a stark example of how speciesism operates in theatres of war.[18]

Webb points out that the novel's attempted engagement with the historical through a depiction of such suffering brings the horse to the forefront of the popularised military narrative form. Building on this line of enquiry, rather than just 'sentience' being the key emphasis in this scene, Robert's experience of shooting the horse is a grotesque subversion of the kind of peaceful material encounter suggested by Haraway. It is one that, through its intimacy and materiality, forces Robert to physically encounter and be complicit in violence towards animals and forms a basis through which he begins to resist such violence.

The novel figures the establishing of kinship with non-human animals, and caring for them through empathetic encounter, as a basis for countering domineering masculinity. Robert's failure to conform to the masculinised image of a military war hero and kill without guilt or empathy differentiates him from the mentality that is needed to survive in the war space. His conflict of duty within the novel brings into question the limits of following orders when they occur at the detriment of lives, both human and non-human. Such a narrative, working within and subverting traditional war narratives that depict overtly masculine protagonists, demonstrates Findley's attempted troubling of this literary genre and the heroic narratives that inhabit it by constructing a protagonist that resists conforming to what is expected of him and is actively distressed by overt displays of masculinity that culminate in violence. In addition, through this narrativization, the novel exposes duty as a means through which patriarchal society reproduces itself, and moreover, demonstrates the corruption of psychology that these forms of heteronormativity produce, normalizing mass killing on the battlefield.

Queer Resistance

As has been established, masculinity and its perceived relationship to military duty is troubled in the novel through the insertion of a care ethics, but it is also repurposed through a queer sensibility that reveals itself both in the form and content of the novel. The weaving of queering and caring in the narrative comes together most notably in a scene in which Robert witnesses one of his military heroes engaging in sexual relations with another man in an act that mirrors a violent interaction of a horse and rider dynamic.

Such a scene dislocates the figure of the masculinised military hero from heteronormativity. In doing so, it indicates to an overarching queer framework that exposes the social and ideological conflicts operating around Robert in his struggle to conform to his military role. In addition, it figuratively displays Robert's distress when faced with violence by means of non-human animal imagery:

> One was lying on his back with his back arched off the mattress while the other sat astride his groin exactly like a rider. The one who played the horse was bucking ... just like the mustangs Robert and the others had broken in the summer. The rider was using a long silk scarf as reins and the horse was biting into the other end with his teeth ... The rider held the reins in one hand and, using a soldier's stiff-peaked cap, beat the horse on the thighs—one side and then the other. And the two—both horse and rider—were staring into one another's eyes with an intensity unlike any other Robert had ever seen in a human face. Panic. (43)

Rather than perceiving this scene as role-play between seemingly consenting adults, indulging in fantasies of dominance and submission, Robert sees only violence. He dehumanises the two men, recognising what he sees as 'panic' in their eyes beyond that which he has ever witnessed in humans before, seen only in the eyes of the horse on the boat. Robert's confusion and distress is heightened by Taffler's role as the submissive horse, complicating his understanding of him as a hyper-masculine, dominant figure.

Terry Goldie argues that Robert's distress stems from his suppressed homosexual identity and the subsequent feelings of desire that surface from witnessing Taffler. Consequently, when, after witnessing this scene, Robert smashes the mirror in the bedroom with his boot, Goldie argues that this plays into Robert's subjective struggle between his homosexuality and his military, masculine identity: 'in an identity game common in descriptions of gay characters, Robert uses this metonymy of his military masculinity to break the image which shows behind him, watching and desiring.'[19] Such an analysis captures the queer workings of the novel, but it doesn't pay attention to the animal imagery at play within the scene and in particular, the choice of horse imagery that works in tandem with the queer content. The importance of this depiction of a seemingly violent sexual enactment of a horse and rider dynamic is such that it provides a de-familiarising of horse riding that also asks us to see horse riding as potentially violent. Through such dominant-submissive role play, the scene implicitly asks us to question whether riding a horse involves this same dominant-submissive dynamic.

The use of the silk scarf as reins is a queer interplay in the material culture of horse riding, femininity, and bondage. In addition, the Swede's use of the 'soldier's stiff-peaked cap' as a whip to beat the horse (Taffler) acts as both as a whip in the ordinary sense of horse riding and also as a phallic signifier of soldier-ness that the Swede ironically flagellates Taffler with, dominating him with a signifier of his own dominance in the military sphere. Such a conflation of violence, between military dominance and this dominant-submissive display of horse riding signifies that human-animal relations like this are violent also. Robert identifies this relationship, as the description of his recoil when handling his boot after the scene evidences a disgust for the violence that surrounds the idea of the 'human': 'he picked up a boot and held it in his hand. Its weight alarmed him and the texture of its leather skin appalled him with its human feel.' (44) In addition to the militarised code of violence represented by the boot as part of a uniform, the leather of the boot is a memento of another kind of violence done to the animal. In recoiling at the boot and throwing it at the mirror, then, Robert rejects his complicity in both systems of violence. His sexual subjectivity and his human subjectivity are ruptured by the suddenly 'human feel' of the boot and he smashes his conception of military heroes, his humanness and his homosexual desires in the mirror. Through such a moment of an intimate homosexual scene played out through a dominant-submissive horse and rider dynamic, the novel demonstrates its concern with queering humanity as a form of utterly entitled control over animal life.

Camp Climatic Heroism

The connection that the novel's protagonist draws between violence against animals and violence in the military sphere escalates to a climactic ending in which Robert decides he can no longer participate in the system that perpetuates violence and sacrifices horses in pursuit of human military victory. This ending plays out in a camp scene of overtly dramatic and hyperbolised heroism that sheds a critical light on the types of themes that have frequented military narratives of nationhood, in which mass murders of "the enemy" have been praised without attention paid to the violent dynamic at play in orchestrating an enemy-hero dichotomy. Applying this queer framework allows Findley's novel to demonstrate that heroism is a fickle term that is moulded to different systems—whilst Robert may be seen as a coward in military terms; abandoning his post and refusing to follow orders, he is positioned as an ethical hero, concerned with rescuing his animal kin who are about to become victims to human warfare.

The camp nature of these scenes is played out in the overtly symbolic nature of the enemy-hero lines that are reconstituted through Robert's actions and that ultimately fail in grandiose displays of mass death. In the penultimate scene of the novel, German forces find Robert's company's location and start delivering heavy gunfire. Consequently, Robert seeks permission to move the horses and mules (thirty of each, the novel states) in a 'strategic retreat ... so that they might be saved'. (200) However, the unironically named character in charge, Captain Leather, refuses his request. Distressed by this, Robert declares, 'I'm going to break ranks and save the animals' (201) before opening the stable gates and releasing them anyway. Such language betrays that Robert's sense of who is the enemy has now radically changed. He sees such a move of rescuing the horses as a defection from his human military company and as an act of allegiance to the horses, switching sides in a new war. However, tragically, the novel reconsolidates the entrenched system of violence to which the horses (and his human colleagues) are continually sacrificed by depicting the total failure of Robert's intentions.

Rather than being released to freedom, the barracks are hit with heavy shelling from the Germans, resulting in a devastating and explicitly violent ending for them all: 'all the horses and mules were either dead or were dying, only Robert had survived.' (203) This overtly symbolic result in which no horses (or men) are able to escape their fate reaffirms their entrapment within the system and reflects the novel's self-conscious battle with inhabiting the violent war-narrative realm. Furthermore, this dramatic, camp self-conscious symbolism is entrenched when Captain Leather is described as struggling to his feet: a surviving image of the endurance of militarised violence. What has changed in this moment, however, is that the Robert who once struggled to kill a horse on a boat and whose only interaction with killing was in the cowboy films of his childhood, is now filled with the confidence of a warped ethical duty. He picks up a gun, intending to euthanize the remaining dying horses, and shoots Captain Leather between the eyes. Such nonchalance demonstrates not only Robert's development from an officer hesitant to take life to an assured man who confidently kills effectively and without contemplation, but also his decided defection to the ranks of the horses who now lay dead. The killing of Captain Leather is a symbolic targeted destruction of a man who represents not only the normalised sacrifice of men on the front line in the name of military duty, but who was also prepared to sacrifice the lives of animals by not permitting Robert to move them (reinforced, of course, through his name, a signifier that his character is a harbinger of animal death).

Although the question as to whether there is a duty to protect the animals rather than kill them has finally been answered for Robert, protecting them is another obstacle that he never overcomes. After defecting in the scene above, Robert's final act of defiance is to lock himself into a barn with roughly fifty horses belonging to the regiment of a Major Mickle. Ironically, it is the very thing that Robert perceives as the remedy to violence, his kinship with the horses, that ultimately dooms him and the horses to a violent end. The narrative notes that 'Robert called out very distinctly (and there are twenty witnesses to this): "we shall not be taken."' (212) Such a statement represents a utopian sense of togetherness that Robert has been striving for throughout the novel and, moreover, his defiance in this unity reflects his determination to protect the vulnerable beings he has repeatedly heretofore failed to protect. The notion that Robert's 'we' could be inclusive of horses is not a point of consideration for Mickle, who, like Captain Leather, is depicted as a product of the humanist, patriarchal military that Robert is opposing in his determination to restore order. As such, Mickle presumes that this 'we' Robert describes refers to human accomplices and orders the barn to be set alight to force Robert and his 'accomplices' out.

The thatch-roofed barn is described as setting alight like a 'tinder box' (212) and collapsing immediately onto the horses underneath it, causing panic in the horses and preventing Robert from opening the doors to free them. Such a rapid escalation into a scene of horror draws upon a camp aesthetic consistent with Sontag's denotation of 'a particular kind of style [with a] love of the exaggerated' that 'incarnates a victory of "style" over "content," "aesthetics" over "morality," of irony over tragedy'[20] The scene erupts into a catastrophic exaggerated display of violence that results in a triumph of stylistic horror over the meaning of the scene itself, in that encapsulating and escalating the melodrama of the military narrative into a scene of chaos means it is hard to pinpoint whether the tragedy lies in Robert's failure—the conditions that led him to attempt to defy orders in the first place or the novel's failure to deliver a coveted heroic ending.

Working within this queer framework of exaggerated camp aesthetic results in an inverted depiction of heroism in which we as readers both literally and figuratively watch an aspiring hero's ambitions burn. Rather than riding his horse kin away to freedom, Robert is instead depicted as trying desperately to regain control of the black mare he is riding, who 'leapt through the flames' with Robert on fire. (213) This dramatized tragic inversion of horse and rider reiterates the 'consciously "stagey", specifically theatrical' concept of camp put forth by Newton and brings us back again to the association between violence and horse riding that has pervaded the novel.[21] Not even in an attempted assertion of empathy and care can Robert ride this horse away from violence because within this military system (and indeed more broadly speaking) by the very nature of its dynamic it is violent. The scene is made even more emotive through descriptions of the horses 'standing in their places while they burned', seemingly reconfiguring a type of military stoicism in which they have accepted their fate. Such mass slaughter, referred to in the novel as a 'holocaust' (207) asserts that the innocence of the victims—the horses and Robert—is sacrificed due to a logic of difference that does not recognise the type of kinship that Robert holds with the horses.

Findley's novel radically inhabits the military mourning mode by depicting a camp stylized tragedy, deadly serious and deeply moral, but meeting the melodramatic cultural logic of the military hero on a similar level. Ending the novel in this way is both tragic in its failure and in the death of so many horses, and it is exaggerated and "too much" in its actualisation of events; it plays into Findley's engagement with the construction of narrative and the self-conscious state of his novel. As we are hearing this account from testimonies of witnesses, through Juliet D'Orsey's account and also through photographs, the camp, exaggerated nature of the scene encapsulates the way in which narratives take on a life of their own when they are retold—they are often built upon, exaggerated, and in particular with war narratives, they hinge upon theatricality, tragedy, empathy and a grandiose mode of mourning.

Robert's defiance of military orders would seem enough to deny him empathy, but through Findley's characterisation of a hero as someone who undermines military duty in favour of ethical duty, he reimagines a military hero as someone who seeks a utopian kinship and commits to a conscience of caring. He thereby commits an awful but necessary act in a dreadful failed attempt to save lives, and attempts to undermine the fixed construction of hierarchy that has been so oppressive. Brydon does not comment on the camp nature of the scene, but she does comment upon the ambiguity of Robert's actions:

> He represents the ambiguity of the beautiful gesture. Is Robert's action beautiful because it is humane, because it is (at least immediately) useless, or because it is doomed to failure and leads inevitably to violence.[22]

It is precisely through the exaggerated camp nature of the scene that such moral categorisation is rendered impossible. There is certainly an underlying sense of heroism and beauty in Robert's militarised logic of 'breaking ranks' in favour of kinship with animals, however, although it is tragic, as Brydon states here, it is difficult to point out precisely that which makes it tragic. In comparison, Webb says of the scene:

> These graphic descriptions reinforce the novel's strategy to shock the readers out of a complacent acceptance of suffering. Findley's outrage at humans "dragging its animals into destruction" finds expression through an articulation of animal suffering in the midst of a conflict they have no stake in and no power to escape, except by death. (234)

Such criticism implies that Robert failed to recognise his and the horses' same entrapment within this oppressive structure of conflict. Webb thus argues that it is through a depiction of 'animal suffering' that Findley attempts to expose the gruesome reality of the arena of war. However, an emphasis on suffering overlooks Robert's controversial and incredible defiance of his military duty in favour of solidarity with animals.

In depicting a man who so explicitly draws lines between his former military company and himself and the horses, the novel suggests that adopting an ethics of care requires the abandonment of the type of heroic nostalgia that has dominated war fiction; it reimagines what constitutes the 'hero' and the stakes that are at play in following one's duty, and forgoes violence in favour of kinship. Findley's novel makes plain that it is difficult to implement such a utopian, sentimental framework, evidenced in the death of the horses and in Robert's injuries. However, the construction of the narrative, in particular by drawing upon the account of Juliet D'Orsey, who admires and cares for Robert, works to depict Robert in a sympathetic and heroic light, underlining the novel's ethics with a kind of sentimental hope that, like the barn, cannot be extinguished. Although the queer hero of this narrative fails to rescue the horses and later dies of his injuries, the anti-heroic heroism of his act, defying military duty in favour of ethical duty, remains the central logic of the novel and its camp climax of heroism. Findley locates within his vision of the heroic an ethics and duty of care that refutes hierarchy and imagines kinship in which queer ways of relating take precedence as a counter to a figured domineering anthropocentric heteronormativity. The queer elements of the novel, such as the camp aesthetic utilised in this particular scene, and Robert's struggle to conform to the masculinised image he associates with soldiers, are coded as entangled within an ethics of care to present a narrative that is radically anti-hegemonic in its way of thinking.

Camp Genesis: Caring for those *Not Wanted on the Voyage* (1984)

The queer techniques of animal representation in *The Wars*, working within a camp framework towards a feminist care ethics, are similarly at work in *Not Wanted on the Voyage* (1984). In *Not Wanted on the Voyage* Findley mobilises anthropomorphism and plays around with gender stereotypes to provide a camp version of the story of the Flood in *Genesis* that exposes and challenges patriarchal authority.

As a story within a central book of Christianity, commonly referred to as "Noah's Ark", and much like Findley's inhabitation of the war fiction genre in *The Wars*, in *Not Wanted on the Voyage* Findley deliberately engages with the types of narratives that have underpinned settler national identity (in this case, the Christian identity) and works to undermine them by demonstrating that violence accompanies them. By framing the narrative with a camp aesthetic, including humour, and playing with character stereotypes, *Not Wanted on the Voyage* presents a self-conscious engagement with narratives about animals, much like that seen in the work of Marian Engel in the previous chapter. However, whereas Engel creates an entirely new story that is self-consciously about writing stories about animals, Findley adopts a process of reconfiguration of established narratives that include animals, inhabiting and taking creative licence with the stories in order to demonstrate the oppression operating under the surface of these narratives.

In Findley's *Genesis* story there are talking animals, layers to the physical ark space that reflect symbolic hierarchies of social standing, and Satan disguised as a woman named Lucy and married to Noah's son Ham. Noah is also referred to as Dr Noyes (his title an ironic nod to his scientific fixation on genetic purity), and his wife is Mrs Noyes. Taking this into consideration, this section of the chapter will reflect on Haraway's aforementioned statement that 'I am convinced that actual encounters are what makes beings' to suggest that Findley's novel, alongside demonstrating the violence and oppression of hierarchical structures, simultaneously imagines a kind of kinship as occurring between its oppressed inhabitants of the ark. It will focus on the intimate kinship that is achieved by Mrs Noyes in comparison to that which Robert in *The Wars* aspired to achieve in his relationship with horses. Such analysis will demonstrate that a new kind of interspecies interaction emerges, which acknowledges these differences and moves beyond them through the establishment of non-violent, non-oppressive relationships. These moments are powerful, deeply emotional scenes that provide profound social commentary on the kinds of relationships we form with humans and non-human animals alike.

Mrs Noyes and Her Feminist Care Tradition

Much like the soldierly hierarchy that governs *The Wars*, in *Not Wanted on the Voyage*, there is an explicit sense of hierarchy between the characters that is evidenced both in the traditional structure of a nuclear family governed by a patriarchal figurehead, and later physically conveyed in the division of space on the ark.[23] The camp nature of the novel is most visible in the dynamic of Mr and Mrs Noyes' marriage, which is depicted as an exaggerated and heavily stylized version of the stereotypical arguing hetero married couple. Such a depiction undermines the ideology underpinning Dr Noyes' patriarchal authority by way of ridicule, creating a theatrical show of 'good' and 'bad' performed by Mr and Mrs Noyes. In rooting for Mrs Noyes to defy her husband, then, we root for a feminist challenge to oppression that is coded as heteronormatively and anthropocentrically patriarchal.

In contrast to her husband who governs the ark with his own comfort in mind, Mrs Noyes is depicted as radically caring, choosing to spend her time in the claustrophobic and dark lower levels of the ark with the animals, rather than conform to her husband's rules surrounding her behaviour and be allowed to live on the higher decks with him. Her relationship with the animals, though perhaps not consciously, is pro-animal and anti-patriarchal. She sees the non-human animals around her not just as sharing a similar experience of oppression, but as her kin; she leverages her position as Dr Noyes' wife to attempt small acts of defiance intended to protect the beings that her husband disregards. In doing so, she demonstrates a sense of duty of care like that displayed by Robert in *The Wars*, finding comfort in relationships with animals outside of a governing patriarchal influence. Thus, in contrast to *Genesis* and dominant cultural understandings of Noah, wherein Noah has been immortalised as a key Godly figure, in this version of the story, it is Noah's wife who takes centre stage in the narrative and shows care to all creatures, even to those *Not Wanted on the Voyage*.

Rescuing those 'Not Wanted'

The title of Findley's novel, *Not Wanted on the Voyage*, is a stark reminder of the gap that the cultural knowledge of the *Genesis* myth fails to fill. For all of the animals that entered "2 by 2", as the famous song goes, there would have been millions that perished in the flood. Although the flood was a biblical event and reportedly the will of God, Findley's novel points out the violence and cruelty in such a notion. One such way that Findley's novel does this is through the depiction of three so-called "ape-children". Whilst their creation nods to the proximity of humans to apes, these children are characterised in the novel as a genetic abnormality because of their visual ape-ness, perceived almost as an evolutionary failure: an underdeveloped human. However, they aren't apes; they are biologically conceived by two human parents, which means that the characterisation of them as "ape-children" is a product of Dr Noyes' ableist way of talking about bodies that do not conform to his anthropocentric edict. This is further reinforced by the fact that they are kept secret by the families they are born into, seen as a marker of shame because they reportedly indicate towards a kind of genetic impurity running within that family. The repulsion at their existence by Dr Noyes in particular signifies the binary he draws between human and non-human, believing that any being that is not wholly human is thereby non-human and a threat to the purity and superiority of the human species. Unfortunately, three such "ape-children" appear in the novel in close proximity to the Noyes family; Mr and Mrs Noyes have a "ape-child" son, Adam, who is born and dies before the novel begins; Emma, who is Dr Noyes's daughter-in-law, married to his son Japeth, has an "ape-child" sister named Lotte; and the third "ape-child" is born to Hannah, the wife of his son Shem, whilst on board the ark, and with whom ironically Dr Noyes himself has spent considerable close (and most likely intimate) time with.

Wendy Pearson links Dr Noyes' obsession with genetics to the queer nature of the novel, arguing that it can only be read 'in light of the Human Genome Project, the search for the gay gene, and the genocidal potential of genetic engineering and biotechnology', and as such:

> Those most at risk from these developing technologies are the ones at the bottom of the social hierarchy, invisible as selves but all too visible—and vulnerable—as objects of study, experimentation, destruction.[24]

Such an analysis centres the "ape-children" as a queering element in the narrative, resulting in a re-writing of a Genesis myth in which Noah's children are homosexual, thereby complicating the repopulation of the earth that is to follow in this creation story. However, this analysis reduces the species element of their characterisation to a symbolic significance. Rather, an intersection of these strands is more effective in acknowledging the relationship between the queer and speciesist elements of the novel. Findley does not privilege one social oppression over another, but rather, through the ambiguous characterisation of these "ape-children", and through the intersection of using them to queer the narrative by the troubling of the question of species that they represent, he problematizes the violence underlying genetics and hierarchy.

Of all the "ape-children", Lotte plays the most significant part in the narrative. When the flood begins, Mrs Noyes discovers Lotte abandoned in the rising waters and is immediately transported back to a memory of her child, Adam: 'Mrs Noyes had never forgotten her unwelcome baby—her pariah—nor how she had lost it.'[25] Working concurrently within this immensely tragic moment, in which a child has been abandoned to her death due to a logic of difference, is a demonstration of a deep sense of care. Giving attention to Haraway's understanding that 'people become kin largely by sharing experiences and generating a sense of belonging'[26] Mrs Noyes decides to rescue Lotte and bring her to the ark in a radical act of kinship that reinforces a sense of belonging ruptured by the exclusionary ark and Noah's speciesist doctrine, refusing to let Lotte become a 'pariah' like her son.

Noting that she is trapped on the other side of a rapidly rising and fast flowing river, Mrs Noyes puts herself at risk to cross and retrieve Lotte, reassuring her 'don't be afraid …' (152) This moment is strikingly sentimental in its symbolic significance because it imagines what it would be like to put yourself at risk out of concern for a member of another species and to literally and figuratively walk through the river together. Philip Armstrong writes of sentimental narratives that they 're-engage literary fiction with the most vital and intimate of contemporary structures of feeling.'[27] Indeed, the kinship that Mrs Noyes demonstrates here, risking herself for Lotte, does reinvigorate the tragic narrative of her abandonment with a sense of care that is deeply moving.

Mrs Noyes' thoughts whilst she is crossing the river reinforce not only her desire to detach herself from the ideologies that permitted Lotte to be abandoned, but also her dislike and distrust of Yahweh for the cruelty of reinforcing this through the deliverance of a flood: 'pray she almost thought, that Lotte will not be afraid when she sees me coming. But I will not pray: not to You, gone mad up there with Your vengeance.' (146) The subversive nature of Findley's characterisation of Mrs Noyes is evident here though her foregrounding of her feelings of maternal protection over her religious duty. In addition, Mrs Noyes does not define her maternal feelings and sense of responsibility within an anthropocentric or genetic framework. In rescuing Lotte, Mrs Noyes gets a second chance at the motherhood role she was denied with her son Adam, actively defying the word of God and of her husband who have deemed them both 'not wanted'. Although Mrs Noyes' efforts are tragically revealed to be in vain when Dr Noyes later kills Lotte on board the ark, by reconfiguring the Genesis story in a way that challenges the figure of a submissive and obedient wife, Findley reimagines a story in which even amongst a catastrophically tragic event perpetuated by a violent speciesist patriarchy, there is a hope that emerges within small radical acts of feminist care. That he does this through a depiction of a camp humoristic depiction of the disobedient wife reinforces the significance of the camp aesthetic to the species politics of the novel.

Caring for the Ark

In this camp exaggerated construction of "goodies" and "baddies" in the novel, Dr Noyes is the perpetrator of violence and Mrs Noyes is the protector, actively working to challenge his patriarchal dominance wherever she can. Her feminist care ethics are a reminder of Donovan's statement that 'what we share—life—is more important than our differences.'[28]

When we think of Noah's Ark, it is common to think of child-like depictions of the animals enthusiastically boarding the ark in their pairs and living harmoniously on board under Noah's protection. However, in Findley's novel, he presents a more realistic depiction of life on board a boat filled with numerous pairs of animal species being governed by a man that shows little care for those who are not human. One such way this is demonstrated is through the division of space on the ark. Noah, Japeth, Shem, and Hannah are permitted to live on the higher levels of the ark, with access to fresh air and space because they follow Dr Noyes' edict unquestionably. Mrs Noyes, Emma, Ham and Lucy must remain locked in the confined lower spaces of the ark with the animals because they repeatedly question Dr Noyes' authority. However, rather than viewing this as the abusive and oppressive dynamic it is intended to be, Mrs Noyes relishes in the freedom from Dr Noyes. In the depth of the ark, Mrs Noyes establishes her kinship with the animals, caring for them with a sense of duty that parallels Robert's in *The Wars*.

It is tempting to read Mrs Noyes' life in the ark as akin to a zoo and zookeeper, given the collection of enclosures within one larger space on board; however, the unique nature of the ark, in which they are all prisoners of the lower decks, provides a stark difference. Rather, the ark functions like a concentrated animal farm; each animal pair confined to a small, inadequate enclosure, being kept alive to ultimately re-populate their species once the flood is over. This microscopic critique of farming conditions and the cruelty of keeping animals imprisoned in this way is offered some relief by Mrs Noyes' care for the animals. She notes that 'she and all these creatures with her shared their captivity in a way that they could never have shared the wood.' (241) It is through being confined together, then, that the dynamics of their relationships have been altered. This is further reiterated in her description of the ark as akin to a baby's cradle:

> Though the ark was absolute hell in so many ways and though all their lives were so appalling—caged and underfed, left without air and daylight, separated from all their kind but one—there was nonetheless some comfort here

in the lamplight, all of them warm together, nesting and being rocked together in this great, fat cradle on the waters. (240)

It is in this sentimental description of 'togetherness' that there is some comfort and peace in an otherwise oppressive and hellish situation. If it is Haraway's contention that 'actual encounters are what make beings', then it is through Mrs Noyes' proximity and material interactions with these animals that a kinship is established that moves beyond species boundaries. The rules that governed their prior relationships and interactions no longer stand because of their unusual proximity in enclosures on board a vessel that is the only means to guarantee their future survival. Confined, as Mrs Noyes notes, to captivity, there is no sense of predator and prey, no active hunting, or any room for the animals to carry out their usual behavioural idiosyncrasies. They swiftly become kin that are sharing both a space and an experience, living more closely aligned lives than ever before. This returns us to Donovan's statement that in an ethics of care, what matters is an acknowledgement and privileging of shared existence over difference.[29] Mrs Noyes's caring for the animals is a recognition of them as her kin, and an acknowledgement of the ways in which she can leverage her humanness and its privileges to the animals' benefit, exercising an ethics of care in accessing and managing food to maintain them through the long duration of the flood.

Most significantly, Mr Noyes recognises the emotional needs of the animals, abandoning the caution that kept her at a distance from species that she hadn't before interacted with. In doing so, she demonstrates an approach to interspecies relationships that recognises and sympathises with suffering in the other through a shared sense of imprisonment and oppression, adopting a 'nurturing and caring' approach to them.[30] Moreover, she finds emotional joy in the closeness that this brings. This interspecies closeness and the emotional value that can be found in these relationships are most closely imagined in a scene wherein Mrs Noyes comforts a weeping bear. She ventures into the bear cage to give comfort to a bear who has become distressed due to a storm, despite admitting that the species both 'terrified and infuriated her.' (223) This encounter is loaded with meaning given that it was written after Canadian author Marian Engel's *Bear* (1975), the subject of the previous chapter of this book. In *Bear*, the animal protagonist refutes all symbolic readings and refuses to conform to the idea of bears that the human protagonist, Lou, constructs of him. Findley's bear, however, does not resist meaning, but it is not symbolic either. Rather, Findley mobilizes anthropomorphism to deliver an emotional politics that feeds into a wider logic regarding the unity of the oppressed and drive for an ethics of care as a means of coping with their confinement.

Whereas Lou fails to initiate an intimate relationship with the bear, Mrs Noyes does not. Through engaging specifically with a woman-bear relationship, Findley depicts a successful, caring, and intimate interspecies relationship with an animal that has famously evaded such depiction in the work of his literary predecessor because he privileges representing kinship and shared life experience over an emphasis of materiality and difference of species. The interaction that occurs within the cage serves as comfort to both Mrs Noyes and the bear through a reciprocated embrace. She offers physical contact to the bear by 'put[ting] her arms to the weeping bear' (223) to which it then 'stepped into the proffered embrace and hung its head on Mrs Noyes's shoulder.' (224) The perceived acceptance of the physical contact by the bear at first leaves Mrs Noyes contemplating her next behaviour, but this doubt is quickly overcome:

> She sat on the floor of the bear cage and held the terrified bear until it fell asleep with its head in her lap …
> In the morning, that was how Ham found them—his mother in her nightdress—snoring in the straw, with a bear on either side, asleep. (241)

The campness of the scene is reinforced through the humour of Ham's discovery, the mundaneness of his mother's nightdress and the 'snoring' undercutting the immensity of emotion that drove her to enter the enclosure in the first place. The camp nature of the scene works to lighten the tragedy of their confinement, reinforcing the beauty of these small caring moments in which Mr Noyes recognises the animal as a being capable of reciprocating her affection. She powerfully notes that 'on the ark, she not only walked amongst bears—she *sat* amongst them and was unafraid' (251) Her use of the words 'amongst' and 'unafraid' speak to the reciprocated, functioning relationship she now has with them, achieving a version of the 'we' that Robert visualised when he barricaded himself in with the horses in *The Wars*.

Queering, Caring, Kinship: Conclusions

In both *The Wars* and *Not Wanted on the Voyage* affection for and kinship with animals is consistently figured as a way of characterising a kind of resistance to domineering masculinity that Findley represents as heteronormative and patriarchal. Resistance to this emerges through a code of ethics that places emphasis on care, reciprocity, and belonging which is consistent with feminist practices outlined by Adams and Donovan.

In *The Wars* Robert struggles with his role as an officer who must carry out normalised killing and visit brothels to maintain the image of masculinised heroism, ultimately choosing to recognise heroism as defying his military duty in favour of kinship with animals. Such a repositioning of heroic duty by way of inhabiting the genre of war fiction contends that through an ethics of care we might abandon such heroic nostalgia that mourns a period of mass violence. In comparison, *Not Wanted on the Voyage* is a more explicitly camp novel that mobilises stereotypes to create humour that undercuts the tragedy of the genocidal disaster happening in the context of the novel. The novel demonstrates that born out of these sites of oppression are opportunities for deep, caring moments spurred by a shared experience.

Much like Robert's struggles with military duty, Mrs Noyes battles with a religious duty. Both ultimately choose to privilege their ethical duty, at times succeeding and at others failing. Mrs Noyes' ability to form meaningful relationships with the animals on the ark does permit more positive and sentimental moments of kinship and togetherness than realised in *The Wars*, wherein Robert's kinship is destroyed in a camp display of violence and death. Despite these differences in the way in which these concepts are played out in each novel, there is evidently a logic at play within both texts that exposes Findley's representational strategy as being a queering of the narrative forms that he is working within to destabilise the masculinised and heteronormative foundations of their construction. In addition, there is an ethics of care at play within both Findley's novels that intersects with a queer ideology and imagines a kinship that moves beyond such socially oppressive constructions. Queer theory and the use of camp is presented as a useful representational strategy within writing about animals because it is dedicated to a radically anti-hegemonic way of thinking, subverting particular narratives, and opening up the possibility for a pro-animal ethics to emerge. Findley's novels, then, build upon the critically self-conscious style of writing adopted by his predecessor, Engel, and introduce a pro-animal element that opens up space for more developed understandings of material relationships between humans and animals.

Notes

1. Timothy Findley (1984) *Dinner Along the Amazon* (Penguin Books) p. IX.
2. Susan McHugh (2000) 'Marrying My Bitch: J. R. Ackerley's Pack Sexualities', *Critical Inquiry*, 27.1, 21–41, p. 23.
3. McHugh, 'Marrying My Bitch', p. 23.
4. Esther Newton (1999) 'Role Models', in *Camp: Queer Aesthetics and the Performing Subject*, ed. by Fabio Cleto (Edinburgh: Edinburgh University Press) pp. 976–109, p. 102.
5. Richard Dyer (1999) 'Its Being So Camp As Keeps Us Going' in *Camp: Queer Aesthetics and the Performing Subject*, ed. by Fabio Cleto (Edinburgh: Edinburgh University Press) pp. 110–116, p. 111.
6. Dyer, 'Its Being So Camp As Keeps Us Going', pp. 110–111.
7. Dyer, 'Its Being So Camp As Keeps Us Going', p. 114.
8. Donna Haraway (2018) 'Making Kin in the Chthulucene: Reproducing Multispecies Justice' in *Making Kin Not Population*, ed. By Adele. E. Clarke and Donna Haraway (Chicago: Prickly Paradigm Press) pp. 67–101, p. 69.
9. Haraway, 'Making Kin in the Chthulucene: Reproducing Multispecies Justice' p. 3) and p. 93–4 respectively.
10. Haraway, 'Making Kin in the Chthulucene: Reproducing Multispecies Justice' (p. 3).
11. Josephine Donovan, 'Attention to Suffering: Sympathy as a Basis for Ethical Treatment of Animals', in The Feminist Care Tradition in Animal Ethics, ed. by Carol J. Adams and Josephine Donovan (New York: Columbia University Press, 2007) pp. 174–198, p. 203.
12. Timothy Findley (2001) *The Wars* (London: Faber and Faber Limited) p. 15. [All subsequent quotations taken from this edition].
13. Shane Rhodes (1998) 'Buggering With History: Sexual Warfare and Historical Reconstruction in Timothy Findley's *The Wars*', *Canadian Literature, A Quarterly of Criticism and Review: Gay and Lesbian Writing in Canadian Literature*, 159, 38–53, p. 39.
14. Brooke charity reports that there is no definitive figure for the number of horses that died during the Second World War, but that estimates vary between 2–5 million. https://www.thebrooke.org/get-involved/every-horse-remembered/war-horse-facts#:~:text=How%20many%20horses%2C%20

donkeys%20and%20mules%20died%20in%20WW2%3F,vary%20between%202%2D5%20million. [Accessed 19 May 2023].
15. Haraway, Making Kin in the Chthulucene', p. 287.
16. Carol J. Adams and Josephine Donovan (2007) *The Feminist Care Tradition in Animal Ethics* (New York: Columbia University Press) p. 2.
17. Webb, '"At War With Nature": Animals in Timothy Findley's *The Wars*', p. 231.
18. Webb, '"At War With Nature": Animals in Timothy Findley's *The Wars*', p. 231.
19. Terry Goldie (2003) *Pink Snow: Homotextual Possibilities in Canadian Fiction* (Ontario: Broadview Press) p. 159.
20. Susan Sontag (1999) Notes on 'Camp' in *Camp: Queer Aesthetics and the Performing Subject*, ed. by Fabio Cleto (Edinburgh: Edinburgh University Press), p. 56 and p. 60 respectively.
21. Esther Newton (1972) *Mother Camp: Female Impersonators in America* (Chicago: University of Chicago Press) p. 107.
22. Diana Brydon, 'A Devotion to Fragility: Timothy Findley's *The Wars*'p. 78.
23. The definition of a nuclear family is, according to Britannica: "**nuclear family**, also called **elementary family**, in sociology and anthropology, a group of people who are united by ties of partnership and parenthood and consisting of a pair of adults and their socially recognised children. Typically, but not always, the adults in a nuclear family are married." https://www.britannica.com/topic/family-kinship [Accessed 19 May 2023].
24. Wendy Pearson (1998) 'Vanishing Acts II: Queer Reading(s) of Timothy Findley's Headhunter and Not Wanted on the Voyage', *Journal of Canadian Studies*, 33.4, 114–131, p. 128.
25. Timothy Findley (2006) *Not Wanted on the Voyage* (Canada: Penguin Canada) p. 142 [All subsequent quotations taken from this edition].
26. Haraway, 'Making Kin in the Chthulucene', p. 3.
27. Philip Armstrong (2008) *What Animals Mean in the Fiction of Modernity* (London: Routledge) p. 225.
28. Josephine Donovan (2007) 'Animal Rights and Feminist Theory' in *The Feminist Care Tradition in Animal Ethics*, ed. by Josephine Donovan and Carol J. Adams (New York: Columbia University Press) pp. 58–87, p. 74.
29. Donovan, 'Animal Rights and Feminist Theory', p. 74.
30. Carol J. Adams (2007) 'Caring About Suffering: A Feminist Exploration' in *The Feminist Care Tradition in Animal Ethics* ed. by Carol J. Adams and Josephine Donovan (New York: Columbia University Press) pp. 198–227, p. 201.

CHAPTER 6

Unsettling Coyote: Engaging with Indigenous Concepts of Care in Gail Anderson-Dargatz's *The Cure for Death by Lightning* (1996)

Canadian settler author Gail Anderson-Dargatz grew up in the Shuswap-Thompson region of British Columbia, an area that she says is engrained with the history and stories of the Shuswap Band Nation.[1] In an interview with *Serendipity* in 2009, Anderson-Dargatz was asked about the inspiration behind her 1996 novel, *The Cure for Death by Lightning*, a novel whose narrative is haunted by imagery and stories of coyotes. She said: 'we live with Coyote every day here in the Shuswap ... [they] have an uncanny ability to appear and disappear out of and into nowhere ...You'd swear they were transformers, magic.'[2] Her reference to their 'magic' is a nod to the narratives surrounding the coyotes that inhabit the landscape with a prowess for being unnoticed, but it also alludes to the elusive trickster figure known as Coyote that appears in many stories belonging to North American Indigenous Nations. Anderson-Dargatz credits her own parents with being talented storytellers, whom she says combined ghosts and magical realism into their stories about the area in which they lived. As a consequence, *The Cure for Death by Lightning* is heavily informed by an awareness of Shuswap–settler relations in the region, including the historical displacement of the Shuswap Band Peoples, ongoing conflict regarding land claims in British Columbia, and the stories that have informed relationships with this land.

The Cure for Death by Lightning follows fifteen-year-old Beth Weeks, who lives on an isolated farm in Shuswap with her mother, brother and her increasingly violent father. After what the local settler community believe to be a bear attack on a young girl, Beth begins to feel that she too is being stalked by something. A local Indigenous matriarch and friend of her mother, Bertha Moses, tells Beth and her mother that a bear is not responsible for the attack, but that it is the trickster Coyote who has possessed the local men. Beth begins to contend with her own knowledge of the landscape and the threats that lurk within now that this new concept of danger has been introduced by the Indigenous characters. In doing so, Beth begins to spend more time with the Indigenous characters, particularly with Beth's granddaughter Nora, viewing Indigenous relationships with the more-than-human world and the time she spends in Indigenous spaces as a 'cure' for the controlling and violent nature of her father and protection from the threat that follows her.

Despite the novel's success in Canada, becoming both a best seller and award-winning piece of fiction, limited critical attention has been given to *The Cure for Death by Lightning*.[3] In particular, little has been said of the text's representation of human-animal relations beyond a symbolic understanding. Heidi Slettedahl Macpherson identifies the novel's use of the Coyote story as a means of offering a feminist critique of male violence, arguing that Coyote is:

> The unnamed "it" who follows Beth Weeks, frightens her, and abuses her ... Coyote is the name of her unmentionable fear: of her father, of other men, of boys ... An adolescent, Beth is at risk of sexual assault both within the home and outside of it.[4]

In contrast, Marlene Goldman's situates the novel within the Canadian gothic tradition and argues that the haunting elements of the text are underpinned by a postcolonial critique:

> [The text] register[s] the uncanny status of Canada and British Columbia, in particular, by representing conflicts between those aligned with the patriarchal, Christian, settler community and those aligned with the unsettling trickster-god Coyote. A transformer-god who provided sustenance for his people, Coyote embodies, for the settler-invader society, the uncanny, Aboriginal claim to the land.[5]

As a non-Indigenous academic, it is neither appropriate nor easy to comment on the specifics of the Coyote figure, however, much has been written on the subject of settler authors utilising and engaging with the trickster story. In *Troubling Tricksters: Revisioning Critical Conversations*, Linda M Morra and Deanna Reder assert that the 1980s was dominated by debates on appropriation. Notably, in 1989 the founding chair of the Racial Minority Writers' Committee of The Writers' Union of Canada (TWUC), Lenore Keeshig-Tobias, stated that 'the stories and cultures of the First Nations (and, by extension, other minorities) should not be appropriated by non-native writers' (Moore).[6] She added:

> You know, in our culture, people own stories. Individuals own stories. Families own stories. Tribes own stories. Nations own stories. And there is a protocol if you want to tell those stories: you go to the storyteller. And if you don't and you start telling those stories, then you are stealing.[7]

To overlook such a particularised relationship to these stories, then, exposes either one's ignorance to cultural differences or one's wilful desire to steal and use these narratives *in spite of* these differences. In more contemporary conversations, the notion of settler writers engaging with Indigenous stories has been seen as a positive move towards the inclusion of Indigenous knowledge within wider cultural understanding. Daniel Morley Johnson states:

> The recent scholarship of North American Indigenous literary nationalist critics has emphasized the need for work that responds not only to the intellectual paradigms of Indigenous nations, but also to the needs of Indigenous communities. Unlike some Native Studies academics, I do not take this call for accountability to mean that only Native people can write about Native literature. In fact, nationalist critics explicitly state the opposite—they simply and rightfully demand a meaningful, informed engagement with Indigenous peoples and their texts. This approach, according to Daniel Heath Justice (Cherokee), "is not a necessarily exclusivist act that seeks an idealized cultural purity," but rather "a deeply realistic and life-affirming act".[8]

For Johnson and Heath Justice the context upon which this engagement with Indigenous stories occurs is a crucial factor in critiquing settler fiction. What is evident from the existing criticism on settler engagements with Coyote stories is that the figure has often been deployed as a blanket means of representing a culture that is "unknowable" to settlers. Kristina Fagan writes that 'the pan-tribal trickster archetype offered a way of managing the issue of Indigenous "difference" without requiring extensive research into the complexity of particular Indigenous peoples.'⁹ It has been, then, an easy tool for settler authors to appear to be making meaningful engagements with Indigenous peoples and stories, but in actuality utilising Indigenous stories to reinforce a stereotypical narrative that fails to acknowledge the depth and diversity of Indigenous cultures and epistemologies.

This chapter will take these complexities into consideration in an analysis of *The Cure for Death by Lightning* to contend that Anderson-Dargatz's novel engages with this notion of the Coyote figure as an archetype of difference. The story of Coyote is deliberately kept vague, introduced elusively by Bertha. Bertha tells Beth and her mother that Coyote is a spirit figure who is repeatedly reborn, possessing the bodies of anyone he chooses. In Bertha's story, like in the majority of Indigenous trickster stories, Coyote is male.[10] However, Bertha fails to provide any further detail or to explain the significance that this Coyote figure has to the Shuswap Band community. Such vagueness not only contributes to the further mysterious coding of the trickster figure in the novel, but it also rescues the novel from falling into a stereotypical settler engagement with Indigeneity, that is, that it is neither Anderson-Dargatz's story to tell and that there is no one Coyote story indicative of all Indigenous cultural values. Franchot Ballinger states:

> A story represents a single storyteller's interpretation of how a story's narrative details open a window on his or her culture's values. Clearly, the cultural value theme dramatized in one telling of a trickster story may not be at all present in another telling.[11]

This chapter therefore does not attempt to suggest that the novel's interaction with Coyote is an entry point into understanding Indigenous culture more broadly, but rather to emphasise that the Coyote story's insertion into the settler community casts doubt on their bear attack narrative, thereby disrupting their knowledge of the human-animal relations in the area. By introducing this narrative of an animal spirit figure that has possessed the local men, *The Cure for Death by Lightning* exposes a gap in knowledge that demands attention: there are Indigenous stories and epistemologies that are valuable and legitimate for understanding the land that settlers have not engaged with. In paying attention to the role of the Coyote story, despite the lack of detail given by Bertha, this analysis demands a broader contemplation of human-animal relations in the novel;

it implores a re-evaluation of the way in which we relate to animals by focusing attention on Indigenous knowledge.

This context informs the praxis of the chapter's analysis itself, which centres Indigenous theories and epistemologies, particularly eco-feminism as defined by Kim TallBear (Sisseton Wahpeton Oyate) and Melissa K Nelson (Anishinaabe/Métis/Norwegian) because, as Billy-Ray Belcourt notes, 'Indigeneity ought to be at the core of any theory of ethical living.'[12] In order to successfully centre Indigenous epistemologies in conversations around human-animal relations, it is imperative that this is approached through a decolonial route which elevates Indigenous voices, particularly in a chapter focused on a settler novel about Indigenous stories.

By focusing on Beth's fascination with the female Indigenous characters of the novel and their relationship with the more-than-human world around them, this chapter will reflect on the feminist care ethics outlined in the previous chapter by examining the representation of the female Indigenous characters and spaces in relation to the settler female characters. In the matriarch Bertha's house, filled only with women, chickens enter freely and lay eggs, signifying an absence of spatial boundaries between determined human and animal spaces that contrasts to Beth's family's farm on which the value of a cow is defined by its existence as a resource for extraction. In addition, attention will be given to Bertha's decision not to re-marry and to Bertha's granddaughter, Nora's, queer identity, both of which offer a sense of female agency that radically contrasts with the strictly patriarchal and heteronormative world of Beth and the settler community. In doing so, the chapter attempts to reconcile the novel's meaningful call for serious engagement with Indigenous epistemologies of non-human animals with its characteristic settler failure to provide a detailed engagement with the specifics of the Coyote story.

Eco-Sexual Spaces and Cross-Species Relations

The traditional heteronormative family-centred lifestyle favoured by settlers is a colonial relic that has not only defined hetero-marital life as the norm, but has also been used to supplant Indigenous beliefs surrounding ways of relating. Scott L. Morgensen writes:

> Colonization produced the biopolitics of modern sexuality that I call "settler sexuality": a white national heteronormativity that regulates Indigenous sexuality and gender by supplanting them with the sexual modernity of settler subjects.[13]

Sexuality and the regulation of it is an influential tool of colonisation because it provides an avenue for retaining a particular form of control over individuals and their bodies.[14] Similarly, Kim TallBear (Sisseton Wahpeton Oyate) has stated that settler concepts of familial relations are deeply grounded in heteronormative monogamous ideals, and that this has been forced on Indigenous Nations globally. In contrast, she argues, Indigenous concepts of sexuality and of forming relations offer a way of relating to both humans and more-than-humans that are less oppressive and more sustainable because they are not determined by maintaining heteronormativity. This latter point regarding sustainability, she explains, stems from her belief that settler colonial relations are 'unsustainable kinship forms' and 'are not sustainable economically or materially' because they turn both the land and its inhabitants into belongings through the ownership of land bodies and water as private property on which to 'settle'.[15] In addition, she terms these kinds of normative, couple centred forms of relationships 'intimate privilege' and says that they go 'hand in hand with discourses of evolution and race and imposition of marriage and monogamy as a technique for state management of indigenous bodies.'[16] It is imperative, therefore, to move away from these colonial frameworks for establishing relations because they are inherently oppressive to non-human and Indigenous bodies and ways-of-being. One such means of doing this is to adopt an Indigenous relationality that TallBear defines as 'eco-sexuality': establishing good relations across familial and other, including more-than-human, relations, that does not divide the erotic between human and non-human bodies. This, TallBear argues, 'might be powerful enough to soothe the pains of colonisation and internal-colonisation.'[17]

In *The Cure for Death by Lightning*, Indigenous spaces and characters are indeed depicted as less subject to a domineering sense of heteropatriarchy. It is important to note that this is the perception of teenage Beth, a victim of her abusive father, who desperately searches for a more caring way of relating to the world and does not understand the colonial history of Shuswap. When spending time with the Indigenous women, Beth witnesses a mode of relating to the more-than-human world that is more caring and less divisive, both spatially in that animals freely enter their home rather than being confined to pens like on Beth's father's farm, and ideologically, in that the Indigenous characters welcome this blurring between human and more-than-human worlds, practising that which this chapter determines to be eco-sexuality. In addition, Beth admires and is envious of the Indigenous women's ability to choose their own clothing and she observes their relaxed attitude to the non-human animals that appear to be attracted to and comfortable around them: 'I followed the women a little way down Blood Road; the birds followed them too, attracted to their glittering jewellery and bright ribbons … Purple swallows zoomed around them.'[18] To Beth, their bright clothing, which contrasts with the 'modest' and neutral way of dressing that she, her mother, and the other women of the settler community adopt, is tied to their relationship with the birds, symbolically reflecting a different and more vibrant way of relating to those around them.

Beth observes the contrast between the way in which her mother wears her hair and the hair of Bertha, her mother's Indigenous friend. Her mother wears 'milking clothes, a brown housedress and gum boots, and her long, long hair was tucked away in a blue kerchief, so you'd think she had no hair at all.' (8) By covering her hair, Beth's mother emphasises her adherence to the patriarchal rules of religious modesty that deem her hair an emphasis of desirable femininity that must be covered. Her clothing denotes her role on the farm and thereby symbolically reinforces a particular relationship to animals that hinges upon the heteronormative regulation of dairy agriculture. In contrast, Bertha's hair is described as 'done up in a single braid that lay down the back of her red dress, and her sleeves were scandalously rolled up to the elbow' and she wore 'black stockings and moccasins decorated with porcupine quills and embroidery.' (8) The incorporation of decorative porcupine quills indicates towards a different kind of relationship with non-human animals: one that operates outside of heteronormativity and incorporates animal skins and feathers into a cultural aesthetic. In addition, Bertha does not observe the same rules of gendered modesty and neither do her daughters. Rather, Bertha's daughters are playful in their clothing choices, mixing gendered clothing and confidently wearing colour. Beth notes that 'one of the daughters' wore boys' jeans and a western shirt that stretched a little at the buttons across her breasts' and 'she wore lipstick and a necklace of bells strung together.' (9) She adds, 'I coveted that necklace … She saw me looking at it and jingled it, and the room filled with tinkling notes that lit up everyone's face.' (9) Beth envies this necklace because of what it represents to her: freedom of feminine expression. It is interesting to note, however, her choice of the word 'covet', which implies that she perceives her envy of this necklace as a sin. Her entrapment within a specifically Christian settler patriarchal doctrine, which determines her expression of her gender to be a sin, means that Beth identifies a more libertarian way of living that is more overtly feminist in its expression to be Indigenous.

This particularised relationship to non-human animals that the novel's Indigenous characters are represented as holding draws upon a common theme within Indigenous storytelling. Melissa K. Nelson (Anishinaabe/ Métis) claims that many North American Indigenous stories depict women as having 'distinct role[s] as mediators between humans and other beings' because 'they are fluid boundary crossers who can enter and maintain erotic intimacy and economic trade with nonhumans.'[19] Indeed this connection between gender and boundary-crossing is evidenced in Anderson-Dargatz's novel when a chicken flies in through the window at Bertha's house:

> The women all laughed ... I started to get up, to help catch the chicken, but Nora held my arm ...We all watched the chicken nestle a place for herself among the magazines and rabbit fur on the mattress, cluck and croon and lay an egg. (116)

Beth instinctively tries to remove the chicken because she understands the space to be a human domestic space and thus not somewhere that animals should enter. Chris Philo and Chris Wilbert have commented on the construction of spatial species boundaries and argue that the transgression of non-human animals into socially understood 'human spaces' renders them 'beastly places'. This is because in crossing into this space, the animal demonstrates an agency that 'count[ers] the proper places stipulated for them by humans, thus creating their own "beastly places" reflective of their own "beastly" ways, ends, doings, joys and sufferings.'[20] It is therefore this transgressive assertion of agency by the chicken that is unfamiliar to Beth, but evidently not so to Bertha and her daughters. Their indifference and the chicken's willingness to 'nestle' in the house indicate that this is a regular occurrence.

In Bertha's house, there are no spatial divisions between human and animal habitation because there are no such distinctions between species and privilege, and indeed Philo and Wilbert recognise that there is often a difference in understanding of human-animal spatial relations in Indigenous cultures:

> With the taking seriously of 'other' knowledges—notably non-Western 'indigenous' knowledges or ethnosciences—which provide a less dualistic

account of the differences between humans and animals, many people (outside the West, but in it too) have started to deconstruct seemingly obvious claims about the privileged status of the human, in contradistinction to the animal, as the source of agency in the world.[21]

It is through this contrast in reaction to the nestling chicken in Bertha's kitchen that the novel is able to demonstrate a difference in knowledge and ways of relating to non-human animals and 'animal spaces'. To the Shuswap characters, all spaces are shared, which means that all spaces are in fact 'beastly places' as much as they are also 'human spaces', thereby eradicating the notion of species spatial boundaries entirely. The agency developed in this distinction is that it is women that are represented as the facilitators of this boundary removal, reinforcing Nelson's aforementioned statement and asserting a type of feminist challenge to settler sexuality.

In bringing together this relationship between species, gender and sexuality, Anishinaabe/Métis critic Nelson comments that she and TallBear share a common interest in '"greening" Indigenous queer theory and investigating how Indigenous stories portray social relations with nonhumans.'[22] Notably TallBear does not specifically focus on non-human animals in her broader definition of eco-sexuality, but Nelson does. Nelson argues that interactions with other beings provide 'contact zones' in which a process takes place that she calls 'getting dirty.' Nelson writes that what occurs in these contact zones is 'a messy, visceral, eco-erotic boundary-crossing entanglement of difference that can engender empathy and kinship and a lived environmental ethic.'[23] 'Getting dirty' with non-human animals, then, as Beth does when she shares Bertha's house with the nesting chicken, endears a way of relating that is grounded in empathy and normalises an 'entangled' sense of living that is not determined by either literal and figurative species boundaries.

There is something inherently feminist in the type of eco-sexual nurturing that occurs in Bertha's kitchen. The chicken that enters is described as nesting, clucking and then laying an egg. The significance of this is such that it codes Bertha's house, governed by Indigenous knowledge and crowded with her granddaughters and Beth, as a space that specifically nurtures cross-species female energy to the extent that even female animals feel comfortable enough to enter it and lay their eggs amongst their female human relations. In this space, no such boundaries between human and non-human space exist and female bodies are celebrated, normalised, and nurtured.

The coding of Bertha's house in this way is made more prominent when compared to Beth's family's dairy farm, wherein the cows are confined within specific enclosures away from the house and their bodies are regulated and governed by specific agricultural expectations. Cows, like humans, only produce milk as a result of being pregnant.[24] Thus the regulation of their bodies on the farm centres around their reproductive capability. Beth's father's control extends across species boundaries in his control of both Beth's clothing and expression of her femininity and the female cows' bodies and their ability to keep producing milk. It is unsurprising, therefore, that despite her non-Indigenous identity, in the context of this shared patriarchal oppression, Beth demonstrates a desire to foster better ways of relating to non-human animals, expressing empathy where her father shows indifference.

This is made particularly visible in a scene in which Beth's father decides to operate on a cow to remove her ovaries, as she is no longer able to become pregnant and must now be prepared to be sold as a beef cow. In contrast to her father, whom she describes as nonchalantly carrying out the surgery 'as if he was carving the Sunday roast', (84) Beth is visibly upset by the cow's distress, noting that 'the cow bawled and bawled … I wanted to stroke her, to offer her some comfort, but I had to keep her head straight.' (84) Once her father finishes his butchery, Beth is able to demonstrate her kindness towards the cow: 'I filled a bucket with water and put it in front of her and smoothed the hair between her horns.' (100) The contrast between her father's 'carving' and her 'smoothing' touch reflects their diverging capacities for empathy. Beth recognises the violence in her father's actions and the pain that this causes the cow, whereas her father only understands the animal within his farming framework—she is his livestock to be managed. It is particularly melancholy that Beth is reminded of her father 'carving the Sunday roast' because this indicates that family life and the preservation of nuclear family ideals, such as sitting at the table to eat a Sunday roast, are founded on inherently violent sources, both colonially through the displacement of the Indigenous Nations who lived on the land that they now farm, but also in relation to animals, through the exploitation and consuming of their bodies.

Understanding Beth's empathy for the cows through this lens of a shared experience of patriarchal oppression emerges also in the practice of milking. Beth describes her father's technique as 'yanking', causing the cows to kick him, and her brother's technique as unhelpfully slow. However, for Beth and her mother, milking the cows becomes a time in which a type of peaceful tactile intimacy between her mother, herself and the cows is realised, akin to Nelson's process of 'getting dirty':

> Mostly it was my mother and I, milking to the rhythms of our own heartbeats, so close sometimes that the milk squirted into the pails in unison, like an iambic drumbeat … My mother sang quietly, and we milked with our heads against the warm flanks of our cows … They knew us enough to trust us. (39)

This calm and intimate encounter contrasts heavily with the aforementioned 'carving' and 'yanking' done by her father. The 'iambic drumbeat' of their milking in unison conveys a sense of effortless musicality to their touch that is mirrored in the calm rhythm of their heartbeats. Moreover, Beth conveys a sense of reciprocity in her description of this intimacy, noting that the cows 'trusted' her and her mother enough to allow them to rest their heads against their flanks. The repeated emphasis placed on touch and proximity reinforces the affinity between Beth, her mother and the cows that is underpinned by their gender but is fostered by these individualised intimate moments that operate outside of a patriarchal logic that seeks to violently control female bodies. These moments, including Beth's kindness towards the cow and her witnessing of Bertha and her daughters' way of relating to the chicken, positions Beth as a character that evidently desires to engage with this more empathetic female-centred way of relating that aligns with Indigenous eco-sexuality.

Queer[ing] Coyote

Beth's exposure to eco-sexuality through the Shuswap characters is prominently visible in her relationship with Nora, Bertha's granddaughter. Nora is depicted as queer, both in her sexuality and attraction to Beth but also through the novel's continual linking of her with Coyote. Such an association ties queer identity and the figure of the trickster Coyote together in the novel through this idea of 'troubling' or disrupting the heteronormative status quo through their unfamiliarity to Beth. As Macpherson writes, 'several critics argue that a coyote aesthetics has at its heart fragmentation, deconstruction and a refiguration of ideas that stretch beyond Western conceptions.'[25] Similarly, of this relationship between Indigeneity and queerness, Jodi A. Byrd (Chickasaw) states:

> The queer in Indigenous studies ... challenges the queer of queer studies by offering not an identity or figure necessarily, but rather an analytic that helps us relocate subjectivity and its refusals back into the vectors of ongoing settler colonialism.[26]

Nora's characterisation feeds into this notion of an analytic and relocation of subjectivity within the context of a settler colonial community because her Indigenous queer identity becomes a marker of her existence outside of the oppressive heteronormative life that characters like Beth are confined within.

Acutely aware of the potential threat posed by Coyote who might be following her, Beth is continually surprised instead by the appearance of Nora. She states, 'I saw a motion in the grass coming towards me, a splitting of the grass as if an animal or a man were running through it.' She then adds, 'the swishing of the grass filled up my ears and came at me faster than anything possible ... Then a hand was on my shoulder ... I swung around and Nora was there.' (129) Nora's ability to appear unnoticed and in the place of an 'animal or a man' contributes to a haunting-like characterisation of her. Goldman concurs:

> Scene after scene aligns Nora with Coyote, rendering her phantom like perhaps because, as Terry Castle asserts, "to love another woman is to lose one's solidity in the world, to evanesce, and fade into the spectral."[27]

Avoiding a reductive and homogenous determination of homosexuality, Nora's sexuality codes her as so unfamiliar to Beth that she appears like a ghostly figure that can operate elusively around the landscape. However, unlike the characterisation of Coyote as a dangerous lurking threat in the novel told by Bertha, Nora's characterisation is nuanced. Nora's presence offers comfort and protection to Beth, appearing in moments like above wherein Beth is experiencing fear. Instead of representing a threat to Beth, then, Nora represents a defiant agency that Beth envies. She moves around and between the communities at her own will and unafraid (like a wild coyote), she wears the clothes she wishes to, and she is overt in her expression of her curious desire towards Beth because she is not determining her value and actions against a patriarchal heteronormative framework. As such, Nora is depicted as an extension of the feminist way of relating that is visible in Bertha's house.

Despite the notion that Nora appears to be stalking Beth in a haunting connection to Coyote, Nora and Beth's interactions are always physically affectionate and engaging on a sensory level, absent of the abuse and coercion that marks her relationship with the men in the novel. Nora inspires a curiosity within Beth through her touch, figured as another example of Nelson's 'getting dirty' through the language that evokes a pet-like dynamic: 'she ran her fingers along the back of my hand, petting me … The thing was so unexpected, so thrilling, so soothing, I just stood there breathless, letting it happen.' (73) Her surprise at the pleasure of being 'petted' by Nora is predictable given that she has grown up in a strict home in which the expression of sexuality or desire is prohibited. It is this kind of sterility and fear of contamination around the white Christian settler mindset that has maintained the absolute distinction between human and animal, and is here confusing for Beth because she has grown up with the distinction that love, affection and desire is shared by married men and women, not women and women. Beth remarks 'looking at her confused me … We were both just girls', but she adds that '[she] kissed me like a lover.' (132) Her phrasing 'just girls' operates on a dual level, simultaneously signifying her immaturity but also her confusion at being kissed like a lover. In determining that Nora is 'like a lover' and participating in this act of 'getting dirty' through touch, Beth acknowledges that their relationship is complicated by a queer sexual curiosity that challenges her understanding of love and relationships.

Commenting on Indigenous stories about women and trickster figures, Nelson (Anishinaabe/Métis) advises that 'Native oral narratives show us the adventures, benefits, risks, and consequences of following women's desires, and trickster stories show how ambivalent and complicated our desires can be.'[28] Nora's association with the trickster figure does seemingly demonstrate an attempt to engage with this type of narrative, becoming a sub-story about desire itself, and specifically queer desire. Shane Phelan has argued that there is a connection between trickster figures and lesbianism more broadly. Both, he argues, involve 'shape-shifting' to survive in a heteronormative society where it is often necessary to disguise one's identity:

> The shape-shifting is the product not of some unique facility of lesbians, but of the rigidity of social codes that make lesbians invisible unless they are conforming to dominant stereotypes. It is in Coyote's "nature" to appear as not-Coyote when it suits his purposes. Some may recognize, or suspect,

Coyote when he is transformed, but Coyote has the ability to fool most people and to get his way. Coyote uses our own expectation to slip under our radar. One implication of this analogy might be that lesbians can gain power from sneakiness and subterfuge, from masking themselves.[29]

Such a connection emphasises that the comparison of Nora to Coyote stems from the fact that, like Coyote who remains elusive and free to roam the wilderness, it is possible for Nora to keep her sexuality personal and hidden; it is not an outwardly visible piece of her identity. In addition, just as Coyote represents an alternative epistemological understanding of animals, Nora's queer identity challenges the patriarchal heteronormativity that governs the settler community. That Nora and Beth are permitted to be alone despite Beth's father's strict control of her sexuality is evidence of the settler ignorance to queer identity, the notion of Nora as a romantic interest is not within Beth's parents' cultural understanding.

It is possible to connect this association between queer identity and Coyote to still important forms of queer critique established in relation to lesbian feminism in the 1980s, in which lesbianism was reclaimed as 'an assertion of sexual agency and feelings, but autonomous from men, a reclaiming of erotic drives directed toward women, of a desire for women.'[30] Nora's lesbian identity figures her as a character that inherently challenges the patriarchal regulation of sexuality by way of excluding them through her sexual orientation. Thus, her alignment with Coyote in the novel symbolically reflects the propensity for the Indigenous 'trickster' figure to shed a nuanced light upon feminist politics. Phelan writes:

> Coyote can refresh lesbian and feminist politics by offering us a less stable understanding of identity and a looser and lighter, and therefore more empowering, interpretation of the political cosmos and human action.[31]

The inclusion of this Indigenous story and queer characterisation within a settler novel positions the Shuswap Band (and more broadly Indigenous) knowledge systems as valuable sources of knowledge for understanding the complexities and multiplicities of feminist approaches. It acknowledges the limitations (or refusal) of settler feminism to incorporate Indigenous women's experiences and to legitimise Indigenous knowledge. Building on this feminist engagement, Nora's alignment with the animal trickster figure incorporates the question of species into the feminist equation, suggesting that Indigenous concepts of feminism include spiritual understandings of human-animal relationships. Through such an engagement with this framework in the novel, so-called Coyote aesthetics are positioned as a necessary and urgent framework for reconfiguring settler sexualities because through the trickster's very nature, cultural hegemonies that enact oppression can be troubled and resisted.

Man, Men, Coyote, Coyotes

The novel's consciously vague engagement with the Coyote story means that the text is haunted by a continual sense of questioning and danger. What really attacked the young settler girl—a bear, a man, a coyote or Coyote? How does one protect oneself from an unidentified threat? This question is never fully answered and, as such, this sense of unknowing contributes to a sinister characterisation of the male characters throughout the novel because we are unable to determine if the men are a threat to Beth.

Rather than attempting to give detailed information on a specific Coyote story, Anderson-Dargatz's novel plays with the notion of Coyote possession through repeatedly shifting descriptions of the male characters, interchanging between man, coyote and Coyote. The introduction of this coyote politics not only builds fear around this idea of Coyote possession, but it muddies species boundaries and troubles the responsibility that was formerly placed on non-human animals in the vilification of the bear at the beginning of the novel. The novel asks us to consider what we (settlers) don't know—settlers do not know about Coyote and trickster stories—but this Indigenous figure, understood through many stories belonging to a wide range of Indigenous Nations—requires the adoption of a new epistemological understanding of relations with the more-than-human world, one in which we might imagine a different type of non-human threat than that of the bear.

Whereas Nora's association with Coyote in the novel marked her defiance of settler sexuality and of Beth's curiosity, the men associated with Coyote (or coyotes) are represented as threatening and predatory. Beth frequently notices coyotes stalking or hovering around the farm and that they appear in proximity to male characters. She describes the way in which 'unseen by [her] father, a coyote skulked through the long grass behind him.' (210) In addition, in an exchange between Beth and Nora, the proximity yet distinction between coyotes and Coyote is evidenced:

"Billy thinks I got Coyote following me," I said.
"Coyotes will follow anything," she said. "They're as curious as dogs."
"No, he means Coyote, that spirit thing your granny talks about." (259)

Nora's reference to curiosity explains the reason why wild coyotes might venture close to both Beth and the farm, but it also sheds light on the reason the trickster figure might present in coyote form. Both are curious navigators of the land, following those that appeal to their curiosity. Macpherson maintains that 'Coyote is a compelling figure, not least because of his connections to the coyote, or Canis latrans, who is stereotypically seen as a wily scavenger, with a sly smile and a mangy appearance.'[32] Similarly, Phelan implicates the historical resilience of the coyote species in comparison to other canine species, such as the wolf, in its' connection to its 'trickster' configuration: 'the coyote is scorned as a pest but it survives.'[33] Indeed this surviving against the odds is what Osage writer and historian John Joseph Matthews also saw as being akin to Indigenous peoples in general. It is additionally relevant that coyotes are wild animals, unlike the cows and chickens on Beth's farm, and their freedom from domestic regulation means that they are well situated to reflect a spiritual figure's challenge to a type of human-animal relationship that is not oppressively governed, instead free to roam the landscape undeterred. The novel plays around with this knowledge of coyotes, using the material characteristics of the animal, and their repeated 'haunting' of the North American plains as wild animals, to narratively breakdown our comprehension of what is haunting Beth, leaving the reader unable to determine for sure whether it is a coyote or Coyote.

In addition to the presence of actual coyotes around the farm, Beth appears to experience visions of men shape-shifting between their human form and a coyote body. Such representations introduce an entirely new epistemological understanding of human-animal relations that muddies clear, anthropocentric boundaries by drawing further attention to the idea of Coyote possession. However, this is the limitation of the novel's engagement with the Coyote story; it is never made clear whether what is stalking Beth is a man, a coyote, or Coyote himself.

Beth's fear is palpable when she states that 'sometimes I think I'm being followed, and I never see it, exactly ... But it leaves footprints ... It's got hands.' (120) This description of 'hands' suggests that what is following her is human, but later, in a more tense moment of haunting, Beth states: 'I saw a motion in the grass coming towards me, a splitting of the grass as if an animal or a man were running through it.' (129) Her inability to distinguish between animal and man contributes to the ghostly and indecipherable conception of the figure that underpins her fear. This lack of clarity surrounding the haunting is further complicated by the fact that these moments of coyote-male shapeshifting, what could be termed Coyote possession, always occur during traumatic encounters with male characters. Whilst this may seem to suggest that the blurring of man and coyote is in fact a trauma response and is therefore imagined, the novel's refusal to provide detailed knowledge about the trickster figure, how he operates, and to ground this knowledge in legitimate reference to a specific Indigenous Nation's story, means that Coyote possession also cannot be ruled out. Beth's inability to decipher what is haunting her operates as an illustration of a knowledge gap—how much of her experiences are born out of imagination (produced by fear) and how much are caused by Coyote, about whom settlers know so little?

This is particularly evident in a scene in which Beth's father sexually assaults her. Beth describes seeing a set of dead coyote skins that are hanging on her bedroom wall come alive. They enter her dreams and attack her, but when they finish their attack, they take the form of her father:

> A darkness crossed the window and fell on my chest. When I cried out, the coyotes put their claws over my mouth. They lifted my nightgown. They rubbed their wet tails between my legs and over my belly. They told me to keep quiet. I hid my dream self in the darkest corner of my room and watched the shadows of the coyotes suck the breath from my body. When they had their fill, the shadows sighed deeply, came together, and took the form of my father. He lifted his weight from my body and left the room. (264)

Beth's description of her 'dream-self' is likely to be a reaction to trauma; to enter a state of self-preservation she detaches her emotional 'dream self' from her physical body and imagines herself as a bystander watching the attack. It is possible to read this scene as Beth's blurring of her fear of a Coyote figure with the reality of her father being a violent paedophile as a method of coping with this trauma. However, the vague introduction of the Coyote story means that this scene is fraught with an underlying haunting possibility that Beth's father has been possessed by Coyote and this is why she is seeing this amalgamation of her father and the coyote skins in one traumatic and violent act, just as Bertha warned. That she sees the skins of the dead coyotes' therefore functions as an image for their propensity to spiritually inhabit her father by way of possession, but it also alludes to the targeted hunting of coyotes on the farmland, who are viewed as a threat to livestock. Their hanging skins, then, signify a form of violence that threatens both Beth and coyotes living in the area.

The notion of shape-shifting, transforming in and out of a human and animal body, contributes to a blurring of the human-animal binary, suggesting that such relations are indeed more complex when they are considered outside of a settler colonial framework. This is particularly pertinent in an encounter with Coyote Jack, a figure named for his reclusive life away from the other settlers and their subsequent fear of him. Coyote Jack attacks Beth when she is walking in the woods and throws her to the ground:

> Suddenly he got up. He twisted, batted the air, and screamed, and the scream became a howl. His body flitted back and forth between man and coyote, then the coyote dropped on all fours and cowered away from me. He bristled and growled. I stood slowly and clapped my hands, as I would to scare off any wild animal. The coyote turned and trotted off and disappeared into the bush. (272)

Unlike her father who is depicted as working in tandem with the pack of coyote skins, Coyote Jack's transformation is depicted as an internal battle of wills—himself against Coyote, 'flitti[ng] back and forth'—struggling between attacking Beth as Coyote and restraining himself in his human form. It is notable that it is when he is in coyote form that she is able to frighten him off the way that she normally scares off wild animals, by making a loud noise, suggesting that there is an inherent violence in male humans that is somewhat easier to challenge when Coyote possession takes hold. Beth's witnessing of this shape-shifting again serves to undermine the bear attack narrative by implicating Coyote possession and offering an alternative understanding of human violence, rather than animal. The notion that the male characters might be responsible for attacking young girls as a consequence of becoming possessed by Coyote interrogates the way in which culpability and violence can be misplaced onto non-human animals when an understanding of human-animal relationships is formed through the anthropocentrism that underpins the settler colonial culture depicted in the novel.

Returning to Macpherson's argument that Coyote's presence in the novel is symbolic in its reflection of Beth's fear of and vulnerability to male sexual violence, such an analysis implies that there is no specific Coyote figure within the novel, but rather that every man is a sexually predatory Coyote. However, Goldman accepts that this opens up onto a disappointing anti-feminist implication, as 'to explain repeated and prolonged sexual abuse away as Coyote possession is to reiterate the worst aspect of an anti-feminist stance: that men cannot control the "beast" within', which then 'absolve[s] men of their sexual crimes.'[34] In addition, considering that Anderson-Dargatz is a settler writer drawing on an Indigenous story, to argue that it is simply for symbolic means ultimately disregards the Indigenous story as a source of knowledge to be handled seriously. It also undermines the implications for species relations that arise through Coyote's disruption of species-boundaries, which trouble the distinction between man and human through his possession of male bodies and through the constant reminder of his existence echoed in the appearance of literal coyotes. Rather, by introducing the story but keeping it underdeveloped, the novel highlights gaps in settler knowledge that frustrate colonial understandings of storytelling, whereby we expect to understand everything. This functions as a methodology that then draws attention to Indigenous stories and serves as a call for engaging with these epistemologies. Echoing Goldman's sentiments, then, understanding Coyote literally means that the novel is better positioned as an intersectional feminist piece of literature. This is because, as Phelan states: 'we can use Coyote's duplicity to become more creative about feminist politics.'[35] The multiplicity, elusiveness, and disruptive nature of the trickster figure that we have not been able to understand fully through the novel's deliberately vague engagement opens up the possibility for considering a multitude of differing perspectives and undermining the status quo in terms of sexuality, species and their intersection.

Conclusion: The Question of Species in Indigenous-Settler Conflict

If considering Coyote in the Indigenous context as a real presence within the novel means that *The Cure for Death by Lightning* depicts a settler character as being haunted by an Indigenous cultural figure of animality and other settler characters as being possessed by him, what are the implications of this in a postcolonial context? The struggle brought on by Coyote possession is reflective of the way in which Indigenous knowledge systems are still at conflict with settler ones. The two characters in the novel that are depicted as being overcome by Coyote are Beth's father and Coyote Jack, both of whom are male, settler characters, and upholders of settler sexuality through their behaviour towards Beth (and other animals in the context of her father). Coyote's possession of them explicitly represents the potential for Indigenous ways of relating to challenge 'settler sexuality' and conversations surrounding species relations. This is reinforced through the way in which Beth's father's dominant personality wanes as the novel develops, culminating in his institutionalisation and later in Beth's standing up to his advances, as she explores feelings of agency inspired by the Indigenous women. The novel therefore attempts to depict Shuswap Band knowledge as capable of destabilising settler foundations of knowledge that are inherently heteronormative and oppressive, and by keeping the engagement deliberately vague, Anderson-Dargatz implores a need for further engagement and understanding of this story from alternative Indigenous sources. In doing so it agrees with the kinds of arguments put forth by TallBear, Belcourt, and Nelson, pre-empting this need for settler writing to be actively decolonial in its incorporation of Indigenous epistemologies into the conversation by engaging with their stories and lifeways in meaningful and respectful ways, not appropriating them by telling them as your own. In this way, Anderson-Dargatz's novel takes a specific interest in Indigenous-settler relationships across literary, cultural, and species boundaries.

Despite this, the novel is not immune to criticism of its representation of Indigenous characterisation and use of the Coyote story; it treads a fine line between positive intention and problematic execution in its methodology of vagueness. The novel encapsulates British Colombia's history of displacement through its very construction: issues over land governance and human-animal relations remain at the core of Indigenous-settler conflict. What emerges from critically examining species representation and the Coyote aspects of the novel, is that settler literature must engage with and destabilise the types of oppressive hierarchies that underpin both species and Indigenous-settler relations, namely settler sexuality and anthropocentrism, if settler culture is to follow. It proposes developing a move towards engaging with Indigenous stories and concepts of animality as a means of thinking through the relationship between literature, species, and the contemporary idea of nation in Canada.

NOTES

1. Shuswap Band is a member of the Secwepemc Nation, who traditionally occupied the south-central part British Columbia, Canada. Source: https://www.shuswapband.net/about-shuswap-band/ [Accessed 20 May 2023].
2. Katy Wimherst, "Interview with Gail Anderson-Dargatz" in *Serendipity*. 2009, http://www.magicalrealism.co.uk/view.php?story=113. [Accessed January 2021].
3. In Canada: shortlisted for the Giller Prize (1996). Awarded the Ethel Wilson Fiction Prize (1997). Bestseller in Canada (selling over 100,000 copies). In the UK: Bestseller & winner of Betty Trask Award (1998).
4. Heidi Slettedahl Macpherson (2004) 'Coyote as Culprit: The Coyote Aesthetics of Gail-Anderson-Dargatz's *The Cure for Death by Lightning*', *British Journal of Canadian Studies*, 17.2, 175–185, p. 178.
5. Marlene Goldman (2009) "Coyote's Children and the Canadian Gothic: Sheila Watson's The Double Hook and Gail Anderson-Dargatz's *The Cure for Death by Lightning*", in *Unsettled Remains: Canadian Literature and the Postcolonial Gothic*, eds. Cynthia Sugars and Gerry Turcotte (Waterloo: Wilfred Laurier University Press), pp. 51–73, p. 53.
6. Quote taken from: Margery Fee (2010) 'The Trickster Appropriation, Imagination in Moment, and the Canada Cultural Liberal', in *Troubling Tricksters: Revisioning Critical Conversations*, edited by Deanna Reder, and Linda M. Morra, (Waterloo: Wilfrid Laurier University Press) p. 163.
7. Quote taken from: Margery Fee, 'The Trickster Appropriation, Imagination in Moment, and the Canada Cultural Liberal', p. 70.
8. Daniel Morley Johnson (2010) '(Re)Nationalizing Naanabozho: Anishinaabe Sacred Stories, Nationalist Literary Criticism, and Scholarly Responsibility', in *Troubling Tricksters: Revisioning Critical Conversations*, ed. By Deanna Reder and Linda M. Morra (Waterloo: Wilfrid Laurier University Press) pp. 199–221, p. 202.
9. Kristina Fagan (2010) 'What's the Trouble with the Trickster?: An Introduction', in *Troubling Tricksters: Revisioning Critical Conversations* edited by Deanna Reder and Linda M. Morra (Waterloo: Canada, Wilfrid Laurier University Press) pp. 3–21, p. 5.
10. Franchot Ballinger discusses trickster figures and gender at length in 'Coyote, He/She Was Going There: Sex and Gender in Native American Trickster Stories' in *Studies in American Indian Literatures*, 2:14:4 (Winter 2000) 15–43. Ballinger notes that the majority of trickster figures are male due to typical understandings of gender characteristics held by different Indigenous tribes and that the telling of trickster stories was often done by men.

11. Franchot Ballinger (2000) 'Coyote, He/She Was Going There: Sex and Gender in Native American Trickster Stories' in *Studies in American Indian Literatures*, 2:14:4, 15–43, pp. 16–17.
12. Billy-Ray Belcourt (2020) "An Indigenous critique of Critical Animal Studies," in *Colonialism and Animality: Anti-Colonial Perspectives in Critical Animal Studies*, ed. Kelly Struthers Montford and Chloë Taylor (Abingdon: Taylor & Francis Group), p. 25 and p. 20.
13. Scott Lauria Morgensen (2010) 'Settler Homonationalism: Theorizing Settler Colonialism within Queer Modernities', *Journal of Lesbian and Gay Studies*, 16.1–2, 105–131, p. 106.
14. Beyond the more systematic imposition of heteronormative monogamy there are, of course, resistance sexual practices at work in Canada. Such are explored in Christopher Lane's *Ruling Passion: British Colonial Allegory and the Paradox of Homosexual Desire* (1995).
15. Kim TallBear (2018) Lecture at the University of Winnipeg's Weweni Indigenous Scholars Speaker series titled "Decolonial Sex and Relations for a More Sustainable World," YouTube Video, 4:9, https://www.youtube.com/watch?v=1ELSwPqjKkE&t=222s&ab_channel=UWinnipeg
16. Ibid., 6:44.
17. Ibid., 19:10.
18. Gail Anderson-Dargatz (1997) *The Cure for Death by Lightning* (Toronto: Random House of Canada) p. 15. [All subsequent quotations taken from this edition].
19. Melissa K. Nelson (2017) "Getting Dirty: The Eco-Eroticism of Women in Indigenous Oral Literatures," in *Critically Sovereign: Indigenous Gender, Sexuality and Feminist Studies*, ed. Joanne Barker (Durham: Duke University Press), pp. 229–261, p. 244.
20. Chris Philo and Chris Wilbert (2000) "An Introduction" in *Animal spaces, beastly places: new geographies of human-animal relations*, edited by Chris Philo and Chris Wilbert (Abingdon: Routledge), p. 13.
21. Philo and Wilbert, "Introduction," p. 15.
22. Nelson, "Getting Dirty," p. 234.
23. Nelson, "Getting Dirty, p. 234.
24. Taken from Compassion in World Farming: https://www.ciwf.com/farmed-animals/cows/dairy-cows/#:~:text=Like%20humans%2C%20cows%20only%20produce,three%20months%20of%20giving%20birth.
25. Macpherson, 'Coyote as Culprit: The Coyote Aesthetics of Gail-Anderson-Dargatz's *The Cure for Death by Lightning*', p. 182.
26. Jodi A. Byrd (2017) "Loving Unbecoming: The Queer Politics of the Transitive Native," in *Critically Sovereign: Indigenous Gender, Sexuality and Feminist Studies*, ed. Joanne Barker (Durham: Duke University Press) pp. 207–229, p. 226.

27. Goldman, "Coyote's Children and the Canadian Gothic," p. 60.
28. Nelson, "Getting Dirty," p. 254.
29. Shane Phelan (1996) "Coyote Politics: Trickster Tales and Feminist Futures" in *Hypatia*, 11: 3, 130–149, p. 139.
30. Teresa De Lauretis (1988) "Sexual Indifference and Lesbian Representation" in *Theatre Journal* 40:2, 155–177, p. 162.
31. Phelan, "Coyote Politics: Trickster Tales and Feminist Futures", p. 123.
32. Macpherson, "Coyote as Culprit," p. 177.
33. Phelan, "Coyote Politics: Trickster Tales and Feminist Futures," p. 134.
34. Goldman, "Coyote's Children and the Canadian Gothic," p. 180.
35. Phelan, "Coyote Politics: Trickster Tales and Feminist Futures," p. 143.

CHAPTER 7

Conclusion

After the publication of Canadian writer Barbara Gowdy's emotive national bestseller novel, *The White Bone* in 1998, Gowdy stated in an interview with Jana Siciliano that 'everything my elephant characters do lies within the realm of the possible. As a novelist I have taken observed behaviour and credited it with a high level of intention.'[1] As this monograph has demonstrated, it is this idea of writing with 'intention' that permeates Canadian animal fiction in the late twentieth-century, directly challenging the nineteenth century 'nature fakers' criticism that bled into discussions about animal writing in the early contemporary period. This new style of writing carved space for consciously stylized animal representation that did not shy away from considering animals as independent agents capable of placing demands back onto human characters.

In addition to refusing to engage with nineteenth century criticism of 'nature fakers', the analysis in this book has shifted discussion from terms that were established in the early twentieth century that sought to claim the "wild animal story" as a peculiarly Canadian genre, visible in the work of Margaret Atwood and James Polk. Such generic definition confines the representation of animals in literature, and the questions about animal lives that fiction provokes, within an anthropocentric nationalist imaginary. Rather, by focusing along intersections of identity, including gender, sexuality and Indigeneity, this monograph and the texts discussed demonstrate a development in writing about animals in Canada across the period of 1960–2000 away from the idea that there is a single, homogenous Canadian identity that is or can be represented through animals. The writing in the latter half of this book therefore marked a new type of animal story in which animals were depicted as reciprocal agents within human-animal relationships, and that non-human animals demand serious and caring engagement, as both literary characters and as material beings.

The analysis that moved chronologically across the period of the late twentieth century and engaged with a variety of texts allowed for perspective on the forms of social identity-based critical approach to representation handled differently in each of the texts. The second chapter argued that the reception received by *Never Cry Wolf* demonstrated the cultural significance that some texts hold in relation to popular understandings of particular animal species. The text itself is an example of the way in which undermining one story about animals often entails constructing another type of story that similarly strives to influence opinion in a particular way. In Atwood's novels, empathy with animals is developed, but it is temporary. As the third chapter noted, it is possible to identify in Atwood's novels a shared logic of representation that codes encountering a dead animal's body as a subjectively transformative experience, allowing for temporary and symbolic refuge from victimisation felt in interpersonal relationships. The consequence of this type of representational engagement with animals is, then, that despite an apparent engagement with violence against the non-human, this is not a critical message that is developed; the animals remain simply literary symbols of the human characters' struggles. Following from this symbolic use of animals, the monograph then identified a distinctive critical turn in the final chapters; in the fourth chapter it argued that Marian Engel's *Bear* is an example of a text that self-consciously engages with the difficulty of writing a story about animals, representing a bear that remains steadfastly incomprehensible to the protagonist. Building on this self-conscious mode of critically engaged writing, the monograph demonstrates that modes of working along particular intersections of identity and species are useful lenses for considering representations of contemporary forms of nationhood in animal writing in Canada. This is visible in Findley's novels, which subvert and camp versions of established narratives. This allows Findley to expose and undermine the hierarchical structures of oppression that underpin these stories and emphasise the beauty in moments of defiance that are born out of this oppression, centring care as integral to kinship. Finally, the last chapter examined Anderson-Dargatz's novel to argue that it builds on the concept of care established in Chap. 5 to re-evaluate the way in which we engage with non-human animals. By introducing an eco-sexual framework that encourages empathy and kinship with all beings, this mode of writing advocates for a move towards centring Indigenous knowledge systems.

By forming an analysis through a triangulation of species, nation and personal identity (namely gender, sexuality and Indigeneity), this book has demonstrated that the representation of animality in the novels intersects and interacts in multiple and complex ways with aspects of both personal and national identity. A particular pervasive configuration identified throughout is that Indigeneity is consistently coded as an identity that can be accessed by settler characters in order to gain a kind of proximity or closeness to animals; perpetuating the dehumanisation of Indigenous people and reinforcing a sense of desire within settler cultural identity to seek out means through which to feel connected to the space on which they have settled. This critical engagement with the nuances that these aspects of personal identity offer to texts that engage with questions of species, and the development that occurs across this period away from homogenous ideas of both Indigeneity and Canadian identity or the Canadian story, demonstrates the value that holding together questions of identity and species has in undermining dominant hegemonies. By incorporating serious—which is to say respectful, appreciative—consideration of non-human lives into a reconfigured notion of social life, these contemporary fictions in Canada present a radically anti-hegemonic way of writing. They refute the idea that by using symbolic representations of animals there is one such way to write from a place of Canadian settler identity and instead demonstrate that stories coming out of Canada in this period are conscious of generic categorisation and the complexity of defining a national genre in a settler country still at conflict within itself and with its Indigenous nations.

Gesturing towards the continuing relevance of the relationship between nation, identity, and species in Canada, in the introduction of this book, I touched upon the relocation of the bear Mali on Hanson Island in British Columbia. There are, though, many more examples of the way in which the types of conversations visible in settler literature about human-animal relationships in Canada have become sites of Indigenous-settler conflict and reconciliation, and through which it is possible to see a definitive turn towards the incorporation of Indigenous voices into wildlife management decisions. In 2017 the Canadian government embraced the formation of the Indigenous Circle of Experts (ICE). One such priority of the ICE has been restoring autonomy and governance back to Indigenous Nations, particularly with regards to conservation. Consequently, Indigenous communities can now request for particular parts of their territories to be named as Indigenous Protected Areas. The aim of IPAs is to restore autonomy to Indigenous communities by establishing areas in which Indigenous governments govern using their own knowledge systems and are given the primary role in caring for the land. For example, in 2018 the Dehcho First Nations established the Edéhzhíe Protected Area in the Dehcho region of the southwestern part of the Northwest Territories. This IPA is co-managed by the Dehcho K'ehodi Indigenous Guardians and the Canadian Wildlife Service, marking a landmark embracing of an important and necessary collaborative effort to conserve the Horn Plateau and its many lakes, rivers and wetlands, the spiritual home for many of the Dehcho Dene community. The Dehcho people consider this IPA to be an extension of Dehcho K'éhodi, which means 'Taking Care of the Dehcho' in Dehcho Dene Zhatié.[2] The Edéhzhíe Protected Area provides a means through which Indigenous communities like the Dehcho Dene are able to reconnect with their ancestral lands by applying their own knowledge systems and stewardship practices, thus marking the beginning of a new type of conservation framework that centres Indigenous ways-of-being. Contemporary settler Canada then, is still engaging in this process of finding a means of reconciling its relationship with Indigenous First Nations through its relationship with the land and the non-human animals that live on it. There is an on-going recognition that there must be a move to centre Indigenous knowledge systems if Canada is to move forwards in the construction of more caring and sustainable personal, national and species relations.

Notes

1. Ella Soper-Jones (2007) 'When Elephants Weep: Reading *The White Bone* as a Sentimental Animal Story', in *Other Selves: Animals in the Canadian Literary Imagination*, ed. by Janice Fiamengo (Ottawa: University of Ottawa Press) pp. 269–290, p.273–4.
2. Information taken from the Dehcho First Nations' Website: https://dehcho.org/resource-management/stewardship/dehcho-kehodi/ [Accessed 1 May 2023].

Bibliography

Primary Sources

Anderson-Dargatz, Gail (1996) *The Cure for Death by Lightning* (Toronto: Random House of Canada).

Atwood, Margaret (2002) *Life Before Man* (Great Britain: Penguin Random House, Vintage Classics).

Atwood, Margaret (1979) *Surfacing* (London: Virago Press Limited).

Engel, Marian (2021) *Bear* (London: Daunt Books).

Findley, Timothy (1986) *Not Wanted on the Voyage* (New York: Arrow Books Limited).

Findley, Timothy (2001) *The Wars* (London: Faber and Faber Limited).

Mowat, Farley (1963) *Never Cry Wolf* (New York City: Back Bay Books/Little, Brown and Company).

Secondary Sources

Adams, Carol J. (2015) *The Sexual Politics of Meat: A Feminist-Vegetarian Critical Theory* (New York: Bloomsbury Academic).

Adams Carol J. (2007) 'Caring About Suffering: A Feminist Exploration', in *The Feminist Care Tradition in Animal Ethics* ed. By Carol J. Adams and Josephine Donovan (New York: Columbia University Press) pp. 198–227.

Adams, Carol J., and Donovan, Josephine (2007) *The Feminist Care Tradition in Animal Ethics* (New York: Columbia University Press).

Aguila-Way, Tania (2016) 'Beyond the Logic of Solidarity of Sameness: The Critique of Animal Instrumentalization in Margaret Atwood's *Surfacing* and Marian Engel's *Bear*', *Interdisciplinary Studies in Literature and Environment*, 23.1, 5–29.

Alberti, Samuel J. M. M (2011) *The Afterlives of Animals* (Charlottesville: University of Virginia Press).

Armstrong, Philip (2008) *What Animals Mean in the Fiction of Modernity* (London: Routledge).

Asma, Stephen T. (2001) *Stuffed Animals and Pickled Heads: The Culture and Evolution of Natural History Museums* (Oxford: Oxford University Press).

Atwood, Margaret (1995) *Strange Things: The Malevolent North in Canadian Literature* (Oxford: Oxford University Press).

Atwood, Margaret (1972) *Survival: A Thematic Guide to Canadian Literature* (Toronto: Anansi Press).

Barnard, Alan John (2023) 'Family: Kinship' in *Britannica*: https://www.britannica.com/topic/family-kinship [Accessed 19 May 2023]

Baker, Katherine (December 13, 1988) *The Associated Press*. New York. Tuesday, PM cycle. Section: Entertainment News.

Baker, Timothy C. (2019) *Writing Animals: Language, Suffering, and Animality in Twenty-First-Century Fiction* (Culemborg: Palgrave Macmillan).

Ballinger, Franchot (2000) 'Coyote, He/She Was Going There: Sex and Gender in Native American Trickster Stories' in *Studies in American Indian Literatures*, 2:14:4, 15–43

Barker, Joanne (2017) *Critically Sovereign: Indigenous Gender, Sexuality and Feminist Studies* (Durham: Duke University Press).

Barrett, Paul (2014) '"Animal Tracks in the Margin": Tracing the Absent Referent in Marian Engel's *Bear* and J. M. Coetzee's *The Lives of Animals*', *Ariel*, 45.3, 123–149.

Belcourt, Billy-Ray (2020) 'An Indigenous Critique of Critical Animal Studies', in *Colonialism and Animality: Anti-Colonial Perspectives in Critical Animal Studies,* ed. by Kelly Struthers Montford and Chloë Taylor (Abingdon: Routledge) pp. 19–29.

Beran, Carol L (1992) *Intertexts of Margaret Atwood's Life Before Man, American Review of Canadian Studies,* 22.2, 199–214.

Bieder, Robert E (2005) *Bear* (London: Reaktion Books Ltd).

Brooke Charity, 'War Horse Facts': https://www.thebrooke.org/get-involved/every-horse-remembered/war-horse-facts#:~:text=How%20many%20horses%2C%20donkeys%20and%20mules%20died%20in%20WW2%3F,vary%20between%202%2D5%20million [Accessed 19 May 2023]

Brydon, Diana (2008) 'A Devotion to Fragility: Timothy Findley's *The Wars*', *Journal of Postcolonial Writing*, 26.1, 75–84.

Brydon, Diana (1986) "It could not be told": Making Meaning in Timothy Findley's T*he Wars*', *The Journal of Commonwealth Literature*, 21.1, 62–79.

Brydon, Diana (1994) '"The White Inuit Speaks": Contamination as Literary Strategy', in *Post-Colonial Studies Reader*, ed. by Bill Ashcroft (Abingdon: Routledge) pp. 136–143.

Byrd, Jodi A (2017) 'Loving Unbecoming: The Queer Politics of the Transitive Native', in *Critically Sovereign: Indigenous Gender, Sexuality and Feminist Studies*, ed. By Joanne Barker (Durham: Duke University Press) pp. 207–227.

Canadiana: Parliament of Canada Records (1950) "House of Commons Debates', 21st Parliament, 2nd Session, Volume 3' http://parl.canadiana.ca/view/oop.debates_HOC2102_03/1016?r=0&s=1 [Accessed 15 November 2017]

Cecco, Leyland (Sunday 19 April 2020) "Indigenous input helps save wayward grizzly bear from summary killing," *The Guardian*.

Colpitts, George (2017) 'Howl: The 1952–56 Rabies Crisis and the Creation of the Urban Wild at Banff', in *Animal Metropolis: Histories of Human-Animal Relations in Urban Canada*, ed. By Joanna Dean, Darcy Ingram and Christabelle Sethna (Calgary: University of Calgary Press) pp. 219–253.

Compassion in World Farming, 'About Dairy Cows': https://www.ciwf.com/farmed-animals/cows/dairy-cows/#:~:text=Like%20humans%2C%20cows%20only%20produce,three%20months%20of%20giving%20birth. [Accessed 1 May 2023]

Clarke, Adele. E. Clarke and Haraway, Donna (2018) *Making Kin Not Population* (Chicago: Prickly Paradigm Press).

Cleto, Fabio (1999) *Camp: Queer Aesthetics and the Performing Subject* (Edinburgh: Edinburgh University Press).

Crown-Indigenous Relations and Northern Affairs Canada (2021) 'Indigenous and Northern Affairs Canada', https://www.aadnc-aandc.gc.ca/eng/1414152378639/1414152548341 [Accessed: 2 June 2019].

De Lauretis, Teresa (1988) 'Sexual Indifference and Lesbian Representation', *Theatre Journal*, 40.2, 155–177.

Dean, Joanna, Ingram, Darcy, Sethna, Christabelle (2017) *Animal Metropolis: Histories of Human-Animal Relations in Urban Canada* (Calgary: University of Calgary Press).

Dehcho First Nations' Website (2016) 'Dehcho K'éhodi': https://dehcho.org/resource-management/stewardship/dehcho-kehodi/ [Accessed 1 May 2023].

Derrida, Jacques (2008) *The Animal that Therefore I Am* (New York: Fordham University Press).

Dickinson, John A. and J. Young, Brian (2002) *A Short History of Quebec* (Montreal: McGill-Queen University Press).

Dodd, Adam, Rader, Karen A., Thorsen, Liv Emma (2013) *Animals on Display: The Creaturely in Museums, Zoos, and Natural History* (Philadelphia: The Pennsylvania State University Press).

Donovan, Josephine (2007) 'Attention to Suffering: Sympathy as a Basis for Ethical Treatment of Animals', in *The Feminist Care Tradition in Animal Ethics*, ed. By Carol J. Adams and Josephine Donovan (New York: Columbia University Press) pp. 174–198.

Donovan, Josephine (2007) 'Animal Rights and Feminist Theory', in *The Feminist Care Tradition in Animal Ethics*, Ed. by Josephine Donovan and Carol J. Adams (New York: Columbia University Press) pp. 58–87.

Doty, William G, and Hynes William J (1997) *Mythical Trickster Figures: Contours, Contexts, and Criticisms* (Tuscaloosa: University of Alabama Press).

Dworkin, Andrea (1980) 'Beaver and Male Power in Pornography', *New Political Science*, 1.4, 37–41.

Dyer, Richard (1999) 'Its Being So Camp As Keeps Us Going', in *Camp: Queer Aesthetics and the Performing Subject*, ed. By Fabio Cleto (Edinburgh: Edinburgh University Press) pp. 110–116.

Fagan, Kristina (2010) 'What's the Trouble with the Trickster?: An Introduction', in *Troubling Tricksters: Revisioning Critical Conversations* edited by Deanna Reder and Linda M. Morra (Waterloo: Canada, Wilfrid Laurier University Press) pp. 3–21.

Fee, Margery (1988) 'Articulating the Female Subject: The Example of Marian Engel's *Bear*', *Atlantis: Critical Studies in Gender, Culture & Social Justice*, 14.1, 20–26.

Fee, Margery (2010) 'The Trickster Appropriation, Imagination in Moment, and the Canada Cultural Liberal', in Troubling Tricksters: Revisioning Critical Conversations, ed. by Deanna Reder, and Linda M. Morra, (Waterloo: Wilfrid Laurier University Press) pp. 59–77.

Fiamengo, Janice (2007) *Other Selves: Animals in the Canadian Literary Imagination* (Ottawa: University of Ottawa Press).

Fiamengo, Janice (1999) 'Postcolonial guilt in Margaret Atwood's *Surfacing*', The *American Review of Canadian Studies*, 29.1, 141–163.

Findley, Timothy (1984) *Dinner Along the Amazon* (Penguin Books).

Fenn, Stewart (2014) 'Grey Owl in the White Settler Wilderness: "Imaginary Indians" in Canadian Culture and Law', *Law, Culture and the Humanities*, 1.1, 1–21.

French, Marilyn (February 3, 1980) 'Spouses and Lovers, Life Before Man by Margaret Atwood' in *The New York Times*

Fromberg Schaeffer, Susan (1974) '"It Is Time That Separates Us" Margaret Atwood's "Surfacing"', *The Centennial Review*, 18.4, 319–337.

Grace, Sherrill E (2007) *Canada and the Idea of North* (Montreal: McGill-Queens Press).

Goldie, Terry (2003) *Pink Snow: Homotextual Possibilities in Canadian Fiction* (Peterborough: Broadview Press).

Goldman, Marlene (2009) 'Coyote's Children and the Canadian Gothic: Sheila Watson's The Double Hook and Gail Anderson-Dargatz's *The Cure for Death by Lightning*' in *Unsettled Remains: Canadian Literature and the Postcolonial Gothic*, ed. by Cynthia Sugars, Gerry Turcotte (Waterloo: Wilfred Laurier University Press) 51–73.

Guth, Gwendolyn (2007) '(B)othering the Theory: Approaching the Unapproachable in *Bear* and Other Realistic Animal Narratives', in *Other Selves: Animals in the Canadian Literary Imagination*, ed. By Janice Fiamengo (Ottawa: University of Ottawa Press) pp. 29–50.

Haraway, Donna (2008) *When Species Meet* (Minneapolis: University of Minnesota Press).

Haraway, Donna (2018) 'Making Kin in the Chthulucene: Reproducing Multispecies Justice', in *Making Kin Not Population*, ed. By Adele E. Clarke and Donna Haraway (Chicago: Prickly Paradigm Press) pp. 67–101.

Haraway, Donna (1992) 'Otherworldly Conversations; Terran Topics; Local Terms', *Science as Culture*, 3.1, 64–98.

Harrod, Howard L. (2008) *The Animals Came Dancing: Native American Sacred Ecology and Animal Kinship* (Tuscon: University of Arizona Press).

Heninghan, Stephen (2002) *When Words Deny the World: The Reshaping of Canadian Writing* (Erin: The Porcupine's Quill).

Howard, Cardinal (1969) *The Unjust Society* (Vancouver: Douglas & McIntyre/ Vancouver).

Howells, Carol Ann (2006) *Cambridge Companion to Margaret Atwood* (Cambridge: Cambridge University Press).

Huggan, Graham (1994) *Territorial Disputes: Maps and Mapping Strategies in Contemporary Canadian and Australian Fiction* (Toronto: University of Toronto Press).

Huggan, Graham, Tiffin, Helen (2010) *Postcolonial Ecocriticism* (London: Routledge).

Hurn, Samantha (2012) *Humans and Other Animals: Cross Cultural Perspectives on Human-Animal Interactions* (London: Pluto Press).

Imgur (2014) 'What the actual fuck, Canada?' https://imgur.com/gallery/uf3YE [Accessed July 2022].

Indigenous Leadership Initiative, 'Indigenous Protected and Conserved Areas': https://www.ilinationhood.ca/indigenous-protected-and-conserved-areas [Accessed 10 January 2023].

Ingerson, Earl G (1992) *Margaret Atwood: Conversations* (London: Virago).

Johnson, Brian (2009) 'Viking Graves Revisited: Pre-Colonial Primitivism in Farley Mowat's Northern Gothic' in *Unsettled Remains: Canadian Literature and the Postcolonial Gothic*, ed. By Cynthia Sugars and Gerry Turcotte (Waterloo: Wilfrid Laurier University Press) pp. 23–50.

Johnson, Daniel Morley (2010) '(Re)Nationalizing Naanabozho: Anishinaabe Sacred Stories, Nationalist Literary Criticism, and Scholarly Responsibility', in *Troubling Tricksters: Revisioning Critical Conversations*, ed. By Deanna Reder and Linda M. Morra (Waterloo: Wilfrid Laurier University Press) pp. 199–221.

Johnson, Lisa (2012) *Power, Knowledge, Animals* (London: Palgrave Macmillan).

Jones, Karen (2003) 'Never Cry Wolf: Science, Sentiment, and the Literary Rehabilitation of Canis Lupus', *The Canadian Historical Review*, 84.1, pp. 65–93.

Jones, Karen (2015) *Epiphany in the wilderness: hunting, nature, and performance in the nineteenth-century American West* (Boulder: University Press of Colorado).

Justice, Daniel Heath (2018) *Why Indigenous Literatures Matter* (Waterloo, Ontario: Wilfred Laurier University Press).

King, Thomas (2012) *The Inconvenient Indian: A Curious Account of Native People in North America* (Minneapolis: University of Minnesota Press).

Kaplan, Lawrence, 'Inuit or Eskimo: Which name to use?', https://www.uaf.edu/anlc/research-and-resources/resources/resources/inuit_or_eskimo.php [Accessed 28 March 2017].

Kirtz, Mary K (2009) "Facts Become Art Through Love': Narrative Structure in Marian Engel's *Bear*', *American Review of Canadian Studies*, 22.3, 351–362.

Lane, Christopher (1995) *Ruling Passion: British Colonial Allegory and the Paradox of Homosexual Desire* (Durham: Duke University Press).

Le Juez, Brigitte, and Springer, Olga (2015) *Shipwreck and island motifs in literature and the arts* (Leiden; Boston: Rodopi).

Lee, Dennis (1974) 'Cadence, Country, Silence: Writing in Colonial Space', *Boundary 2*, 3.1, 151–168.

Loo, Tina (2006) *States of Nature: Conserving Canada's Wildlife in the Twentieth Century* (Vancouver: UBC Press).

Lopez, Barry Holston (1978) *Of Wolves and Men* (New York: Charles Scribner's Sons).

Mackey, Eva (1998) 'Becoming Indigenous: Land, Belonging, and the Appropriation of Aboriginality in Canadian Nationalist Narratives', *Social Analysis: The International Journal of Anthropology*, 42.2, 150–178.

MacPhee, Katrin (2014) 'Canadian Working-Class Environmentalism', 1965–1985' in *Labour / Le Travail*, fall:74, 123–149.

Macpherson, Heidi Slettedahl (2004) 'Coyote as Culprit: The Coyote Aesthetics of Gail-Anderson-Dargatz's *The Cure for Death by Lightning*', *British Journal of Canadian Studies*, 17.2, 175–185.

Mart, Michelle (2009) 'Rhetoric and Response: The Cultural Impact of Rachel Carson's Silent Spring' in Left History, 14:2, 31–57.

McClintock, Anne (1995) *Imperial Leather: Race, Gender and Sexuality in the Colonial Contest* (London: Routledge).

McHugh, Susan (2000) 'Marrying My Bitch: J. R. Ackerley's Pack Sexualities', *Critical Inquiry*, 27.1 (The University of Chicago Press) 21–41.
McKay, Robert (2005) '"Identifying with the animals": Language, Subjectivity, and the Animal Politics of Margaret Atwood's Surfacing' in *Figuring Animals*, ed. by Mary Sanders Pollock and Catherine Rainwater (London: Palgrave Macmillan) pp. 207–227.
Mohtadi, M. F (1980) *Man and His Environment: Proceedings of the Third International Banff Conference on Man and his Environment* (Exeter: Pergamon Press Ltd).
Morley Johnson, Daniel (2010) '(Re)Nationalizing Naanabozho: Anishinaabe Sacred Stories, Nationalist Literary Criticism, and Scholarly Responsibility', in *Troubling Tricksters : Revisioning Critical Conversations*, ed. By Deanna Reder and Linda M. Morra (Waterloo: Wilfrid Laurier University Press) pp. 199–221.
Morgensen, Scott Lauria (2010) 'Settler Homonationalism: Theorizing Settler Colonialism within Queer Modernities', *Journal of Lesbian and Gay Studies*, 16.1–2, 105–131.
Moss, Laura F. E (2003) *Is Canada Postcolonial? Unsettling Canadian Literature* (Waterloo: Wilfrid Laurier University Press).
Murray, Heather (2013) 'Women in the Wilderness (1986)' in *Greening the Maple: Canadian Ecocriticism in Context*, edited by Ella Soper and Nicholas Bradley (Calgary: University of Calgary Press) 61–85.
Nelson, Melissa K. (2017) 'Getting Dirty: The Eco-Eroticism of Women in Indigenous Oral Literatures', in *Critically Sovereign: Indigenous Gender, Sexuality and Feminist Studies*, ed. by Joanne Barker (Durham: Duke University Press) pp. 228–260.
Newton, Esther (1972) *Mother Camp: Female Impersonators in America* (Chicago: University of Chicago Press).
Newton, Esther (1999) 'Role Models', in *Camp: Queer Aesthetics and the Performing Subject*, ed. By Fabio Cleto (Edinburgh: Edinburgh University Press) pp. 976–109.
Parson, Edward A. (2000) 'Environmental Trends and Environmental Governance in Canada' in *Canadian Public Policy / Analyse de Politiques*. 26, 123–143.
Pearson, Wendy (1998/99) 'Vanishing Acts II: Queer Reading(s) of Timothy Findley's *Headhunter* and *Not Wanted on the Voyage*', *Journal of Canadian Studies*, 33.4, 114–131.
Phelan, Shane (1996) 'Coyote Politics: Trickster Tales and Feminist Futures', *Hypatia*, 11.3, 130–140.
Pick, Anat (2011) *Creaturely Poetics: Animality in Literature and Film* (New York: Columbia University Press).
Piercy, Marge (1973) 'Margaret Atwood: Beyond Victimhood', *The American Poetry Review*, 2.6, 41–44.

Philo, Chris, Wilbert, Chris (2000) *Animal Spaces, Beastly Places: New Geographies of Human-Animal Relations* (London: Routledge).

Plumwood, Val (1995) 'Human Vulnerability and the Experience of Being Prey', *Quadrant*, 39.3, 29–34.

Poiana, Peter (2013) 'The Traumatic Origins of Representation', *Continental Philosophy Review*, 46.1, 1–19.

Polk, James (1972) 'The Lives of the Hunted' in *Of Heavenly Hounds and Earthly Men. Spec. issue of Canadian Literature*, 53, 51–59.

Raincoast (2015) 'Alberta slaughters more than 1,000 wolves and hundreds of other animals', https://www.raincoast.org/2015/01/alberta-wolf-slaughter/ [Accessed 30 November 2017].

Reder, Deanna, and Morra, Linda M. (2010) *Troubling Tricksters: Revisioning Critical Conversations* (Waterloo: Wilfrid Laurier University Press).

Rhodes, Shane (1998) 'Buggering With History: Sexual Warfare and Historical Reconstruction in Timothy Findley's *The Wars*', *Canadian Literature, A Quarterly of Criticism and Review: Gay and Lesbian Writing in Canadian Literature*, 159, 38–53.

Robles, Mario Ortiz (2016) *Literature and Animal Studies* (Abingdon: Routledge).

Rothberg, Michael (2012) '"Ensnared in Implication": Writing, Shame and Colonialism in Contemporary Literature', *Contemporary Literature*, 53.2, 374–386.

Sainato, Michael and Chelsea Skojec (5 January 2017) Chelsea, *The New York Observer*.

Sandlos, John (2000) 'From Within Fur and Feathers: Animals in Canadian Literature', *TOPIA: Canadian Journal of Cultural Studies*, 4, 73–91.

Scholtmeijer, Marian (1993) *Animal Victims in Modern Fiction: From Sanctity to Sacrifice* (Toronto: University of Toronto Press).

Shore, Randy (2019) 'B.C. predator cull would target 80 per cent of wolves in caribou recovery areas', https://vancouversun.com/news/local-news/b-c-predator-cull-would-target-80-per-cent-of-wolves-in-caribou-recovery-areas [Accessed 12 January 2022]

Shuswap Band Nation, 'homepage': https://www.shuswapband.net/about-shuswap-band/ [Accessed 20 May 2023].

Shukin, Nicole (2009) *Animal Capital: Rendering Life in Biopolitical Times* (Minneapolis: University of Minnesota Press).

Simmons, Matt (2021) 'B.C. Funding caribou extinction through fossil fuel subsidies and tax breaks: study': https://thenarwhal.ca/bc-caribou-habitat-fossil-fuel-subsidies/ [Accessed 12 January 2022].

Sliwinski, Sharon (2011) 'The Gaze Called Animal', *CR: The New Centennial Review*, 11.2, 61–81.

Smith, Julie A. Mitchell, Robert W (2013) *Experiencing Animal Minds: An Anthology of Animal-Human Encounters* (New York: Columbia University Press).

Sontag, Susan (1999) 'Notes on 'Camp'' in *Camp: Queer Aesthetics and the Performing Subject*, ed. By Fabio Cleto (Edinburgh: Edinburgh University Press) pp. 54–66.

Species at risk public registry, https://species-registry.canada.ca/index-en.html#/species?sortBy=commonNameSort&sortDirection=asc&pageSize=10&keywords=caribou [Accessed 3 March 2022].

Stanton, Kim (2011) 'Canada's Truth and Reconciliation Commission: Settling the Past?', *International Indigenous Policy Journal*, 2.3, 1–18.

Stewart, Fenn (2014) 'Grey Owl in the White Settler Wilderness: "Imaginary Indians", Canadian Culture and Law' in *Law, Culture and the Humanities*, 1.1, 1–21.

Sugars, Cynthia (2004) *Unhomely States: theorizing English-Canadian Postcolonialism* (Peterborough: Broadview Press).

TallBear, Kim, lecture at the University of Winnepeg's Weweni Indigenous Scholars Speaker series in October 2018 titled 'Decolonial Sex and Relations for a More Sustainable World' [Accessed on YouTube September 2019].

Taylor, Sunaura (2011) 'Beasts of Burden: Disability Studies and Animal Rights', *Qui Parle*, 19.2 (Durham: Duke University Press) 191–222.

Taylor, Verta; Rupp, Leila and Gamson, Joshua (2004) 'Performing Protest: Drag Shows as Tactical Repertoire of the Gay and Lesbian Movement', *Research in Social Movements, Conflicts and Change*, 25, 105–137.

Tolan, Fiona (2007) *Margaret Atwood: Feminism and Fiction* (Leiden: Brill).

Tiffin, Helen (1988) 'Post-Colonialism, Post-Modernism and the Rehabilitation of Post-Colonial History', *The Journal of Commonwealth Literature*, 23.1, 169–181.

Tumblr, www.dirtyriver.tumblr.com [Accessed July 2022].

Vintage Ad Browser: http://www.vintageadbrowser.com/airlines-and-aircraft-ads-1980s/8 [Accessed 10 March 2020].

Wakeman, Pauline (2008) *Taxidermic Signs: Reconstructing Aboriginality* (Minneapolis: University of Minnesota Press).

Walsh, Sue (2015) 'Nature Faking and the Problem of the "Real"', *Interdisciplinary Studies in Literature and Environment*, 22.1, 132–153.

Webb, Peter (2007) '"At War With Nature": Animals in Timothy Findley's *The Wars*', in *Other Selves: Animals in the Canadian Literary Imagination*, ed. By Janice Fiamengo (Ottawa: University of Ottawa Press) pp. 227–244.

Western Wildlife Outreach, 'Gray Wolf Biology & Behavior' http://westernwildlife.org/gray-wolf-outreach-project/biology-behavior-4/ [Accessed 6 November 2017]

Wimherst, Katy (2009) "Interview with Gail Anderson-Dargatz" in *Serendipity*: http://www.magicalrealism.co.uk/view.php?story=113.

Wolfe, Cary (2003) *Zoontologies: the question of the animal* (Minneapolis: University of Minnesota Press).

Wolfe, Cary, Elmer, Jonathan (1995) 'Subject to Sacrifice: Ideology, Psychoanalysis, and the Discourse of Species in Jonathan Demme's Silence of the Lambs', *Boundary 2: An International Journal of Literature and Culture*, 22.3, 141–70.

Wright, Laura (2010) *'Wilderness into Civilized Shapes': Reading the Postcolonial Environment* (Athens: University of Georgia Press).

Yeung, Heather H (2015) 'Adventures in Form: The Hebrides and the Romantic Imaginary', in *Shipwreck and island motifs in literature and the arts*, ed. By Brigitte le Juez and Olga Springer (Leiden; Boston: Rodopi) pp. 85–97.

Pictures

Qantas advert (1982) http://www.vintageadbrowser.com/airlines-and-aircraft-ads-1980s/8 [Accessed 10 March 2020] Used with permission.

Index[1]

A
Ackerley, J R., 94
   My Dog Tulip, 94
Adams, Carol J., 96, 99, 116
America/United States of America, 4, 22, 37, 50, 57, 59, 72n11
Anderson-Dargatz, Gail, 4, 14, 15, 119–138, 145
Anthropocentrism, 14, 89, 90, 136, 138
Anthropomorphism, 33–38, 43, 44, 50, 81, 89, 108, 115
Atwood, Margaret, 3–5, 7, 9, 12, 13, 16, 17n8, 42, 49–72, 76, 77, 88, 91, 143, 144
   Survival, 4, 9, 17n8, 50, 54, 58, 76, 77, 88
Australia, 32, 82

B
Banff, 6
   Banff Conference 'Man and His Environment,' 6
Bear (Engel), 3, 13, 14, 75–91, 114
Bears
   grizzly bears, 1, 2, 16n1
   teddy bears, 77, 82, 91
Beaver, 2–4, 60
British Columbia, 1, 20, 44, 119, 120, 139n1, 145

C
Camp
   aesthetic, 13, 95, 97, 106, 108, 109
   Notes on Camp, 118n20
Care, 13, 14, 16, 55, 93–117, 119–138, 144, 145
   feminist care ethics, 108, 113, 123

---

[1] Note: Page numbers followed by 'n' refer to notes.

© The Author(s), under exclusive license to Springer Nature Switzerland AG 2023
A. Higgs, *Animal Fiction in Late Twentieth-Century Canada*, Palgrave Studies in Animals and Literature,
https://doi.org/10.1007/978-3-031-42612-4

INDEX

Caribou, 12, 19, 20, 22, 23, 35, 36, 38, 39, 41
Carson, Rachel, 21
  Silent Spring, 21, 43
Chicken(s), 123, 126, 127, 129, 134
Churchill, Manitoba, 11, 22–25, 27, 36, 38
Conservation, 2, 6, 39, 43, 44, 146
Cows, 123, 128, 129, 134
Coyote/coyotes, Coyote the trickster, 15, 119–138
Cultural appropriation, 14

D

Disney
  The Legend of Lobo, 8
  Never Cry Wolf, 8, 22, 144
Duty, 41, 96–102, 105, 107, 108, 110, 112, 113, 116

E

Eco-sexuality, 14, 124, 127, 129
Environmentalism, 6, 9, 21
  environmental movement in North America, 20, 21

F

Feminism
  feminist, 66, 96, 100, 109–110, 112, 116, 120, 126, 127, 130, 132, 137
  Second Wave feminism, 66
Fiamengo, Janice, 7, 52
  Other Selves, 7
Findley, Timothy, 3, 13, 15, 93–117, 144

First Nations, 1–3, 15, 17n3, 18n28, 39, 52, 121
Fur, 2, 5, 17n8, 54, 79, 84, 126

G

Gender, 4, 11, 15, 34, 63, 64, 96, 108, 123, 125–127, 129, 139n10, 145
Grey Owl syndrome, 60

H

Haraway, 76, 96, 98, 101, 109, 112, 114
Heteronormative/heteronormativity, 69, 93–96, 101, 102, 108, 110, 116, 123–125, 129–132, 138, 140n14
Horses, 25, 94, 97–109, 115, 117n14
  horse riding, 103, 106
Hunting, 22, 34, 35, 38, 39, 46n16, 51, 53, 55–57, 114, 135

I

Indigeneity, 3, 11, 14, 15, 40, 42, 60–63, 69, 122, 123, 129, 145
Indigenous
  identity, 4, 40, 60
  Indigenous Circle of Experts (ICE), 145
  Indigenous Protected Areas (IPAs), 146
Island(s), 1, 2, 17n3, 76, 79–81, 85, 87, 90, 91

J

Jones, Karen, 9, 19, 20, 43, 53

K

Kinship, 2, 13–15, 39, 41, 93–117, 124, 127, 144, 145

L

Life Before Man (Atwood), 3, 12, 49–72
Loo, Tina, 6, 20, 37, 39, 43, 60

M

Martel, Yann, 7
  Life of Pi, 7
Masculinity, 33, 53, 65, 66, 96, 101–103, 116
McHugh, Susan, 8, 10, 11, 94
McIlwraith, Thomas, 7
  Birds of Ontario, 7
Moose, 51, 53, 65
Museums, 8, 12, 50, 51, 63–71, 78

N

Nationalism, 37, 52, 58
Nature fakers, 3, 7–9, 45, 143
Never Cry Wolf (Mowat), 3, 9, 11, 12, 19–45
Not Wanted on the Voyage (Findley), 3, 13, 15, 93–117

P

Patriarchy, 55, 69, 96, 112, 124
Polk, James, 4, 5, 7–9, 143

Q

Qantas, 82
  advert, 83
Quebec, 12, 61, 73n25
  the Quiet Revolution, 61

R

Rabies, 23, 25, 30
Reconciliation, 2, 145
Roberts, Charles G. D., 5, 7–9, 13, 16, 45, 76, 78, 88, 91
Robles, Mario Ortiz, 10

S

Sandlos, John, 5–9, 76
Scholtmeijer, Marian, 9
Seton, Ernest Thompson, 5, 7–9, 13, 16, 45, 50, 76, 78, 88, 91
  Wild Animals I have Known, 8, 9
Settler colonialism, 58, 130
Sexuality, 4, 11, 15, 94, 95, 97, 123, 124, 127, 129–133, 137, 138, 145
  homosexuality, 95, 102, 130
Shuswap
  region, 119
  Shuswap Band Nation, 119
Story
  the Canadian animal story, 4, 8, 13, 45, 75–91
  Indigenous stories, 14, 15, 121–123, 127, 131, 132, 137, 138
  storytelling, 2, 8, 29, 78, 91, 126, 137
Surfacing (Atwood), 3, 12, 49–72

U

Unjust Society, The, 58

V

Victimhood, 3–5, 50–52, 55–60
Vulnerability, 25, 28, 31, 32, 50, 54, 58, 137

W

Wars, The (Findley), 3, 13, 93–117
White Paper, The, 58, 59
Wilderness, 22, 23, 34, 37, 40, 41, 49–72, 76, 101, 132

Wolves
   culling, 20, 21, 24, 38, 41
   wolf gaze, 22, 27, 29–32, 56
Women's writing, 50